MARGARET ST. GEORGE

HAPPY NEW YEAR, DARLING

Harlequin Books

TORONTO • NEW YORK • LONDON
AMSTERDAM • PARIS • SYDNEY • HAMBURG
STOCKHOLM • ATHENS • TOKYO • MILAN

Published January 1992

ISBN 0-373-16421-1

HAPPY NEW YEAR, DARLING

Chapter One

New Year's Eve, 1980

Having no date at all for New Year's Eve was probably worse than going out with your roommate's fiancé. But Bailey Meade wasn't sure.

"At least you have a date," said the girl in the red cap. She glared up at Radcliffe's administration building, then shifted her picket sign to her other shoulder and scowled at Bailey through the snowflakes swirling out of the darkness.

"Pity dates don't count. My roommate is out of town, so she fixed me up with her fiancé." Bailey frowned and made a face. She didn't know why she had let Pam talk her into spending New Year's Eve with Cole Tarcher. "Going out with your roommate's fiancé is about as exciting as dating your cousin."

"It's your own fault," one of the Lit majors said. She stepped out of the picket circle, leaned on her sign, and cast a dejected glance toward the solitary light burning over the steps of the deserted administration building. "You shouldn't have broken up with your boyfriend just before the holidays. That was dumb, Bailey. Really dumb."

Lois, a junior who worked with Bailey on the *Radcliffe Underground*, stopped marching and heaved a sigh toward the snow-shrouded campus before she glared at Bailey.

"Speaking of dumb—why are we doing this? What's the point of protesting if no one is around to read our placards? I thought you said we'd have media coverage."

Bailey bit her lip and scanned the unbroken field of snow carpeting the night-dark quad. There wasn't a soul in sight and hadn't been since they started picketing two hours ago. Like the others, she was cold, tired of marching in a circle, and starting to feel depressed.

"I sent out thirty-two press releases," she said finally. "I thought at least one reporter would pick up the story." She glanced at the snowflakes tumbling out of the black sky, sticking to caps, coats and eyelashes, then she spread her mittens. "Five committed Radcliffe women give up the best parties of the year to make a statement against injustice, chauvinism and blatant discrimination. I thought someone would be interested." Her mouth pressed in a line and she resumed circling in the track they had tramped in the snow, waving her picket sign for the benefit of a nonexistent audience. "Our effort is not in vain. I promise I'll run the story in the *Radcliffe Underground!*"

"If you do, for God's sake don't mention my name," Lois insisted. "I don't want anyone to know I was this stupid."

Bending, she smacked her picket sign on the ground to dislodge a sheet of snow. "I can't believe I let you talk me into this, Bailey Meade. Instead of being out here cold and depressed, I could be in my apartment—warm and depressed."

Murmurs of agreement grumbled along the circle, and Bailey released another sigh.

The girl in the red cap opened a thermos of hot chocolate and passed it around. "I can tell you this. The minute your pity date shows up and you leave, I'm leaving too." She waved a shapeless glove at the administration building. "No one's home. We're wasting our time."

An hour ago the same thought had occurred to Bailey. Pushing back her coat sleeve, she glanced at her watch. If Cole Tarcher didn't show up soon, she would join the mutiny and leave with the others.

"I hate men," someone complained. There was more fervent emotion in the chorus of agreement than the picketers had shown all evening. "I was dating this Yalie, see, until three months ago. Then he..."

Bailey checked the deserted quad. It wouldn't break her heart if Cole Tarcher spaced her out and didn't show. Then she could go back to the apartment, take a hot shower, snuggle into her faded old robe, and watch the big ball drop in Times Square on her TV. It would be the worst New Year's Eve in her entire twenty-two years. But it had to be better than trying to make conversation all night with Pam's fiancé.

All she knew about Cole Tarcher was that he was an MBA candidate at Harvard, came from some podunk town in Wyoming, and Pam's parents were appalled by him. Which delighted Pam, of course. And he was great-looking. When Cole arrived at the apartment to pick up her roommate, Bailey had to remind herself not to stare. He and Pam made a terrific-looking couple.

She decided to give him three more minutes, then she'd leave.

COLE LOCKED THE DOOR of his pickup, thrust his hands into the pockets of his topcoat and bent his head against the eddies of flying snow. Pam had warned him that Bailey Meade was "different," and that was sure as hell how it was turning out.

All afternoon, since the snow started falling, he had waited for Bailey to phone and tell him to pick her up at the apartment instead of meeting her in front of Radcliffe's administration building. But she hadn't phoned so he assumed she was, for some reason, waiting in front of the administrative building at night in the middle of a snow-storm. She was different all right.

To be fair, Cole supposed he was, too. Pam liked to say she collected unique people. He was never entirely comfortable when Pam talked about her unique people. She made herself sound like the rallying point for the world's outsiders, people like Bailey Meade—and himself—who didn't quite fit the image of the Ivy League schools, those who didn't have the proper accent, the Mayflower background or a generational list of social and financial credentials. The very people, in other words, that parents such as his, and presumably Bailey Meade's, sent their children back East to meet.

Raising his head, he squinted past the snow-sugared trees and white walkways toward the administration building, then stopped short. In the glow of the light shining above the steps, a small group of bundled, miserable-looking women marched in a tight circle carrying picket signs. Even if the light had been stronger, he couldn't have read the messages on the signs. Melting snow had blurred the words.

Approaching slowly, Cole wondered what issue was so burningly important that these women would come out on a bitterly cold New Year's Eve to march in protest. The trackless snow suggested no one but himself had witnessed their effort. He also wondered which of the shapeless bundles of parkas, caps and gloves was Bailey Meade.

He had met Bailey two or three times in the hallway outside the apartment she and Pam shared, or for a few minutes inside, but he hadn't paid much attention. He retained a vague image of a pretty girl with intense blue eyes and a Kansas accent, always with a stack of books under her arm, always wearing some kind of protest button on her lapel. He recalled Pam mentioning Bailey was the editor of the *Radcliffe Underground,* an unofficial campus tabloid that some labeled a rabble-rousing rag and others lauded for confronting issues more important and controversial than those addressed by the official campus publication.

When he approached to about twenty yards of the group, the picketers lowered their placards and stopped marching. A half-dozen cold unhappy faces turned toward him with expressions of relief, except for the rosy-cheeked young woman who stepped forward to meet him. That, of course, would be Bailey Meade. He didn't notice any relief on her face, only indifference. For the first time it occurred to him that she was probably no more enthusiastic than he about Pam's arrangements for this evening.

"Cole?" When he nodded, she turned back and shouted to the others. "Okay, ladies, let's call it a night. Remember, we weren't protesting for the benefit of an audience. We came here tonight because we believe the issue is important! We won't give up. We'll picket again when classes resume."

One of the women took Bailey's placard, wished everyone a happy new year, then joined the others hurrying toward the parking lot. Bailey brushed the snow from her shoulders and cap and fell into step beside him.

"God, it's cold!" She rubbed her mittens together and stamped her feet. "Have you ever been to Monaco? I'll bet Pam is sunning herself on her father's yacht right now, laughing her head off at us poor fools freezing back here in Boston. Are you parked nearby?"

"I'm parked under those maples. What were you protesting? I couldn't read your signs." She was taller than Pam and had what his parents' generation had called a whiskey voice, lower in register than most women's, rich, warm and full-bodied. He suspected she had a wonderful laugh.

But she wasn't laughing now. She cast a scowl over her shoulder at the administration building, then shook her head.

"We're protesting pay toilets in the women's johns."

He stopped and stared down at her. "You came out on a night like this to protest pay toilets?"

"If you had to pay a dime to use the john, you'd protest, too!" The flash in her bright blue eyes warned him the issue was not trivial to her. "But there are no pay toilets in the men's johns, right? And there shouldn't be pay toilets in the women's johns, either! We won't stop until justice and equality have been achieved!" Her intense gaze dared him to argue.

Smiling, Cole raised his gloves in a gesture of surrender. "Hey, I'm in favor of justice and equality. Down with pay toilets in the women's johns. Yea team."

She eyed him suspiciously, then her shoulders relaxed and she offered a thin smile. "Okay, so it isn't Vietnam or Watergate." A sigh sent a plume of vapor out before her lips. "I was born too late. All the really good issues are behind us."

"Not all of them," he said, nodding toward the two buttons she wore on her coat lapel. One of them showed a death's head surrounded by the words: Three Mile Island. The other shouted Ban the Bomb in fluorescent letters.

She gave him a sidelong look, trying to match his stride. "Then you've joined the crusade against nuclear destruction?"

"Nope," he said cheerfully, touching her elbow to direct her toward the curb. "Nuclear capability is a powerful incentive for peace. Plus, someday we're going to run out of fossil fuels. Nuclear power is the hope of the future."

"Dead people don't need electricity," she said tartly, tapping a mittened finger against her Three Mile Island button. Then she noticed the vehicle at the curb and looked at him with interest. "I'd forgotten Pam said you drove a pickup. You must be the only MBA candidate at Harvard who drives a pickup."

"I think there's one other maverick. But his is ten years newer than mine." After unlocking the passenger door, he leaned to open it.

"Oh, please, I can open my own doors."

"I'm sure you can." He met her eyes. "But when you're with me, you don't have to." He opened the door and waited while she tried to decide how to respond. "It's still warm inside. But it's not going to stay that way unless you get in now."

Frowning, Bailey pulled herself up and inside, and he shut the door. In a minute he reappeared on the driver's side and bent forward to brush the snow off the windshield. The idea of driving a pickup to the Boston Symphony tickled Bailey. It was exactly the kind of thing that drove Pam's parents wild and made them disapprove of Cole Tarcher as a future son-in-law. It was also exactly the kind of thing that appealed to Bailey.

While she waited for him to finish clearing the windshield, Bailey pulled off her stocking cap and fluffed her hair, peering in the tiny mirror attached to the back of the visor. Wet snow had smudged her mascara. She had chewed off her lipstick an hour ago. While she effected hasty repairs, she peeked at Cole Tarcher through the windshield.

He was as handsome as Bailey's roommate, Pam, was gorgeous. And Cole's dark, rugged Marlboro Man type of looks contrasted wonderfully with Pam's delicate beauty. What appealed to Bailey, and probably to Pam, was that Cole Tarcher didn't look as though he was East Coast born and bred. To Bailey's midwestern eye, men from the East seemed too too. Too well dressed, too well groomed, too cliquish, too sophisticated, too *GQ* perfect.

Cole Tarcher didn't fit that mold. He wore the obligatory tweed topcoat and wool muffler, and she could tell he'd had his dark hair styled rather than just cut. But there the resemblance ended. No one who drove a battered pickup that still smelled faintly of hay and tack could lay claim to polished perfection or a withering sophistication. And when he looked at her, he didn't gaze through her, his eyes connected.

Plus he was drop-dead handsome—dark hair starting to curl from the melting snow, warm dark eyes, premature smile lines at the edges of his eyes and framing his mouth. Cole Tarcher exuded self-confidence, and there was something unyielding about his attitude and posture. Intuitively Bailey sensed Cole Tarcher was the type of man other men would trust but find intimidating. Women would see him as dangerous, a heartbreaker, but they would fall for him anyway. As Pam had. As Bailey might have if she had met him first.

And that would have been a disaster, because there were plenty of cowboy types in Oakley, Kansas; she hadn't come East to meet a man she might have stumbled over in her own backyard. Plus she didn't warm to the dangerous, heartbreaker types. Girls like Pam could have them and be welcome. When the time came, Bailey hoped to find a comfortable man, a safe man, a man who would anchor her own volatility and modest ambitions.

"You're right. It's freezing out there," Cole said as he slid behind the wheel. He rubbed his hands together and looked at her fluffed hair and fresh lipstick. "Whatever you did you look beautiful."

His tone indicated surprise as if he had never noticed her before. Which was probably true. By and large, roommates were invisible.

"Look, I know Pam had this dumb idea that we were both going to spend New Year's Eve alone and miserable, so she insisted we get together." Bailey drew a breath and ran her palm over the sheepskin seat cover. "But we don't have to. You could just take me back to the apartment..."

"Is that what you want?"

Bailey watched fresh snowflakes drifting over the windshield he had just brushed clean, then looked down at the new velvet pantsuit she had bought for this evening before she broke up with Brad the Rat. A small sigh tugged her lips.

"What I'd really like to do is go to President Dilson's cocktail party and run into Brad the Rat. In this fantasy he's alone and dying for me." She stared out the windshield. "I sweep in with you and cut him dead. And he starts the new year thinking I've already found someone else and he hasn't. He wonders what I would have given him for Christmas. He wonders how he's going to live without me. And his first resolution is to jump off President Dilson's roof." She sighed again.

"Brad the Rat? Ex-boyfriend, right?" Cole smiled. "So what would you have given him for Christmas?"

"You really want to know?"

"Yes."

"I was going to give him a leather attaché case with brass fittings." They looked at each other in the light from the dashboard. "I can tell from your expression, Brad would have hated it, wouldn't he?"

"An attaché case is like a saddle," Cole said finally. "Each man should select his own."

Bailey collapsed against the sheepskin seat cover and spread her hands. "That's what I was afraid of. He probably wants one with a designer label and gold fittings, something that costs the earth. But thanks for not lying about it. From now on, no attaché cases—or saddles—as gifts."

Cole eased the pickup away from the curb and into the deserted street. Light filtered through the bare branches onto the snow-packed lanes. "I don't have an invitation to President Dilson's cocktail party or I'd take you. Do you have an invitation?"

"Me? Get serious. To attend that party you have to be able to trace your ancestors back to the Garden of Eden. Even if I could produce documents signed by God, I'd still be persona non grata. Officialdom—and that means President Dilson—frowns on the *Radcliffe Underground*. Our Pres doesn't relish being taken to task over pay toilets or lecherous professors or grades for sale or tacky things like the awful truth.''

"You've done a good job with the paper."

Bailey shifted on the seat and looked at him in surprise. "You've read it?"

"Every now and then Pam gives me a copy. I liked your piece about student involvement in government. Although I thought your portrayal of Carter was one-sided."

"What?" She sat up straighter. "Are you a Republican?"

He grinned. "Absolutely. I think Reagan is going to win the election this fall."

"You're crazy," Bailey said hotly. "California may be nutty enough to draw some connection between acting and politics, but I think the rest of the country has better sense!"

They argued the issue during the drive to the symphony and again throughout the walk from the parking lot to the symphony hall. At one point they stopped on the sidewalk, waving their gloves and talking at the same time. Bailey loved it. It was exactly the release she needed after the frustration of the failed pay toilet protest. And discovering that Cole Tarcher was willing to argue politics—and was good at it—was a pleasant and stimulating surprise. By the time they entered the symphony hall, Bailey had begun to relax.

And she was looking at Cole Tarcher with more interest than she had when he appeared out of the snowstorm to pick her up. Maybe tonight wasn't going to be as dismal as she had dreaded it would be. In fact, to her great surprise, so far she was enjoying herself. She hadn't really expected to.

"I like the way you argue," Cole commented as he helped her out of her parka and laid it across the back of her seat. "You stick to the issue and you don't personalize."

Pleased by the compliment, Bailey smiled at him. His damp hair was drying in dark waves around his face. And she could tell by the distracted look in his eye that he was still thinking about the issues they had been discussing. While she listened to the symphony's first selection, she peeked at him from the corner of her eyes and decided Pam had been right. Spending New Year's Eve with Cole was a lot better that sitting alone in the apartment feeling sorry for herself.

At the intermission they sipped hot mulled wine and nibbled tiny cardboard cookies, standing before the lobby doors looking out at the snow.

Cole observed several interested glances scan Bailey's wild hair and slender figure, although Bailey didn't seem to notice. Pretending an interest in the thinning snow, he observed her, too. She was not beautiful in a classical sense like Pam, but Bailey Meade was a striking young woman. The ruby-colored pantsuit molded a noteworthy figure and enhanced her vibrant coloring. A cloud of long, unruly dark hair surrounded an oval face and a sweep of bangs dropped toward thick dark eyebrows. Her cheeks and mouth were naturally rose-colored.

But it was her eyes Cole noticed first, large heavily lashed eyes of an unusual blue. He couldn't pin down the exact color, possibly because the color seemed to change from cornflower to aquamarine almost to navy depending on the light and, intriguingly, on her mood. Largely her eyes drew attention because of their expressive liveliness. She saw everything and was interested in everything, and her bright eyes reflected her curiosity and pleasure.

Cole decided Bailey Meade lacked the cosmopolitan polish of young women like Pam, but aside from a wholesome freshness that suggested the Midwest, he could also see that she was no longer representative of Kansas. For an instant he glimpsed the woman she was evolving toward and drew in a breath. Bailey was the type of woman who would become more beautiful with time. By age thirty she would be breathtaking; stunning at forty. Her striking features and expressive eyes would eclipse more standard beauties.

"Are you enjoying the concert?" she asked, looking around for a place to set her empty wineglass.

Ordinarily he would have answered yes. Certainly that's how he would have replied if Pam had asked the same question. But he felt a Wyoming-Kansas connection with Bailey Meade, an outsider's kinship that banished any impulse toward pretense.

"The truth? I haven't quite acquired a passion for classical music. I enjoy it, but..." He shrugged.

Surprise lighted her eyes, then she laughed. And her laugh was as rich and husky and wonderful as he had imagined it would be.

"You're the first person I've met recently who actually admits classical music isn't his first preference. Except me."

"You too?" he asked, grinning down at her. "Let me guess. You like Willie Nelson, Waylon Jennings and Johnny Cash."

Her eyes sparkled and she looked in both directions before leaning near enough that he caught a whiff of a clean woodsy perfume. "Good Lord, does it show?"

"Just a little," he said, laughing. "Look, I made dinner reservations at Tante Maison's. It's within walking distance from here. Would you like to ditch the second half of the symphony and see if we can get into Tante Maison's early?"

"You're on."

After retrieving their coats and caps, they ducked out a side door, chuckling like conspirators, then Cole offered his arm and Bailey accepted it. They strolled along the sidewalk, admiring the Christmas decorations, waving at cars that passed honking in the new year. When they approached a bookstore that was still open, Bailey's steps slowed and she stopped to peer in the window.

"Books are my weakness," she apologized. "I can't bear to pass a bookstore without going inside." She pointed at the window display. "Have you read that one? David Attenborough's *Life on Earth?* It's terrific."

"How do you find time to study, edit the *Radcliffe Underground,* and read for pleasure?" he asked, opening the door for her. When she hesitated, he gave her a mock frown. "Yes, I *am* going to open doors tonight. You can be a macho women's libber with other guys, okay? Not with me."

"All right," she agreed, letting him see her reluctance before she passed beneath his arm into the bookstore. "I guess I can stand to be pampered for one night."

They examined the bestseller racks together, then drifted apart. Cole headed for the business books section; Bailey stopped before a new offering of dictionaries and writers' hints.

"Find anything?" Cole asked when they met again near the front counter.

"Not really. But I hate to leave a bookstore without buying something. It's bad luck."

He noticed a rack of astrology booklets and moved to inspect them. "How about this? The stars see all, know all. Are you curious what the new year will bring? Here's your answer."

"Oh, come on," she said, smiling and rolling her expressive eyes. "You don't believe in that stuff."

"Nobody does. But do you know anyone who can resist reading their horoscope in the daily newspaper? Don't you want to know what kind of year you'll have in 1980? What sign are you?"

"Gemini," she admitted, watching him pull a Gemini booklet out of the rack. "What sign are you?"

"Scorpio."

"Oh, no!" Pressing the back of her hand to her forehead, she staggered backward and pretended to swoon. "Scorpios are the sex maniacs of the zodiac! You Scorpios have an extra six-pack of hormones. Quick, call me a cab!"

"Faker. You do know about astrology." He grinned at her. "Okay, let's see what it says about you Geminis." Opening the booklet, he flipped to the character analysis section. "'Creative and intelligent, interested in literature and art.' Okay, I can see that. 'Charming, quick-witted.' Uh-oh, here's trouble." He gave her a suspicious squint and she grinned. "'Can be duplicitous. Sees both sides of an issue and therefore may seem indecisive or wishy-washy. Tries too hard to please.'"

"Where does it say that!"

The woodsy perfume enveloped him as she leaned to read over his arm. "Good God, I'm doomed. Look at that. It says I'm a great starter, start millions of projects, but I seldom finish anything." Turning, she pulled out the booklet for Scorpios. "Okay, cowboy, let's see what it says about you sex maniacs."

He assumed a Napoleonic pose. "It says I am a prince of a fellow. Brave, courageous, and bold. A paragon of manly virtue."

Bailey groaned and smiled at his grin, then read a few sentences. "I can't believe this. It does say something like that. You are definitely a finisher—nothing but nothing deters you from your goal. Obstacles don't exist for you Scorpios. Aha! Here we go. It says you can be ruthless and arrogant, you don't care diddly what other people think." Twinkling blue eyes sized him up. "Heaven help the poor sucker who crosses you. It says you'll seek revenge. *And*—" she jabbed her finger at the page "—it says here in irrefutable black and white that you Scorpios often display an excessive interest in sex!"

"Yeah, but it's great sex," he said, grinning. "Come on. We're buying these booklets. I want Pam to see the part about great sex."

Bailey laughed and followed him to the register, trying not to think about Cole Tarcher and great sex. But once the idea was in her mind... "The part about arrogance was right on target. The booklet didn't say a thing about 'great' sex, just sex."

"It also said we Scorpios are sincere and loving. Our relationships are profound and not superficial. Whereas you frivolous Geminis are natural flirts." Lifting his head, he gave her a superior gaze down the length of his nose. "Shame on you. You toy with affections and leave a trail of broken hearts behind you. It's enough to make a man cry."

She batted her eyelashes in a parody of old-fashioned flirtatiousness. "Good. I hope Brad the Rat is suffering."

Laughing and wiping snow from the pages, they read aloud from the booklets as they continued down the street toward Tante Maison's. The light in the lounge where they had to wait for their table was too dim to read by and they put the booklets away with reluctance.

"That was fun," Bailey said, tasting her daiquiri. "From now on I'm going to start each New Year with an astrology book. I'll mail it home to my folks, then I won't have to write letters. They can just check my horoscope to find out what I'm doing."

"Do you ever feel homesick for Kansas?" Cole asked.

"I did during my freshman year, but not so often now that I'm a senior. I don't know. When I was home for Christmas everything looked so small and flat." A sad smile touched her lips. "Main Street runs from the school on one end to the railroad tracks on the other end. The kids drag Main, jog around the old depot, then go down past the new stores toward Highway 40, and the whole ritual doesn't take fifteen minutes. Oakley's a terrific town, and I'm glad I grew up there. It still has a Norman Rockwell kind of feel."

"But?"

She met his eyes, then poked at the ice in her glass. "But I don't want to spend the rest of my life stuck in a small Kansas farm town. I want something more."

"Is your father a farmer?"

"I have an uncle who raises wheat and maize, but my dad publishes the Oakley Graphic. He started in the newspaper business in Chicago but he always wanted to own a paper in a small town. We moved to Oakley when I was three." Tilting her head, she studied him across the tiny table. And tried not to think about great sex. "How about you? Do you miss Wyoming's sage and open range?"

"Hell, no." Cole shook his head and signaled for another daiquiri and Scotch and water. Bailey thought a cloud crossed his expression. "I'm back East to stay. My dad runs about two thousand head on the Tarcher ranch. It's a third-generation spread. My great-grandfather homesteaded the land, my grandfather expanded it, my father is working himself to death to preserve it." He looked toward the dining room. "I don't want it."

"A three-generation legacy is a lot to turn your back on," Bailey said carefully. Sympathy flickered in her gaze. "I imagine your father isn't too pleased."

"You imagine right," Cole said. "But this cowboy doesn't want any part of hard winters, animal diseases and fluctuating beef markets. There's something about land that satisfies a man's spirit, but land doesn't pay the bills. What does it matter if a man owns a fortune in land if he can't pull up the cash to buy a new truck when the old one starts to fall apart? Or if sending his son to Harvard means taking out a large mortgage, then fearing the payments for however many years?"

Bailey studied his face as he spoke. Cole Tarcher was not at all what she had expected. Certainly she had not expected to like him this much, or to enjoy spending the evening with him. She absolutely hadn't expected to feel a stirring of attraction. When she realized she was staring at his sexy mouth, she dropped her eyes, frowned, and tried to push aside the recognition of her attraction.

Part of their affinity could be attributed to similar small-town backgrounds; as she described Oakley she sensed Cole was seeing Rawlins, Wyoming, in his mind's eye. And part of her pleasure in the evening came from the discovery of common tastes. Neither were wild about the symphony, they both liked the look and feel of books. Obviously he enjoyed a stimulating argument as much as she did. She didn't share Pam's aversion for Cole's old pickup, and Cole didn't seem to mind that Bailey jumped from subject to subject with unsettling speed.

Letting her mind drift for a moment, Bailey tried to imagine what tonight would have been like if she hadn't broken up with Brad the Rat. She wondered if she would have enjoyed herself as much as she was enjoying the evening with Cole.

First Brad would have raised hell about her picketing the administration building and so they would have arrived at President Dilson's cocktail party in the middle of an argument. There they would have stood around an antique-stuffed room, angry at each other, listening to old-line Boston Brahmins discussing the deplorable state of today's art and literature, listening to Mozart playing softly in the background while Revolutionary War-era candlesticks reflected heirloom pearls and conservative ties.

After the cocktail party, she and Brad the Rat would have driven to his club for dinner and the dance afterward. Bailey's new pantsuit would have been wrong somehow and Brad would have let her know it. He would have warned her beforehand not to discuss politics or nuclear anything. He would have reminded her not to start any sentence with: "Back in Kansas..."

Feeling out of place and vaguely lonely, Bailey would have spent the evening watching Brad the Rat get steadily drunker while he and his stuffy friends remembered better New Year's Eves with Buffy and Muffy and Winston and Bunny and all those other people who numbered among the in-crowd who really counted.

Part of her would have loved being included. Part of her would have wished she were somewhere else.

"It's true," Cole said, smiling at her. "You Geminis really do have a short attention span. You're spacing out."

"Sorry," she murmured, feeling a blush rise on her cheeks. "I was just thinking what a genius Pam is." Pushing back a wave of springy hair, she met his warm dark eyes. "Thanks, Cole. I've really enjoyed this evening."

"It's not over," he said. "I haven't fed you yet. The way I hear it, you Kansas girls can put away half a cow. I'm looking forward to discovering if that's true. Eastern girls don't eat, have you noticed? They curl their lips at real food and order salads. They don't understand the word dessert."

Bailey laughed. For the first time since she had met Pam, she felt a genuine twinge of envy for her roommate. Cole Tarcher was as terrific as Pam insisted he was. And Bailey had decided at least an hour ago that he had the sexiest mouth she had ever seen.

When their table was called, they stood at the same moment, standing close together in the crowded lounge. Bailey's mouth dried and she felt her stomach tighten when Cole looked down at her. In his steady speculative gaze she saw a reflection of her own feelings: interest, pleasure, attraction, and surprise at these unexpected emotions.

Guilt and excitement shivered down her spine. She didn't have to consult her horoscope to know that the magic happening between them might feel wonderful—but it was dead wrong.

Chapter Two

"Tell me about Brad the Rat," Cole said when the dessert plates had been cleared and their coffee and cognac were served. "What went wrong?"

Bailey added the cognac to her coffee, then sighed. "What can I tell you?" She waved a hand, wishing she had polished her nails. "It's your standard culture clash of East meets Midwest. Sometimes that works beautifully," she added hastily as she remembered Cole and Pam. "But sometimes it doesn't."

"Tell me about it."

"Brad has a lot of the qualities I want in a man," Bailey said, frowning across the candle-lit dining room. "He's solid and dependable. He's predictable. He wants a family as much as I do. He'll be a good husband and father."

"The guy's a regular Boy Scout."

She glared at him. "Do you want to hear this or not?"

"I want to hear it. What went wrong between you and this dependable but dull creature?"

"Comfortable, not dull. Anyway, I have an idea Brad looked at me as a fix-it project. He was continually telling me what to wear, what to eat, what to say, how to think." She shrugged. "I didn't mind in the beginning. Maybe I needed a lot of fixing. But a steady diet of criticism undermines a person's confidence, and confidence isn't my long suit to begin with. After a while I began to wonder why he started dating me in the first place.''

"Have you looked in the mirror recently?"

Cole knew exactly what had sparked Brad the Rat's interest. What mystified him was how he himself had managed to overlook her vivaciousness for so long. He wondered if Bailey had any idea how marvelous she looked with that cloud of dark hair and her expressive smile, or if she knew how her face lighted when she spoke of her pet projects.

He suspected the astrology booklet was right; Bailey Meade could charm any man. She was easy to talk to, really listened when other people talked, and she projected a wholesome sexiness she seemed to be unaware of—but he was not. With every passing minute Cole became more acutely cognizant of Bailey Meade as a sexy and exciting woman. The unexpected realization made him slightly uncomfortable.

"Thanks for the compliment, I needed that," she said. A blush tinted her cheeks. "Anyway, eventually I got tired of playing Eliza Doolittle to Brad's Professor Higgins. We had a big fight about it after Thanksgiving break, and, well, you know the rest. Brad's phoned a couple of times since, but what's the point? There's no way we'll ever be on an equal footing."

"He sounds like a jerk. You were right to give him the heave-ho." Cole studied her face, watching the candlelight caress her throat and mouth. He touched his tie and cleared his throat. "So. What are your plans after graduation?"

The evening had turned into an enormous surprise. When Pam first mentioned that she wanted him to take Bailey out for New Year's Eve, Cole had groaned and tried to beg off. The idea had impressed him as a waste of time. Plus, he had received several other invitations that sounded infinitely more appealing than entertaining Pam's lonely roommate. He had anticipated long silences, had imagined himself struggling to make conversation with a personality about as stimulating as vanilla pudding. Not once had he imagined instant chemistry or that he would feel so attracted to Bailey. He hadn't guessed their conversation would snap and spark or that he would listen to her marvelous voice and wonder how it would feel to kiss her.

This last thought was disturbingly disloyal to Pam, and it wasn't his only disloyal thought. Suddenly Cole wondered how things might have turned out if he had met Bailey first.

"I'd like to find a position in publishing," Bailey answered. "That's my dream." It took Cole a moment to recall what they had been talking about.

"A crusading newspaper woman?" he asked, smiling. With that low husky voice, everything she said sounded sexy.

"What's wrong with that?"

"Now don't go prickly again. I'm in favor of crusading newspaper women. I'm the guy who supports free toilets in the women's johns. Remember?"

Her eyes narrowed—cornflower blue now—then she relaxed. And he could have sworn she was staring at his mouth as if it fascinated her, before she bit her lip and looked away. "Actually I'm more interested in publishing books. I'd like to edit serious books, the kind of books that have the potential to alter the world." In a lightning change of mood, she grinned. "A modest little dream, but my own."

He laughed. "Modest indeed. Why do you aspire to be an editor instead of a publisher? Think big, Kansas. Aim high."

She shook her head. "No way. I'm not falling into that trap. I set goals I have a prayer of achieving."

"Where does the next Brad the Rat fit into this dream of modest success?"

"Eventually I'll find the right Brad the Rat." She met his eyes, then quickly looked away before she spread her hands. "I want a successful career and a wonderful husband and a house full of terrific kids. Especially kids. I want lots and lots of children. Actually," she said brightly, "I want it all."

"Good for you. The world's waiting for you to grab it."

She grinned. "I'm not planning an assault on the whole world. I'll be satisfied with one small corner that I can call my own." She tilted her head. "How about you? What will you do after graduation? Aside from marrying Pam, I mean."

"I've already received a couple of offers from Wall Street."

Bailey sniffed and raised her eyebrows. "The crass pursuit of financial gain."

"Absolutely." He grinned at her. "Where else can a Wyoming cowboy get rich quick? I want to be a millionaire before I'm thirty, thirty-five at the outside. That's my dream."

A blend of admiration and resistance widened her eyes. She flicked another glance at his mouth. "That's a pretty ambitious goal for a guy from a wide spot in Wyoming, isn't it?"

"Come on, Kansas. That's small-town thinking. You and I can do anything or be anything that anyone else can do or be."

"A Wall Street whiz kid will certainly please Pam's family, but is that what you really want? What about the old Tarcher homestead?" Leaning forward, Bailey argued for tending the land, for responsible environmental care, for family legacies. She argued against materialism and stressed the importance of preserving traditional values.

"I agree with a lot of what you're saying. But unfortunately, overseeing the Tarcher holdings means doing it in Wyoming," he said when she finished speaking. "Like you,

I want something bigger, better, and more than Wyoming has to offer.''

"Maybe my own conflicts are showing." Frowning, she pulled her napkin through her fingers. "But there is a tug, isn't there? You and I grew up with open spaces, with land and sky and breathing room, with a strong sense of community." She gave him a lopsided smile. "Those items are in short supply here in the East. Sometimes I miss them. Maybe you do, too."

It was impossible not to contrast Bailey's remarks with Pam's. Not once had it occurred to Pam that Cole's decision to build a career on Wall Street might conflict with his father's wishes or his own loyalties. Or that the decision might have been difficult to make. But Bailey keyed immediately on his doubts and conflicts. She understood the almost visceral appeal of land and what it represented to farmers and ranchers. It wasn't easy to break free of tradition and choose a different path.

They stared at each other across the table, knowing they had connected in some profound, hard-to-define way. They didn't agree on several issues, but they understood each other on a level not usually achieved on such short acquaintance.

A silence opened and stretched, unnoticed by either of them. They continued to study each other, finding pleasure and excitement in each other's presence. It was amazing to them both that they hadn't noticed each other before.

"I can't believe this," Bailey whispered.

"Can't believe what?" But he understood what she was saying and what she was feeling. He saw it in her wonderful blue eyes, felt an answering reverberation in the pit of his stomach.

Color flared in her cheeks and she smiled to lighten a moment that had become intense. "That you're a Scorpio." It was the first thing that came to her mind, and more comfortable to state than the truth. The truth was Bailey looked at him and felt that she couldn't breathe. When he spoke, she stared at his sexy mouth and forgot what he was saying.

"Ah yes, great sex," he said lightly, trying to follow her lead.

But it was a mistake. The issue of sex was suddenly there between them, as if it hadn't been before. Speculation leapt into their eyes, unwanted and unanticipated and producing feelings of guilt on both sides. But it was there, and the curiosity was strong. At some point a slow fire had ignited. Now the flames inched higher.

Bailey gave him a helpless, troubled look, then touched her fingertips to her forehead. "What were we talking about?" she asked in a low voice.

"Ranches," Cole said after a moment, still staring at her. He sought for something to say that had nothing to do with sex or the color of her eyes or the way her husky voice made him think of moonlight and sultry nights. But he came up blank.

"Less than five minutes to go!" someone shouted. Smiling waiters passed among the tables, handing out noisemakers and paper hats, serving trays of foaming champagne.

"Can you believe it's midnight already!" Bailey dropped her gaze and turned a silver-and-red paper hat between her hands. "Why don't they make these things in an adult size? They don't even fit kids."

"The idea is to look silly." Cole snapped his hat onto his head and smiled at her. "See?"

"Where does it say we have to start the new year looking like goofballs? Well, okay, if you're going to wear yours." After putting on the hat and adjusting the rubber band, she made a resigned face into the mirror behind the table. "Oh, argh."

Then they both stood beside the table as the houselights flickered and another waiter hastily passed out small bags of confetti. Bailey looked up at him and bit her lip, intensely aware of his closeness and his after-shave, and a fluttering tension that drew her nerves tight. The maitre d' moved to the front of the room holding a large-faced clock. "Four," he shouted. The crowd took up the chant. "Three...two...one! Happy New Year!" Confetti exploded into the air.

Cole turned to her, looked down into her thick-lashed eyes, and touched the rim of his champagne glass to hers as brightly colored streamers showered around them. "Happy New Year, Bailey Meade."

"Happy New Year, Cole Tarcher."

Bending forward, he placed a chaste kiss on her lips. And felt as if he'd been rocked by lightning. The touch of her soft yielding lips ignited an explosion that consumed his body with sudden fierce desire. Bailey stared up at him with a stunned expression as if she, too, suddenly found herself in the grip of something powerful and urgent.

Oblivious to the celebration erupting around them, they gazed into each other's eyes, assessing, questioning, unaware of the raucous whir of noisemakers and the shouts and clouds of confetti spilling from the ceiling. Cole felt as if he couldn't breathe. Bailey's eyes had darkened almost to navy, and the corners of her lips trembled.

He removed the champagne from her hand and placed both glasses on the table. Then he wrapped his arms around her waist, felt her hands circle his shoulders and slide around his neck. She had the kind of eyes a man could drown in; her body was warm and pliant against his, trembling slightly. For a long moment he gazed into her magnificent eyes, then he kissed her again. This time their kiss was not chaste, but deliberate and exploratory.

He held her firmly against his body, felt her hands in his hair, on the back of his neck. Her lips opened beneath his and he tasted the exciting sweetness of her, felt her returning his kiss with a helpless eagerness that matched his own.

When they broke apart, they stood close together, fighting to catch their breath, not moving but staring at each other with new recognition, new thoughts. They were both as breathless and as shaken as if they had just made love instead of sharing a kiss.

Almost at the same instant, they swiftly stepped backward, pretending not to notice the brush of hands as they hastily retrieved their champagne glasses.

"To Pam," Bailey said in a breathless whisper, raising her glass. Her cheeks were fiery red and she didn't look at him.

"We wish she was here." Cole spoke with difficulty, still staring at her lips. The excitement of her kiss lingered on his mouth. He continued to feel her yielding body against his torso and thighs, fitting against him as if they were matching pieces of a jigsaw puzzle. And he experienced the same confusion that he saw mirrored in Bailey's troubled eyes when she glanced up at him, then quickly looked away again.

"When will Pam return from Monaco?" she asked quietly.

"The day after tomorrow." Undoubtedly Bailey knew this. But Cole was grateful for the question. Right now, he needed to be reminded of Pam, and the realization was disturbing.

"Pam's a wonderful girl," Bailey said.

"The best," he agreed, frowning. "None better."

"The problem with New Year's Eve," she said after an awkward pause, the first such awkwardness they had experienced, "is that everything after midnight seems anti-climactic."

Cole agreed. But he didn't feel ready for the evening to end. "What would you have done at this point if you were still seeing Brad the Rat?"

"I don't know. I guess we would have gone back to the apartment and put on a stack of Doobie Brothers or Billy

Joel records.'' She looked into her champagne glass. ''That is, if you and Pam hadn't already staked out the apartment.''

Raising a hand, Cole caught their waiter's eye and signaled for the check. ''Then that's what we'll do. Unless you're tired or would rather—''

He almost hoped she would offer an excuse and decline. They were playing with fire, and he sensed Bailey knew it, too. But even knowing this was a dangerous situation, he couldn't bring himself to say goodbye to her. Not yet.

''I'd like that,'' she said finally, speaking slowly as if she, too, acted against her better judgment. She held his gaze, then bent for her purse and the paper sack containing the astrology booklets. When she straightened, she drew a long breath and gave him the most artificial smile he had ever seen. ''Tell me about Pam. How did the two of you meet?''

THE APARTMENT WAS SMALL, cozy and reassuringly cluttered with reminders of Pam. Snow melted down the dark windows above the comfortable hiss of the radiators. A braided rug cushioned the chill hovering along the floorboards.

After a brief hesitation, Bailey opened the bottle of French brandy she had been saving for graduation day, then she went into her bedroom and changed into a pair of jeans and a green sweatshirt, a safe unsexy outfit that she hoped would calm her thoughts. And his. When she returned to the living room, wrapping her hair into a ponytail, Cole had thrown off his tie and rolled up his shirt-sleeves.

He gestured to the jelly jars holding her special brandy before he returned to his inspection of album titles. ''Those are the only glasses I could find.''

''We have some decent crystal for special occasions, but it's stored in the lockers downstairs.''

''I like jelly jars. They feel like home.'' He winked at her. ''Don't tell Pam I said that.''

If Bailey had imagined for a moment that she would invite Cole back to the apartment, she would have dug out the crystal. And she would have run a dust rag over the apartment. Sweeping aside a pile of books, she settled into the corner of a faded chintz sofa. "Find anything you like?"

They glanced at each other, suddenly aware of double meanings. Then Cole smiled. "A couple of great Waylon Jennings cuts," he said. "Okay with you?"

"Perfect."

He stacked the stereo, then sat on the floor with his back against a garage-sale chair. For a long moment they didn't speak, gazing at each other with contemplative expressions, thinking about the kiss in Tante Maison's. And wondering. Then they both spoke at once, laughed and began again, talking about everything except a kiss that had been explosive and wildly exciting—although that kiss was uppermost in each of their minds.

They talked about music instead, compared classes, and argued politics, before drifting into more personal areas.

A subtle difference ran like an undertow beneath the currents of conversation. Unlike earlier in the evening, now they searched for differences rather than similarities. And they found them. Bailey hated crowds; Cole found crowds exhilarating. She wanted to save the world; he wanted to own it. She was not motivated by money; he was. She hoped to have it all; he expected to have it all. Cole was a risk taker, a Mississippi gambler born into the wrong age; Bailey tended to play it safe, gambling wasn't her forte.

"Life is a gamble," Cole insisted. "It's a giant toss of the dice, and each roll is more exciting than the last."

"Not my life," Bailey disagreed. "I would hate to live like that. I need stability. Predictability. An anchor that's always there and doesn't shift."

"This from the crusader?" he teased, raising an eyebrow.

"I know, it doesn't fit." Smiling, she nodded toward the astrology booklets. "But remember the Gemini duality? We can want two opposing things at the same time. I want to change the world, yes. But I don't want *my* world to change too much."

Mention of the astrology booklets made them both think of great sex and a short silence ensued. Cole fiddled with the stereo, and Bailey was glad when he turned aside and she didn't have to see his sexy mouth and white, white teeth.

"I can't wait for my real life to begin," Bailey said when he sat back down. She pulled her legs up and looked at him over the tops of her knees. "Does it ever seem to you like there will always be one more class to take, one more exam to pass, one more paper to write? That we're never going to get to our real lives?"

"One more hill to climb? But that's what life is all about."

Bailey looked at him. "What if we reach the top of the hill then discover we made a mistake? What if our real life isn't as wonderful as we think it's going to be?"

He studied her expression. When he spoke again, his voice was gentle. "Are you afraid to go out into the real world, Kansas?"

They had switched to coffee an hour ago and Bailey poured another cup before she answered. "Sometimes I'm scared to death of the big world out there," she admitted in a low voice. "Other times I feel as if I can't wait to finally be on my own, to get on with my real life." She couldn't believe she was confiding this. She hadn't even discussed these feelings with Pam. "I have so many dreams, and right now I don't see any obstacles to having everything I want out of life."

"But?"

"But I see other people, like my parents maybe, and I know they had dreams once, too. But somewhere along the years, life got in the way." She frowned into her coffee cup.

"I'm afraid that could happen to me, too. Maybe there's a rule we don't know about that says no one gets to have it all."

"I don't believe that. If the first job doesn't work out, you find another, better job. If you marry the wrong person, you get a divorce and start over. You keep trying, you keep searching."

"I don't believe in divorce," she said. "My parents got a divorce when I was ten. It's confusing as hell to grow up in a small town with two sets of parents living a few blocks apart. I'm never going to get a divorce." A shudder passed down her spine. "I'm not going to do that to my children."

Cole was silent for a minute. "I'm sorry that happened to you, but people make mistakes. Divorce is a way to correct the mistake." Standing, he stretched and looked at the pearly dawn glowing against the windowpanes. On the stereo behind him Johnny Cash sang of trains and rain and broken hearts.

Cole spoke about his own growing-up years, and occasionally an anecdote engaged his full attention. More often he found his mind wandering, focused on Bailey. She listened and she understood the tug between his father and himself about the ranch. He felt as if he could have talked to her forever and it still wouldn't be long enough.

Their eyes met across the room and more than anything in the world he suddenly wanted to take her into his arms. He wanted to hold her and caress her and tell her what it meant to him to be able to talk about these things with someone who understood. He wanted to carry her into the bedroom and discover if their differences were as exciting there as in other areas. He wanted to know what she thought about God and socialism and quiche and ants and Paris. He wanted to know what books she read and what she dreamed about at night. He wanted to taste her mouth and drink a hundred kisses from her lips. He wanted to hear her call his name in that deep whiskey voice that sent a thrill down his spine.

"Oh God," she whispered, returning his stare. She wet her lips in a nervous gesture, and her hands made a fluttering motion. "We're in trouble here."

"Then you feel it, too?" Knots ran up his jaw.

"I feel like we've compressed five years into this night. I feel as if I've known you all of my life." She slowly stood from the sofa. "Right now I'm confused and shaky inside, as if I'd shatter if you touched me. I don't know what's happening here, but I know you scare the hell out of me, Cole Tarcher."

A man who could make her forget Brad the Rat so totally and who could make her consider betraying her roommate's trust was a dangerous man. Bailey had guessed that the moment she slid into his pickup, and now she knew it for a certainty. She couldn't look at him without remembering his lips on hers, without feeling a sudden rush of blood to her head. At this moment she couldn't remember what they had talked about all these hours. Whatever it was, it hadn't been as important as just being together.

"You scare the hell out of me, too, Bailey Meade," Cole said in a husky voice. "I've never met anyone like you."

They faced each other across the room, feeling a magnetic swell of attraction, staring helplessly at each other in the salmon glow of dawn. And both of them were aware the bedrooms were but a few short steps away.

"It wouldn't be right," Bailey said in a whisper. She knew what he was thinking, because the same thoughts burned in her mind, too. All night the tension between them had been winding tighter and tighter. Each glance, each accidental brush of fingertips, each movement had assumed an importance and an urgency that left her with trembling hands and feeling dizzy and breathless.

"No, it wouldn't be right," Cole said slowly, frowning, unable to look away from her. "We'd regret it," he added, wondering if that was true.

Her shoulders lifted, and she expelled a long breath. "Wow." Finally, reluctantly, Bailey tore her gaze away from him and pressed her fingertips to her cheeks. "Look, are you hungry? I think...I think we should get out of here."

"There's a twenty-four-hour place about three blocks from here called—"

"Mama Wilson's café. I know it."

But neither of them moved. They continued to stare at each other across the old lacquered trunk that served as a coffee table as if they knew this chance would not come again and they were reluctant to walk away from it. Five minutes might have passed, or an eon, and during that time the tension snapped and flashed between them, promising magic. Finally Bailey swallowed hard, gave her head a shake and forced herself to turn aside.

"I'll get my parka," she said. It was difficult to speak in a normal tone. "Don't forget your tie. And your astrology book."

At the door they were careful to stand well apart, but they continued to respond to the powerful electricity crackling between them and knew the danger still existed. A single touch was all that was required to ignite an explosive passion that good intentions could not have withstood.

"Pam asked me to be in your wedding," Bailey said abruptly, stepping backward and away from him. She looked at the floor.

Cole paused with his hand on the doorknob. His gaze was almost black. "Bailey, something happened here tonight. No, let me say this." In the dim opalescent light he watched her large troubled eyes turn up to him. "You're important to me, Bailey Meade. I like you. A lot. We started a friendship tonight that's going to last for the rest of our lives. That's a promise.''

"It's not going to be easy," she said slowly, staring at his mouth. "I'm not sure Pam would understand. I'm not sure *I* understand." Her gaze lifted to his eyes. "But you're important to me, too. And I like you. A lot."

He managed a smile, trying to ease the tension. "Come on, Kansas, I'll race you to Mama Wilson's."

Bailey led the way outside, then stopped and drew in a breath of delight. Mounds of powdery snow glowed salmon and lavender in the hazy light. The air was sharp and cold. A woman bundled like an Eskimo walked a terrier on the far side of the street, otherwise the block was deserted, magical in the pastel glow.

"Oh, Cole," Bailey breathed. "What a perfect way to begin the new year! Isn't this wonderful?"

"Wonderful," he agreed, smiling at her bright eyes and blooming cheeks.

They fell into step together, resonating to the powerful awareness flashing between them, listening to their shoes squeak against the new snow. Before they reached the corner and the streetlight, Bailey drew a deep breath, then she darted to one side and scooped up a handful of snow. With a shout, she threw it at him, then bent to scoop up another snowball.

"What was that for?" Cole asked, wiping the snow from his face.

"To cool you off, you sex-crazed Scorpio!" She grinned at him and hurled another snowball, which he dodged. "I know what you were thinking back there!"

Laughing, he ducked the next snowball and lunged forward to tackle her. When he had her on the ground, he rubbed a handful of snow across her lips. "You were thinking it, too, don't tell me you weren't."

"No I wasn't!" Rolling out from under him, she hurled snowballs at him as fast as she could pack them. "You're the ugliest, most boring man I've ever met!" She grinned and aimed for his crotch. And missed. "You don't turn me on at all!"

"Good, because you remind me of my sister. I'd rather write a doctoral thesis than make love to a plain girl like you!" Laughing, he chased her around a maple trunk, managed to push a snowball down the collar of her coat before she shrieked and twisted away.

Finally, gasping for breath, covered with snow and laughing, they staggered to the stoplight. But they were friends again. The attraction that sparked so powerfully between them receded to a safe corner. When Cole bowed and offered her his arm, she curtsied and took it. They were still grinning when they peered through the steamy windows of Mama Wilson's, then went inside.

Over a huge breakfast they argued about socialism, longed for Paris, and talked about the books they had read recently.

"Ants?" Bailey repeated, staring at him over her coffee cup. "You want to know how I feel about *ants?"* She burst into fresh laughter.

He smiled and spread his hands. "Is there anything else we haven't discussed?"

"Oh, Cole," she said finally, looking at him with soft eyes. "I've loved every minute of this evening. Thank you. Pam is a lucky girl."

He reached past the maple syrup to squeeze her hand. "I'm already envying the safe comfortable dullard who is going to snap you up."

Bailey shook her head when the waitress would have refilled her coffee cup, and she stifled a yawn. It was 1980, and it was time to go. Traffic had thickened outside the fogged windows of the café. A pale winter sun glowed behind a high thin haze.

They returned to the apartment in comfortable silence and stopped beside Cole's pickup. Cole pushed his hands into his pockets and leaned against the door, smiling at her.

"When's the next pay toilet protest?"

Bailey made a half circle in the snow with the toe of her boot. "Maybe the week after next. Have you decided which offer you'll accept? Chase Manhattan sounds good."

"I'm leaning toward Drexel. Or maybe First Guarantee Trust."

They had already asked these questions, had already given these answers. Cole glanced at his watch; Bailey looked up at the windows of her apartment.

"Well," they both said at the same moment, then grinned.

"Thanks again," Bailey said in her low husky voice. "It was wonderful."

Cole clasped her hand. "I hope 1980 is everything you want it to be. I hope you find a fabulous job in publishing and set New York City on its ear."

"I wish you and Pam every happiness. I know you're going to take Wall Street by storm."

They continued to hold hands, standing close to each other and smiling farewell. Bailey didn't move when he finally opened the door of the pickup and slid inside. The engine coughed, then took hold, but Cole didn't reach for the gear shift. He looked at her through the windshield as if memorizing her face, then rolled down his window.

"If I wasn't engaged to Pam . . ."

"Forget it," Bailey said in an unsteady voice. She tried to smile. "We bring out the small town in each other, cowboy. Together we wouldn't stand a chance of fitting in. I represent everything you're trying to escape, dummy. And that's what you are to me. Don't you realize that?"

"Bright women are a pain in the butt." He grinned at her.

"So I've been told. Goodbye, friend."

"I'll see you in a couple of days."

"I know."

She also knew it wouldn't be the same. To spare Pam any discomfort they would return to the casual relationship they had shared before tonight. They would pass each other in the hall outside the apartment and say hello in bright artificial voices. Cole would exchange a few words with her when he arrived to pick Pam up or when he brought Pam home. Bailey would listen to Pam talk about him and feel her loyalties divide in two.

Right now she wished with all her heart that she had met Cole before Pam had. Cole Tarcher made her forget about safe and comfortable and think about the thrill of roller coaster rides. That was the danger of men like Cole.

He blew her a kiss, waved, and coaxed the pickup into the street. Bailey stood on the curb and watched until his taillights turned toward Charles Street.

"Happy New Year," she whispered.

It was going to be a great year, one of the most significant years of her life. She would graduate in June, and afterward her real life would begin. She had been working toward this year and anticipating it for as long as she could remember.

So why did she feel so sad?

Chapter Three

New Year's Eve, 1983

Ordinarily Cole enjoyed the excitement generated by large crowds. But the tens of thousands of revelers packed into Times Square waiting for the ball to drop were wild and loud enough to make him wish for saner surroundings. The icy drizzle pelting the back of his neck didn't help, either. Nor did it improve his spirits to realize he didn't have a prayer of finding the Excaliber executives. Half an hour ago the Excaliber people had been swept away in the crowd.

Rising on his toes, Cole shielded his eyes from the drizzle and scanned the thousands upon thousands of shouting people jamming Times Square. It was hopeless. The odds of finding the Excaliber executives were one in a million. The odds of locating any familiar face in the midst of this chaos were probably—

He did a double take and leaned forward, squinting against the drizzle for a better view of a profile he suddenly spotted and thought he recognized. "I'll be damned." Waving a hand, he shouted. "Bailey! Bailey Meade!"

Though they stood only a few yards apart, there was no possibility that she could hear him. The intense noise was deafening, a rising wave that rolled over the massive crowd and swelled as the big ball glowed and flashed and began its descent. Cole's shout was drowned in an ocean of sound.

Shoving forward, holding Bailey in sight, Cole struggled to reach her through the tightly packed bodies. Her hair was shorter than he remembered, curling in wet tendrils beneath the assault of the cold drizzle. Smudges of mascara lay beneath her uncomfortable gaze. Her pale expression suggested the exuberant crowd made her intensely uneasy, and he wondered why she was here. But he was glad she was.

When he had crowded, pushed and bullied his way to her side, Cole clasped her arm and grinned when she turned an annoyed expression toward him. Then a delighted smile danced across her face and he saw her lips form his name before she embraced him. He inhaled the scent of a musky perfume and felt her warm breath on his cheek as she shouted near his ear.

"I can't believe it's you!" Leaning back, smiling up at him, she touched her gloved fingertips to his face. "You look wonderful. How are you? You won't believe this, but I was just thinking about you!"

Unable to stop grinning, he clasped her shoulders and looked down at her, thinking she was more beautiful than he remembered. "I've thought about you more times than you would probably believe." Which was an understatement, if anything.

Forgetting the sea of people tossing and shouting around them, they held hands and studied each other's smiles, looking for changes, looking for the reassurance of those things that had not changed. When Cole's gaze dropped to her mouth, Bailey gave herself a little shake as if returning to the present.

She shouted up at him. "I want you to meet my fiancé, Brendan Hanson." Leaning away from him, she scanned the people packed around them, then hurriedly rose on tiptoe and tried to peer over the sea of bobbing heads. "Oh, no! He's vanished!"

The crowd surged forward with an excited roar, beginning the chant, and if Cole hadn't gripped her hands tightly, they would have been swept apart.

A quarter of a million voices screamed. "Four...three!"

Bailey looked at him with those magnificent long-lashed, aquamarine eyes and shrugged at the futility of trying to speak, then she grinned. Abandoning any effort to talk, they faced each other, holding hands, and joined the countdown to 1983.

"Two...one...Happy New Year!"

Cole had believed the noise couldn't intensify, but it did. Whistles blew, horns honked, noisemakers buzzed and everyone screamed. Bailey covered her ears and laughed at the madness exploding around them. She mouthed the words "Happy New Year," and so did he. An elbow knocked her forward into his arms, and he kissed her.

He intended the kiss to be gentle and casual, and so it was when his lips first touched hers. But someone shoved Bailey up against his body and he felt an instant flash of igniting chemistry. Startled, he gazed into her surprised eyes and understood she, too, had experienced the same explosive reaction. As they couldn't move anyway, Cole closed his arms around her waist and held her tightly against his body. Curiosity as intense as his own flamed in Bailey's gaze as he surrendered to a sense of unfinished business and lowered his head to kiss her again. Instantly he felt her response, as immediate and powerful as his own. Standing in the middle of Times Square, unable to move, they experienced the burst of passion they had kept in careful check three years ago. When Cole released her, he saw his kisses had shaken her as badly as they had shaken him.

For a long moment they stared at each other, then Cole caught her hand in a firm grip. "Let's get the hell out of here," he shouted, his voice hoarse.

She shook her head as if to clear away the confusion in her eyes, then she lifted on tiptoe, straining to see over the people shouting and surging around them. "Brendan," she mouthed, giving Cole an apologetic look. Crimson burned on her damp cheeks.

He put his lips close to her ear and yelled. "Brendan is a big boy, he can take care of himself. You and I have some catching up to do."

Indecision flared in her gaze. Then she scanned the crowd again before she shrugged, laughed and nodded. Feeling happier than he had all night, Cole tightened his grip on her gloved hand and fought toward the edge of the madness. When they emerged, feeling battered and bruised but triumphant, he made a beeline toward the nearest all-night coffee shop and ushered Bailey into the crowd jamming the overheated interior. After a short wait they slipped into a two-person booth practically on the laps of the people trying to vacate it.

"I can't believe I found you!" Cole stared at her in delight. "I thought you hated crowds."

"Tonight was Brendan's idea. He says everyone should experience one New Year's Eve in Times Square. Once in your life, then never again," Bailey explained, smiling. "I'm half-frozen and I think I've gone deaf." After digging in her purse, she produced a packet of Kleenex, handed him one, and they both mopped the drizzle from their faces and throats. She pushed at a tangle of wet curls then shrugged at the hopelessness of the task and grinned at him. "Hi, cowboy," she said in that marvelous whiskey voice.

"Hi, Kansas."

She was beautiful. Maybe it was the shorter hairstyle or the thinned eyebrows—whatever it was, Bailey no longer looked like a student. Even damp and cold she was as polished in appearance as the female executives at First Guarantee Trust. Except Cole didn't recall any female executives of his acquaintance who could have endured two hours of cold and drizzle and emerge looking as great as Bailey

Meade. The shorter hairstyle emphasized terrific cheekbones and her flawless skin. Her smile lighted up the booth.

"This is unbelievable running into you again," she said after shrugging out of her coat. "It's so good to see you. I've thought about you a hundred times and wished we'd kept in touch."

"I've thought about you, too. I tried to find you in the phone book, but you aren't listed."

For a long moment they didn't speak. They held hands across the sticky table and grinned at each other, enjoying the moment.

Bailey decided Cole was more handsome than she remembered, if that was possible. She remembered thinking Cole looked like a movie star, and he still did. With those chiseled features and that sexy mouth, he should have been in film. She suspected he would only get better-looking as the years unfolded. The intriguing lines crinkling his dark eyes and framing his mouth would deepen. A feathering of silver would distinguish his temples. She would have bet everything she owned that all the women he knew were wildly in love with him.

"That's a Savile Row suit, isn't it?" she inquired after they pulled apart to order coffee along with the free champagne the café was offering. "I'd say you're well on your way to wrestling Wall Street into submission."

He laughed and toasted her with the plastic cup of champagne. "I'm making progress. I've been promoted into Mergers and Acquisitions. That's where the action is—the eighties are shaping up as the takeover decade. It's an exciting time to be in investment banking. And you wouldn't believe the money involved. The commissions are almost obscene."

"They must be if you can say that," she teased.

"Tell me about you. Where are you working? What's your telephone number? What's going on in your real life?"

She laughed her wonderful throaty laugh and glanced over her shoulder. "I'm sorry we lost Brendan. Right now he's the biggest part of my real life. I'm eager for you to meet him."

Genuine affection lighted Cole's smile. "You're still changing the subject midsentence." He winked. "I'm not sorry we lost Brendan the Rat. His loss is my gain."

"We agreed on a backup plan in case we were separated. We'll meet later at a party we're invited to." Narrowing her eyes, she gave him a look of exaggerated severity. "And he isn't Brendan the Rat. He's Brendan the Terrific. Look."

Extending her hand, she wiggled her ring finger, showing off a gorgeous engagement ring. The stunning aquamarine surrounded by diamonds was as brilliant as her jeweled eyes.

"It appears Brendan the Rat is not only besotted by your charms but he's as wealthy as Midas. You can rave about him in a minute, but first I want to know everything you've been doing since I saw you last. Besides saving baby seals and remembering Love Canal," he said, smiling at the buttons on the lapel of the coat she had thrown over the back of the booth. "The last I heard of you was from Pam, about two weeks before we called off the wedding. She mentioned you were interviewing publishing houses."

Bailey's expression sobered. "I'm sorry things didn't work out for you and Pam."

"It would have been a mistake." He met her eyes. "But that's ancient history. So tell me—which publishing house was lucky enough to hire you? Are you editing earthshaking books?" He couldn't take his eyes off of her. "God, you look great!"

She laughed and the people standing in the aisles waiting for a table smiled down at her. She had that kind of laugh, the kind of spontaneous warmth that drew people into sharing her delight and pleasure.

"I lasted six months at Random House. Are you sure you want to hear this sordid tale?"

"Every word," he insisted.

"As my second project I was assigned to work on Senator Thurston Mahoney's book, *On The Floor,* but I was so far down the chain that no one would ever have known I was part of the project. I got the scut work, the stuff no one else wanted to do." She rolled her expressive eyes. "You can spin your wheels for *years* in publishing before you get anywhere. You wouldn't believe it. Anyway, one day the senior editor was supposed to meet Senator Mahoney for lunch, but she broke her ankle on the way into the city. By the time she could reach a phone, all the other editors were out or were already committed for lunch. I was the only one left."

Cole smiled. "I can see this coming. You had lunch with the senator and impressed the hell out of him. I haven't forgotten—you Geminis can charm the socks off any man."

She laughed again, pleased by the compliment. "The senior editor told me to show up at 21, praise the book to the sky, pay the bill and don't screw up. As it turned out the senator and I hit it off immediately. We had lunch, talked through the entire afternoon, had dinner and finally left 21 about midnight. By that time Senator Mahoney had offered me a job on his staff and I accepted."

Cole tilted his head and studied her flushed cheeks and the excitement sparkling in her eyes. "Then you moved to Washington, D.C.? No wonder I couldn't find you."

"Oh, Cole, I just love it! Every day is exciting and different. Sometimes I answer the phones, sometimes I answer letters from the senator's constituents. Some days I review bills or write memos. Some days I sit in on debates and take notes for the senator. Next month I'll start editing a bimonthly newsletter. It's so exciting to be part of making the world a little better!"

"That's a matter of opinion," he commented wryly. "Some people wouldn't agree that more government makes the world better. If I remember correctly, you used to be one of them."

He wondered if she knew how her eyes lighted and her expression grew radiant when she talked about something that excited her. It seemed to him that she cast off sparks of excitement as she talked. He had to believe that every man in the restaurant envied him. But he couldn't look away from her long enough to judge.

"You wouldn't say that if I had time to explain all the bills our office is working on."

"Careful now, Kansas. Is this the same do-gooder who once castigated me for hypocrisy? So how did the last of the good guys end up defending Washington, D.C., home of the hypocrite? Square that, if you can."

Her eyes sparkled and flashed, and she laughed then threw herself into the argument. More champagne appeared, then more coffee. The crowds began to thin. And Cole couldn't remember when he'd enjoyed himself more. They argued the hypocrisy of Washington versus the ethics of Wall Street, their words rushing and tumbling, ideas sparking between them.

"So when are you going to run for Congress?" he asked, grinning.

She blinked then spread her hands and laughed. "There aren't any limits with you, are there? I just told you how much I love my job, but you're pushing me out of it and onward and upward. Take my word for it, I'm happy where I am. I'll leave the lofty ambition to guys like you."

"Don't you want to know how far you could go if you tried? Or are you still intimidated by the big-city slickers?"

"Good God," she said suddenly, pushing back her sleeve to stare at her watch. Her engagement ring winked in the bright café lights. "Look at the time! Brendan will be

wondering what happened to me." Raising her head, she
gazed at him, biting her lip. "Look, are you doing anything? If you don't have plans to catch up with the Excaliber executives, come with me. I'm long overdue at a party
on the East Side, very, very posh." She grinned. "I really
do want you to meet Brendan. You'll like him."

"Honestly?"

"Probably not," she admitted. "But make an effort for
my sake. Okay?"

Good sense warned him to decline her invitation. But his
delight in finding her again urged him to accept. It might
be a long while before he saw her again. "All right, you're
on. Someone has to check out this guy and make sure he's
good enough for you. It's a dirty job, but someone has to
do it." He sighed heavily and grinned at the face she made.
"As one of your most devoted friends, I accept the call to
duty."

Smiling, Bailey allowed him to assist her on with her
coat. And she pretended she didn't feel a thrill shiver down
her spine when Cole's hands brushed her shoulders. At
some point during the last hour and a half, she had reluctantly admitted a powerful attraction still sparkled between herself and Cole Tarcher. Three years had changed
nothing on that count. She gazed at his sexy mouth and remembered those crazy kisses in Times Square, and her
stomach tightened and she suddenly felt overly warm.

But she also accepted that Fate knew best. And this time
Fate had arranged that she was engaged. Also, she was
three years older and two years smarter than the last time
she and Cole had reacted to the chemistry igniting between
them. She was mature enough to understand that a powerful physical attraction was not enough on which to base
a relationship. Moreover, Cole Tarcher still scared the hell
out of her. Or rather, he would have if the possibility for
anything more than friendship had existed.

Cole was one of the wheelers and dealers, the princes of commerce. He tossed out multimillion-dollar figures the way she talked about loose change. When Bailey joked about fitting into a posh party on the East Side, it truly had been a joke because Cole Tarcher would easily blend into that milieu. No traces of Wyoming were apparent in his elegantly tailored suit or his air of self-assurance. The rough edges were gone.

When he hailed a cab in front of the café, he did so with the aggressive carelessness reminiscent of a born New Yorker, with the authority of a man who knew where he was going and possessed the innate authority to impose his view on others. It didn't surprise Bailey that the cabbie passed another couple and stopped for them. Cole Tarcher was evolving into that kind of man. Inside the taxi, she slid a look in his direction and experienced a quick bittersweet flash of regret. Though she understood his desire to obliterate his small-town background—because she felt it, too—there was something a tiny bit sad about his success in doing so. As there was in her own.

"How's your family?" she asked after a minute.

"My dad had a minor stroke before Thanksgiving, but he's doing fine now. My sister, Beth, got married last spring. She and Harlan are living on the ranch, helping out. Now—" he dropped an arm around her shoulders and peered into her face "—tell me everything about Brendan the Rat."

She sighed and let her head fall back against his arm. "You're determined to dislike him, aren't you? You aren't even going to try to like him. And he's wonderful, Cole, really."

"Let's have the whole story. You met him where?"

"At an embassy party in D.C." She narrowed her eyes. "Brendan is a successful attorney. He's thirty, has never been married, had an ancestor who helped settle Long Island." She ignored Cole's groan. "He's exactly the man I hoped to find."

Cole grinned down at her with teasing eyes. "Let me guess. He's safe, comfortable and dull as toast. He probably has a routine you can set your watch by. He's never committed an impulsive act in his entire life."

A rush of pink colored her cheeks. "He's solid and dependable. A Rock of Gibraltar."

"Let's see, corporate law, right? Criminal law would be too stimulating."

"Very funny. Brendan wants children as much as I do, and the sooner the better. In a year or two we'll move back to the New York area and he'll accept a partnership in his father's firm." She turned the aquamarine on her finger. "Cole, be happy for me. I love Brendan. All right, he's not like you. He's not wildly ambitious, and he doesn't feel a need to set the world on fire. Brendan is never going to climb a mountain just because it's there. But that's part of why I love him. He's my anchor."

"Poor little Gemini," Cole said softly, brushing a curl back from her cheek. "You really do want it all. You want the exciting chaotic life you thrive on in Senator Mahoney's office, and you want a nice safe refuge, too."

"There's never been a divorce in Brendan's family," she said simply.

"I see. Are you looking for guarantees, Kansas?"

"Let's say I like the odds stacked in my favor." She gazed at him, her eyes almost navy in the dim interior of the cab. "I'm not a gambler like you are, cowboy. If I can minimize the risks, I'll do it. Whereas you, every day you hang yourself out on the line, playing with millions of dollars of other people's money, gambling on risks that make me shudder to think about. I don't know how you stand it. Do you push the limits in your personal life, too?" she asked curiously. "Do you drive too fast? Play too hard? Date dangerous women?"

"Dangerous women?" he laughed.

"You know what I mean." She raised an eyebrow. "You're dangerous yourself. You probably attract dangerous women." Interest brimmed in her gaze. "You haven't told me—is there anyone special in your life?"

He leaned across her to open the cab door, then reached for his wallet to pay the driver. "I haven't taken a vow of celibacy if that's what you mean. But sometimes it feels as if I have." He gave her a wry grin. "Getting established on the street requires single-minded determination. Most social events are looked on as opportunities to hustle new clients, not new women."

"Hey, cowboy, this is me you're talking to, remember? Your old friend? The Wyoming-Kansas connection? I can't believe you've been too busy to break a few hearts. Not a sex-crazed Scorpio like you." She stood beneath a striped awning giving him a disbelieving frown that was so utterly Bailey Meade that he laughed as he guided her past the doorman and inside a beautifully luxurious building.

"It's pathètic, isn't it? Here it is, New Year's Eve, the biggest night of the year, and earlier I was squiring clients around town, and now I'm tagging along with some guy's fiancé. Doesn't sound much like a Scorpio, does it?"

"I'm not giving up until you confess everything. Who do you date when you aren't working your brains to the bone?"

"You Geminis can be relentless." He sighed. "I see Marsha Haversham, a client's daughter, more than anyone else." A shrug lifted his topcoat.

"Tell me about her," Bailey insisted as they stepped into the elevator. The interior smelled like whiskey sours and champagne. Confetti layered the carpeted floor.

"It's not a serious relationship."

"Give! I told you everything."

"What can I say? Marsha is . . ."

"Beautiful," Bailey prompted. Cole seemed to fill the elevator, making her acutely aware of his size, the scent of his after-shave, the fact that they were alone. Neither of them had mentioned the wild kisses in Times Square, and Bailey hoped they wouldn't. But she couldn't glance at his mouth without remembering. She swallowed and decided it was urgently important to keep him talking about Marsha.

"Marsha is charming and funny. And spoiled and used to getting her own way," Cole said, smiling. "She loves horses like I do and rides like she was born in a saddle."

Bailey's mouth curved in a smile. "Aha. You managed to find a cowgirl in the midst of the rich and famous!"

"A cowgirl?" He choked on a burst of laughter. "Not on your life. Not unless cowgirls have taken to wearing de la Renta and Gucci. Marsha rides in the show circuit, not on the range."

"What does she do?" Bailey asked as they stepped into a hallway littered with streamers, confetti and squashed paper hats. They followed the noise toward a door opening into the penthouse apartment.

"Do? She has lunch, hosts charity balls, shops…I don't know. She does whatever debutante types do." He shrugged. "This isn't a grand passion." He smiled down at her. "Not like you and Brendan the Rat."

"Stop calling him that, damn it." Lifting an arm, Bailey elbowed him in the ribs. "Behave yourself. I'm already having second thoughts about bringing you with me." She glanced into the darkened room beyond the open door. People were dancing in the foyer; the noise of laughter and conversation and music spilled into the corridor. "Suddenly I have this awful idea that you and Brendan are going to loathe each other on sight. And it would be a lot easier to explain why I'm late if you weren't so damned handsome."

"I already loathe Brendan, meeting him can't make it any worse." Pushing his hands into his pockets, Cole examined the couples dancing inside the door with an innocent expression. "Jealous type is he, old Brendan?"

"Of course not."

"I'd be jealous if you belonged to me."

"First, I don't 'belong' to anyone. I haven't changed *that* much. And second, Brendan is too civilized and too secure to be jealous," she said with a sniff. "Our relationship is thankfully free of theatrics."

"No passion, huh? Too bad." Cole slid a twinkling look toward her exasperated expression. "Does this guy have a pulse?"

She sighed, frowning up at him and trying to see him as Brendan would. Cole was heart-stoppingly handsome. Not the kind of man another man would want his fiancé spending time with no matter how secure he was. "Why couldn't you be ugly and timid? Brendan is going to have difficulty understanding that we're just friends."

"I thought you said he was too civilized to be jealous."

"He is. He's going to skip jealousy and move right to anger. Of course Brendan is too refined to get really angry," she said in a distracted voice, peering through the penthouse door. "He'll get tight-lipped and silent until I have a chance to explain why I'm so late."

"Old Brendan sounds like a swell guy. I can see why you're crazy about him. Let's see . . ." Cole lifted his hand and started ticking down his fingers. "He's unexciting, too rich to be ambitious or show any gumption, too lethargic to be jealous, the silent type, a sulky kind of anger...yep—" he smiled at her "—this bozo is definitely one terrific catch."

"Shut up, Cole, I'm trying to think this out." It was as if the year and a half since they had seen each other had vanished. Their affinity and their friendship was strong enough, warm enough, to pick up as if they had seen each other yesterday. Bailey gave him a speculative look. "You wouldn't consider just saying goodbye now and—"

"Not a chance. I'm here to check out this shyster, and I'm not leaving until I've met him," Cole said cheerfully, his smile widening when she swore under her breath. A more serious note entered his voice. "Look, Bailey. We lost touch once, it's not going to happen again. You and I are friends. Important friends. It's time Brendan knew about me because I'm not going to disappear. I intend to keep in touch with you. With both of you if that's how it has to be."

"That's how it has to be, Cole," she said in a low voice.

"Okay," he said lightly, linking arms with her. "Then let's go in there and find the lucky stiff."

They entered an opulent apartment that was beginning to look a bit worse for the evening's wear. Despite the hour, the noisy penthouse was nearly as crowded as it must have been at midnight. Most of the dancing couples still wore their silly paper hats. More than a few were in advanced stages of happy intoxication. Twists of silk ribbon and gaily colored balloons decorated every room. Holiday greenery and twinkling Christmas lights added to the festive air.

Bailey gave Cole a little push toward a lavish buffet manned by white-coated servants. "See if there's anything left to eat while I find Brendan," she said.

"I do like a girl with strong appetites." His gaze lingered on her mouth. Then he lifted his palms and backed away, smiling. "I'll behave. I swear."

Bailey popped into a nearby powder room and repaired her makeup and did what she could with the tousle of curls that had dried in a wild tangle. She stared at the flush on her cheeks and the sparkle in her eyes, then she sighed. And wondered if Cole Tarcher would always have this effect on her nervous system. Probably. He was that type. Somehow he made their differences seem stimulating and exciting.

But right now she needed to think about Brendan. He was probably worried to death, wondering what had happened to her. After straightening her shoulders, Bailey pushed through the crowded dancers, not finding him, and began to check the various rooms. Eventually she located her hostess, Mrs. Lydia Peckinpaw, introduced herself, and inquired about Brendan.

"Oh my dear, you're as lovely as Brendy promised!" Mrs. Peckinpaw held Bailey's hands at arm's length and inspected her with unabashed curiosity.

"Brendy?" Bailey repeated in a faint voice. She hadn't known anyone called him Brendy. Brendy and Bailey. It had a Ken and Barbie ring to it, she thought, trying not to groan aloud.

"The dear man is frantic," Mrs. Peckinpaw said. She wore a fuchsia Mary McFadden gown with the trademark pleats, garnished with diamonds and garnets at ears and throat. Mrs. Peckinpaw was one of those incredibly thin, incredibly polished New York women whose age was impossible to guess. Her husband, Wiley Peckinpaw, had been a diplomat and now chaired a dozen *Fortune 500* boards.

"Where is Brendan? I can't locate him." Bailey pulled her lower lip between her teeth. Guilt darkened her eyes.

"He was here for an hour or so, then he left to search for you."

"Oh dear. Maybe I should—" She darted a glance toward the door but Mrs. Peckinpaw clicked her tongue and shook her head.

"Now don't you go dashing off, too. I promised Brendy I'd keep you here until he returns. Do you know anyone? I'll introduce you to a few people, and—"

"I brought an old friend with me. I hope you don't mind. I want him to meet Brendan."

"Then I won't worry about entertaining you. There's food in the library, and bars everywhere. Make yourself comfortable, my dear. It's difficult to really talk at this kind of party but I'm sure we'll have an opportunity to get acquainted soon. Everyone is thrilled that Brendy is finally settling down. And with a girl from Kansas, too. It's all so surprising and wonderful.''

"Yes. Well." Suddenly Bailey felt like a gawky schoolgirl in her off-the-rack black silk and her drizzle-splashed pumps. She would have given anything to get her hands on a curling iron. At least she wasn't wearing her coat. She had a suspicion Mrs. Peckinpaw would have considered her protest buttons amusing and a trifle gauche.

Dispirited, she found Cole in the library and absently plucked a fat shrimp off his plate. "Brendan's out looking for me. I feel terrible." Brooding, she chose another of Cole's shrimps. "Our hostess is warm and nice and everything I want to be when I grow up." She released an elaborate sigh. "If you notice a vision in fuchsia floating by, that's her. She looks like the roof could fall in and she wouldn't lose her composure. While I was talking to her I tried to imagine her wearing a ratty bathrobe and her hair in curlers. I couldn't." Leaning, she inspected Cole's plate, poked around the olives before selecting the only green one. "Why didn't you get more green olives? Meanwhile Brendan is out there in the ice and drizzle, running around the city probably worried out of his mind, thinking a mugger got me. God, I hate this."

Cole watched the food disappearing off his plate. "I hate it when people eat off my plate. Why do women do that? I'd be happy to get you a plate of your own."

"Thanks, but I'm too upset to eat," she said, taking another of his shrimps. She watched the couples dancing to a Ray Charles song performed by a live band. "Brendan is going to be mad and I deserve it. I should have called at least. This is your fault."

"My fault? Look, take this plate and I'll get another."

"I told you, I don't want anything. Just that pickle. And yes, it's your fault. When I'm with you the time flies. I get so interested in what we're arguing about that I forget everything else.''

What she had forgotten this time was her fiancé, Brendan.

The realization hung between them as if she had spoken aloud. Feeling her heartbeat accelerate, Bailey stared into Cole's steady gaze. It upset and confused her to recognize how attracted to him she was.

"We're in trouble, Kansas," he said in a low husky voice, staring at her lips. "All I can think about is kissing you again."

Chapter Four

Bailey watched her engagement ring sparkle and flash as she turned it around her finger. "Please, Cole," she whispered. "Don't say things like that." But similar thoughts plagued her, too. She gave him a warning glance but saw his firm, well-shaped mouth, and something hot and crazy exploded in the pit of her stomach.

Because they had discreetly refrained from mentioning the exchange of passionate kisses in Times Square, she had assumed they were tacitly agreed to pretend the incident never happened. A flush of annoyance and embarrassment colored her cheeks, and she looked away from him.

"I think it's clear that we need to talk, Bailey. Have dinner with me tomorrow night."

"You know I can't do that," she said, making herself meet his eyes. While they weren't specifically discussing the exchange of kisses, it appeared they needed to deal with the implications. After drawing a breath, Bailey faced him directly and confronted the issue. "All right, Cole. I admit I feel a certain attraction to you," she conceded with obvious reluctance. "But you know as well as I that all we're ever going to be is friends."

"Our relationship can be whatever we want it to be." The warmth in the room enhanced the provocative scent of Bailey's perfume. Cole watched the tiny twinkling lights reflected in her eyes. "Don't you think we should at least explore the possibilities?"

"For heaven's sake, Cole. I'm planning to be married. We don't even live in the same state. And last but not least, you and I don't agree on anything. Doesn't all that tell you something? Such as, you and I make terrific friends, but we wouldn't make terrific partners? Partners should at least agree on the basics." The word partners sounded a little stilted, but she couldn't bring herself to say lovers.

"Come on, Bailey, look a little deeper. We do agree on the basics. As for our opinions, you find our arguments and our differences as stimulating and exciting as I do. It would get old pretty fast if we agreed on everything."

A startled look constricted Bailey's expression. She and Brendan agreed on nearly everything. Until this moment she had considered their similar views as one of their strengths as a couple. But Cole's comment made it sound as though common views were about as exciting as dental floss.

"Most people consider harmonious viewpoints as a sign of compatibility rather than a signal that the relationship is going stale," she pointed out, her voice wry.

Cole shrugged. "I imagine that depends on what you're looking for. If you want a nice safe extension of yourself, then I suppose it's comforting to know in advance that you'll agree with whatever remark falls out of Brendan's mouth." He lifted one dark eyebrow. "But I had the impression you enjoy a stimulating difference of opinion."

"I do find our differences stimulating," she agreed slowly, frowning. And the tension between herself and Cole was exciting. It sharpened her mind and enhanced her awareness. Unfortunately Bailey's heightened awareness did not end with mental stimulation. She was also acutely, tinglingly, aware of Cole's body and her own. "But a steady diet of arguments and differences doesn't sound appealing, frankly, it sounds exhausting. That isn't what I want,

Cole." She drew a breath and faced him directly. "We might as well lay it out and put this question to rest once and for all. You and I are simply incompatible as anything more than friends."

"Since I don't agree, you're going to have to be more explicit." He ate the rest of his shrimp before she could steal the last one. "Exactly what is it that you hate about me?"

"I don't hate anything about you and you know it," she said, taking his last olive. "I just don't think we'd mesh well as anything more than friends. As friends our differences are interesting. The same differences would be annoying if we were more than friends. For one thing, your life-style is unsettling. I couldn't be comfortable with the pace you keep."

It seemed to her that Cole Tarcher sped after the future like a sleek updated version of the Orient Express, whereas Brendan Hanson was more like a well-seasoned Bentley. With Brendan there would be time and leisure to enjoy the scenery. "With you, there's no such thing as thinking small, no room for modest success. Take for instance that comment you made about me running for Congress. But me, I like to know my parameters. I'm happy with small attainable goals, small triumphs. Because you don't recognize obstacles, you make people who do feel guilty. You make me feel deficient somehow because I'm satisfied with my life as it is, like there's something wrong with me because I don't want to hurl myself into battle to achieve some ambitious goal that *you* think is more worthy than what I'm doing now."

After putting down his plate, Cole framed her shoulders between his large hands. "You're sounding like a small-town girl, Kansas."

"I think we're both past that, Cole. Small-town attitudes don't figure in this anymore. If they ever did. I'm simply telling you how I feel."

"You're playing it safe, driving in the slow lane. And you aren't giving yourself enough credit." He peered intently into her large eyes. "Maybe you're afraid to discover just how far you can soar. With a little help from your friends."

"Brendan says—"

"You aren't going to soar with Brendan, Bailey. What you've described is a slippers-by-the-hearth marriage." He tilted her face up to his. "What happened to the women's libber who wouldn't let a man open her doors? Does that sound like the same woman who's willing to settle into a traditional wife's role?"

"That isn't fair." But she felt a rush of heat flood her cheeks. "Look, Cole. From the beginning I wanted a home and family. Plus, you don't know Brendan. Our life isn't going to be as conventional as you make it sound. Brendan doesn't expect me to surrender my independence and start baking cookies and clipping recipes to the exclusion of all else."

"Every day I meet a hundred guys like Brendan. He's the type who rolls his socks in balls and lines them up in his drawer. He's a gentleman, a good sport. He wouldn't dream of creating a scene, right? He wouldn't be caught dead making a spontaneous move, it's a point of honor to give serious and sober consideration to every decision no matter how small. There's a place for everything and everything should be in its place. Including his wife. And—this is his worst fault—he doesn't understand Waylon Jennings or Willie Nelson, and he never will."

Despite herself, Bailey laughed. "Go ahead, make all the lousy jokes you want to. But I love Brendan, and I'm going to marry him. That's how it is, cowboy. So do us both a favor and stop being so damned pushy."

"That's it, huh? You've made up your mind and you're giving me the kiss off?"

"That's it."

Cole stared at her with a forlorn expression, then spoke with a heavy sigh. "Well, what can I say? You've driven a stake through my heart. I'll never love again."

A burst of laughter broke from Bailey's lips, and she rolled her eyes toward the ceiling. "You Scorpios are relentless. If persuasion doesn't work, try guilt, right?"

He grinned. "I do love a challenge. Come on, let's dance. Maybe physical proximity will succeed where reason has failed." Taking her hand, Cole led her into the crush of dancers, guiding her into his arms. For a long moment he didn't move. He held her close, gazing down into her eyes, molding the contours of her body to his. Just when Bailey thought her knees would collapse and her nerves would explode, he finally stepped forward. They danced as if they had danced together for years, she noticed with a sigh. She moved her hand across his broad shoulder and tilted her fingers so she could see Brendan's engagement ring. Damn it, she didn't need this kind of complication. She loved Brendan, she really did.

Cole murmured against her ear. "If Brendan Hanson walked in the door right now, he'd find his fiancé in the arms of a man who has been half in love with her for three years." His arm tightened around her waist, and an explosion of warmth coursed through Bailey's trembling body.

"Cole, we have to stop this. The joke has gone far enough." Beneath her black silk dress Bailey's skin tingled and her legs felt shaky. Her voice was unsteady.

"But old Brendan won't make a scene, will he?" Cole murmured in her ear. "He'll be a good sport. Then he'll punish you with a few hours of silence for enjoying the company of an old friend."

"That isn't true," she protested. But it probably was. Still, Cole's comments made her nervous. Bailey darted a look over his shoulder toward the door. Where was Brendan anyway? "You're making him sound pompous and stuffy."

Cole grinned as if she had gotten the point, and tucked her hand against his chest. His breath flowed over her lips and his mouth hovered an inch above her own. Bailey felt as if she had stepped on an elevator that just dropped twenty floors. Her heartbeat accelerated; her breath caught in her throat.

Abruptly she stopped dancing and stepped away from the hypnotic heat of his body. With a wild glance, she scanned the room seeking something she could use to change the subject. Her gaze settled on a display of beribboned baskets holding party favors. Taking Cole by the hand, she pulled him through the dancers, past a couple necking on a brocade settee, and stopped in front of the baskets.

"Mrs. Peckinpaw is giving away astrology booklets." Bending, she sorted through the basket's contents until she emerged with a booklet for Gemini and one for Scorpio.

"Exactly what we need here," Cole said, taking the Gemini booklet from her hands. "Let's see what the stars have to say about beautiful exciting do-gooders marrying dull uptight lawyers."

Bailey rolled her eyes incredulously as he leaned toward a table lamp. "You are amazing. You just don't quit. No wonder you're a success on Wall Street."

"Here we are. Listen to this, Kansas, and take heed. 'The Gemini woman should avoid stodgy attorneys at all costs. They are definitely not for you. If you see one coming, run like hell.'"

"You have no shame."

He flipped a page. "Now here's something interesting in your immediate future. Pay attention, will you? 'A rising star on Wall Street, a prince of a fellow, has recently reappeared in your life. He's your friend but could be much more if you'd give him a chance. Follow your baser instincts.'" Raising innocent eyes, he tilted his head and listened to her wonderful laugh. "Hey, it's in the stars. What can I say? It says right here that you're supposed to give us a chance."

Bailey waved the comment aside. "What does my horoscope predict about children? Brendan and I want to start a family immediately. You'll notice I said '*Brendan* and I.' Brendan like in Brendan my future husband, the man I love, the father of my children, the man I intend to spend the rest of my life with. That Brendan."

Cole didn't glance at the booklet in his hands. His gaze held hers. "It says you're making a mistake if you marry Brendan Hanson. It says that you and I have been given a second chance and we should explore it thoroughly before you make any long-term decisions."

For a lengthy heart-stopping moment, they stared into each other's eyes. Bailey felt her pulse pound and recognized she was having difficulty controlling her emotions. Question marks blinked in her mind, undermining everything she had believed was settled. One thing was certain. She shouldn't be feeling what she was feeling toward Cole Tarcher, not when she was engaged to marry someone else.

She wet her lips with a nervous gesture. "Cole, let's be serious for a minute."

"I've never been more serious in my life."

Bailey released a slow breath, then straightened her shoulders. "I'm glad I ran into you tonight. I value your friendship and I'm happy we've found each other again. But—"

"I don't think I'm going to like this."

"But if you're really my friend, you won't complicate my life on the basis of a chance encounter. If our friendship is going to continue we need to establish some rules and agree to abide by them."

She was so beautiful. So vivacious and earnest and intense. As always she gave the issue at hand her full concentration, speaking slowly, working it out as she spoke. Cole could almost read her thoughts by studying her lovely expressive face.

"We've admitted a dangerous attraction exists between us." Her troubled eyes examined his expression. "We have to agree it goes no further. That's the only way we can continue to see each other, Cole. We have to agree we're friends, and that's all. And," she added in a gentler tone, "that's all we're ever going to be."

He kept his voice light and teasing, but his eyes were serious. "Give me one bottom-line reason why you've decided we can't be anything more."

She stared at him, then spread her hands. "I can give you several reasons." A long breath lifted her breast. "You don't see me as I am, you see all the things I could be if I were as ambitious as you are. That scares me. It makes me feel as if I'm not living up to my potential."

"Maybe you aren't. I see you as bright, beautiful and capable. Is that so wrong?"

"Next, you're in the fast lane and loving it. But I'm a behind-the-scenes type. I don't think I'm in the slow lane as you suggested, but the middle lane suits me fine. And next, you're willing to give up your personal life, your social life and heaven knows what else in the pursuit of money and success. I don't understand that thinking. I believe you're glad there are people like me who are willing to confront injustice, who are willing to carry picket signs and lend real support to causes like saving baby seals, but you aren't one of them." She paused for breath. "Need I go on?"

"You don't agree that differences can enrich and enliven a relationship?"

"In some instances, yes. But Cole, the timing is lousy here. Neither of us needs to settle for a relationship that would require a lot of compromise and adjustment. More importantly, I've found Brendan and we love each other.

We'll have a satisfying, comfortable life without a lot of strain or serious differences."

"You're absolutely sure that's what you want?" he asked softly. Cole had said a lot of things in jest tonight, but he genuinely believed it would be a mistake if Bailey married Brendan. He couldn't make himself believe she felt the same electricity, this same charged tension with Brendan Hanson. His sixth sense told him that he and Bailey Meade could be terrific together if she would only give them a chance.

"I'm sure," she said quietly. Her husky voice gave the words a depressing finality. "Please, Cole, if we're really friends, then don't complicate things for me."

For a lengthy moment he didn't speak. "All right," he finally agreed. Regret deepened his voice. "You're correct about one thing, our timing has been lousy in this life. You have to promise that in our next incarnation, you'll give us a chance. Agreed?"

"Agreed," she said, laughing. After a brief hesitation, she placed her fingertips on his sleeve. "It will be more comfortable for both of us if we don't make suggestive remarks or talk about might-have-beens, or things like that." Her eyes narrowed and flashed a warning. "And if we don't make lousy jokes at Brendan's expense. Agreed, cowboy? You stop putting down Brendan and I promise not to criticize Marsha or whoever you end up with."

"You Geminis drive a hard bargain," he said, leading her back into the crowd of dancers. To show he accepted her terms, he made a point of holding her at arm's length, smiling down into her wonderful jeweled eyes.

"Stop looking at me like that!" she said, making an exasperated face.

"Hold on, Kansas. There's nothing in the rules that says I can't look at you." He grinned.

"But not like that. You're looking at me as if— Brendan!"

Bailey didn't see Brendan until his hand dropped on her shoulder. Startled and feeling as if she'd been caught doing something wrong, she stumbled over Cole's feet. While Brendan watched with cool eyes, Cole caught her by the waist and steadied her on her feet. Quickly, Bailey stepped backward and turned a guilty smile toward her fiancé.

"Brendan! I'm so glad you're—"

But Brendan interrupted the tumble of words by increasing the pressure on her shoulder. He extended his other hand to Cole. "I'm Brendan Hanson, Bailey's fiancé. And you are..."

Biting her lip, Bailey stifled a sigh. Brendan couldn't have arrived five minutes ago when she and Cole were standing well apart, talking. No, Brendan had to arrive and find her dancing with a man who happened to be dashingly handsome and intensely attentive. And Brendan would have to be a grim good sport about it. While she performed the introductions, she exchanged a quick glance with Cole and knew exactly what he was thinking. He was thinking Brendan was stuffy and sulky.

It was true that Brendan wasn't at his best. The drizzle had plastered his sandy hair to his skull; he looked pale and chilled. And of course he was angry. This would have been their first New Year's Eve together, and he had spent it lost in the crowd at Times Square, then running around in the drizzle and cold slush searching for her. And Bailey had spent their first New Year's Eve in the arms of a man who made her blood race and befuddled her thoughts, who confused the hell out of her and made her feel like a different person.

She slipped her arm around Brendan's and gave his chilled palm a squeeze. He didn't return the pressure of her fingers.

"Cole Tarcher—that name sounds familiar. Are you the Cole Tarcher in Acquisitions at First Guarantee Trust?"

Brendan still hadn't glanced at Bailey. His refusal to look at her signaled the depth of his anger.

One of Cole's dark eyebrows lifted. "Yes, have we met?"

"I'm with Colquist, Colquist, and Percheron."

"CC&P did the Washington legals on the Star Ride buy-out. Were you involved in that deal?"

"You two know each other?" Bailey asked in amazement, looking back and forth between them.

The bottoms of Brendan's glasses were still fogged, and his hair was soaked. He reminded Bailey of a kid who had just come inside from playing in the rain. Brendan was no rugged Marlboro Man like Cole; he didn't resemble a film star. He was good-looking but not exceptionally so. The first time Bailey met Brendan Hanson she hadn't thought about racing pulses or passionate bedroom scenes. She had taken one look at his solid features and his assured demeanor of quiet self-possession and thought about qualities like dependable, steady and reliable. Instinctively she had known he would be a devoted husband and a caring, affectionate father.

Responding to a burst of warmth, she moved closer to Brendan's side and lifted her chin in Cole's direction, feeling defensive and protective. It wasn't Brendan's fault that he didn't make a powerful first impression.

Cole met her eyes and again she knew what he was thinking. It had not escaped his notice that Brendan had yet to glance at her. Cole was aware that Brendan was furious and straining to be polite. To Bailey's irritation, Cole's raised eyebrow said: I told you so.

Cole cleared his throat with a tactful sound. "I'm sure you two would like a moment alone. If you'll excuse me, I'll track down drinks for everyone." Bailey cast him a look of gratitude that swept aside her earlier irritation. "What's your preference, Hanson?"

"Scotch on the rocks." The minute Cole disappeared into the crowd, Brendan tugged her to a spot near the floor-to-ceiling windows overlooking the lights twinkling across Manhattan. Staring down at her through his fogged glasses, he spoke in a tightly controlled tone. "What the hell happened to you? One minute you were right beside me, the next minute you were gone. I came directly here as we'd planned, but one hour passed, then two and you didn't appear. I was worried half out of my mind!"

"Oh, Brendan, I'm sorry, I didn't mean to worry you. I would have called, but there was a line in front of the telephones that stretched half way through the café." It wasn't exactly a lie. There probably had been a line in front of the telephones.

"What café? And how do you know Tarcher?"

Speaking rapidly, hoping to fill in the background before Cole returned, Bailey sketched her friendship with Cole Tarcher, then explained how they had run into each other after she lost Brendan in Times Square.

"There didn't seem any harm in sharing a cup of coffee while we waited for the traffic to clear. It would have been impossible to snag a cab immediately. I . . . I didn't realize how long we were in the café, and I apologize for that lapse. We were catching up on people we both know, what we've been doing the past three years . . . I insisted Cole accompany me here because I wanted him to meet you."

Brendan directed a frown toward one of the bars where Cole was talking to Wiley Peckinpaw. For a moment Brendan didn't say anything, digesting what Bailey had told him. "Did you ever date Tarcher?"

"I told you, Cole and I are good friends, but *just* friends." Bailey drew a breath and met his eyes. "Now Cole will be *our* friend."

"Tarcher would be a good business connection," Brendan said thoughtfully. He was still irritated and disappointed in how the evening had turned out, but he was beginning to relax. "The way I hear it, Cole Tarcher is the man to know at First Guarantee Trust. He's made a name for himself in a remarkably short time." The fog had lifted from his glasses, and Bailey could see he was beginning to regain his equilibrium. He hadn't forgiven her for worrying him, not yet. But at least Cole wouldn't be a problem.

"This friendship could be beneficial for both you and Cole," Bailey said brightly. She suspected she was leaving the impression that business considerations had been her primary reason for wanting Brendan and Cole to meet. It seemed prudent to allow the impression to stand. But dishonest. "More importantly," she said after a moment, looking up into his eyes, "Cole is my friend. I hope the two of you will be friends, too."

Brendan cast a speculative glance toward the bar. Cole was smiling and shaking hands with Wiley Peckinpaw. The two men exchanged cards. "What's Tarcher's background?"

"As undistinguished as mine," Bailey said in a level tone. Although she hated it, this question always arose. "But he graduated cum laude from Harvard, and you said yourself he's a rising star at First Guarantee Trust."

Brendan turned the look of speculation on her. "You don't need to sound so defensive. I just asked a simple question."

"Maybe that question isn't valid in today's world, have you thought about that? Every time you ask about someone's background, I wonder how I managed to pass the test!"

Bailey's shoulders dropped in dejection, and she touched her fingertips to her eyelids. Tonight wasn't remotely similar to the New Year's Eve she had envisioned. First she and Brendan had become separated. Now they hovered on the verge of having an argument.

Brendan stared at her, then opened his mouth, but Bailey interrupted whatever he had been about to say.

"I don't want to fight with you. Look, I'm sorry the evening didn't work out as we wanted it to. We're both disappointed and maybe a little irritable." Her gaze pleaded with him. "Can't we put the unpleasantness behind us and salvage what's left of our evening?"

He glanced at his wristwatch, his expression sour. "It's three o'clock. There isn't much of the evening left."

Bailey spread her hands. "We could go out to breakfast, watch the sun come up . . ."

"Do you really want to do that?" Brendan asked in a voice that suggested he would rather call it a night but would go along if Bailey insisted.

Cole reappeared. "I brought you a daiquiri. I hope that's what you wanted." He studied the pink circles on Bailey's cheeks and lifted an eyebrow.

"A daiquiri is just what I wanted, thank you," she said brightly, knowing both men heard the artificiality in her tone. "We were discussing whether or not to go out to breakfast and watch the sun come up on a new year. What do you think, Cole?"

"Absolutely," he agreed promptly. "That's exactly what you should do. It's practically tradition. The best place to watch the sunrise would be from atop the World Trade Center."

Brendan frowned at his Scotch and water. "I imagine the place will be packed. Frankly, I've had enough of crowds for one night. But if Bailey . . ."

"I know the maitre d' at the Trade Center. If you like, I'll be happy to make reservations for you."

Bailey noticed the phrasing and realized Cole had excluded himself. Biting her lip, she too gazed into her drink. "Thank you, but on second thought it's probably a dumb idea. We're meeting Brendan's parents for brunch at ten-thirty and we're going to be asleep on our feet as it is."

Bailey told herself she didn't mind not watching the sun rise on 1983. Staying up all night was a thing college kids did, and people like Cole Tarcher who apparently could exist on minimal sleep. She and Brendan had matured beyond the need for magical thinking; that old saw about having good luck if you watched the sun come up on the new year was kid stuff. Nineteen eighty-three promised to be a fabulous year whether or not Bailey was present to cheer the first sunrise.

Having conquered her disappointment, she raised her head and fixed a smile on her lips as she listened to Cole and Brendan discuss business trends.

After twenty minutes Bailey noticed Brendan stifle a yawn. The conversation lagged.

"It was wonderful seeing you," Cole murmured, glancing at his watch. "My resolution for 1983 is not to lose touch with you."

"Good." Bailey smiled. Although Cole looked at his watch the way people did when they were tired, he looked as fresh as when they had arrived. Like her, he was a night person. "I'm glad you and Brendan met."

Bailey watched the two men shake hands and agree to have lunch the next time Brendan had business in Manhattan. Then Cole turned back to her and opened his arms.

As Cole embraced her goodbye, he whispered in her ear. "You're making a mistake, Kansas. Give me one weekend in the Bahamas and I promise you'll change your mind."

She laughed and kissed him on the cheek. "I've already made up my mind. You Wall Street cowboys scare me."

When she turned back to Brendan, who watched with a tight smile, she was shaking inside as if she had just made a momentous decision. The odd feeling didn't make sense. It was hardly an earthshaking decision for a woman who was about to be married to turn aside a pass from another man. But running in to Cole again had unleashed a prickle of doubt.

"You have a peculiar expression on your face," Brendan said, stretching his neck against his hand. "What did Tarcher say to you?"

"I was just thinking what a strange New Year's Eve this is." Tilting her head, Bailey studied his face. "Brendan, you do love me, don't you?"

"What kind of question is that? Of course I love you. You wouldn't have to ask if you knew what I went through trying to find you."

Frowning, she continued to examine Brendan's face as he related the aggravations he had encountered during his search for her. And she wondered if she and Brendan were really as right for each other as she had believed before she ran into Cole Tarcher again.

For an instant she gazed at Brendan's mouth and realized his lips were well formed for sulking. It occurred to her that his attitudes were as rigid as his posture. It upset him when events didn't unfold precisely as he'd planned. Flexibility did not number among Brendan's strong qualities. Suddenly Bailey wondered if Cole was right. Maybe Brendan did want a conventional slippers-by-the-hearth marriage.

Confusion flickered in her gaze.

Then he looked down at her with a tender, almost timid smile and said in a gruff voice, "I was so worried about you. I don't know what I'd do if anything happened to you..."

And suddenly he was Brendan again, the man who loved her and whom she loved. A predictable man, unchanging. A man she could count on, could lean on, the man with whom she would share children and the rest of her life.

"Happy New Year," she said softly, resting her head on his solid wide shoulder, needing to touch him.

"Happy New Year, Miss Meade." Raising her fingers, he kissed her hand above her engagement ring and smiled. "Next year, I'll be celebrating with Mrs. Brendan Hanson."

"We're going to have a wonderful life, I just know it."

"The best."

Bailey would have submitted to torture before admitting that for one fleeting instant Cole Tarcher had flared in vibrant primal colors while Brendan had faded to dull pastel. She didn't intend that such a bewildering comparison would happen again.

While they waited for their coats, Brendan touched her cheek and asked if she still wanted to have breakfast at the World Trade Center. "We'll stay until the sun rises if that's really what you want to do," he said.

"I know." Leaning close to him, she pressed his arm. And she surrendered to her Gemini duplicity and offered a white lie. "It was a silly idea. I know you're tired and so am I. Let's call it a night."

In the back of her mind, she heard Cole laughing. "Brendan isn't dull," she protested silently, defensively. "He's mature."

She followed Brendan down the elevator and into the rest of her life. The romantic imagery made her smile. It was the kind of overstatement that would have made Cole groan and roll his eyes.

Cole Tarcher's warm smile and teasing gaze lingered in her memory, but she had the memory under control now. She clasped Brendan's arm close to her side and hoped Cole found someone who would make him as happy as Brendan made her.

Chapter Five

To:Mr. Cole Tarcher
85 East 70th Avenue
New York City, N.Y.

Mr. and Mrs. William Bailey Meade
and
Mr. and Mrs. Jack Robert Amesley
request the honor of your presence
at the marriage of their daughter
Bailey Marie
to
Mr. Brendan Hanson
on
Sunday the twelfth of June
at one o'clock in the afternoon
at St. James Church
New York
Reception to follow
at the Sherry Netherland
The favor of an answer is requested

July 1, 1983

Dear Cole,
Thank you for the lovely Waterford vase. Brendan and I love it. Your vase occupies the place of honor on the mantelpiece. At present it's brimming with fresh flowers and looks lovely with the morning sunlight striking the crystal. I included a sprig of sage in remembrance of my favorite cowboy.

We had a wonderful time in Paris! Paris is as exciting as you and I hoped it would be when we talked about going there way back when. Brendan had friends in Montmartre and we were treated to out-of-the-way spots that tourists don't usually visit. Naturally I insisted on touring the touristy sites, too. Versailles is a long way from Kansas, cowboy! We hicks were awestruck.

Warm regards,
Bailey

To: Mrs. Bailey Hanson
    256 Cherry Lane
    Georgetown, D.C.
    December 14, 1983

Hi Kansas,
Sorry you had to stay behind in Washington and couldn't join Brendan and me for lunch last week. You were missed. Brendan says you are happily jumping from one project to another in Senator Mahoney's office, and still finding time to picket for your causes. Made me think of the good old days before you liberated all the pay toilets.

I'll be spending the holidays in Wyoming so I'm sending your horoscope for 1984 with this Christmas card. It looks like Geminis are going to have a prosperous year. You can send my horoscope—and a long chatty letter—to my folks' address in Wyoming. (You do intend to reciprocate, don't you? You wouldn't leave me dangling in suspense over what

1984 holds for us poor Scorpios. We've established a tradition here, Kansas; I expect you to honor your part.)
Have a merry Christmas and a wonderful new year!

Cole

February 27, 1984

Dear Cole,

I'm sorry we didn't have more time to visit at the valentine benefit or during the dinner afterward. I know you're busy with the biggest buyout of your career and I would have enjoyed hearing all the juicy details. And I would have liked to tell you about a bill I helped write for Senator Mahoney. Maybe next time.

I'm also sorry your Marsha was in Europe and we missed an opportunity to meet her. (I promise not to mention that ravishing model when we finally do meet Marsha. Was the model really as dumb as she sounded?)

I promised to tell you the results of my latest pregnancy test. I wish it was good news, but it was another false alarm. Each time the disappointment is more intense. I tell myself I won't let my hopes soar too high, but I always do. I suppose it's too soon to start worrying, but . . .

I'm happy, cowboy. Honestly I am. So the next time I see you, will you please stop giving me those deep penetrating looks as if you're trying to glimpse the misery beneath the smile. There is no misery. Honest. The only blot on an otherwise blissful state is my failure to get pregnant. As soon as I get pregnant—and I have faith it will happen any day—I'll have it all, just like we talked about four years ago. A wonderful job, a wonderful husband, a wonderful life.

Now it's your turn. When are you going to settle down and stop breaking hearts all over Manhattan?

With affection,
Bailey

P.S. I peeked at your horoscope before I sent it to you at Christmas. The stars have you scheduled for a big event in May of this year. ???

To:Mr. and Mrs. Brendan Hanson

Mr. and Mrs. Winston Pershom Haversham III
request the honor of your presence
at the marriage of their daughter
Marsha Anne
to
Mr. Cole Tarcher
on
Friday the eleventh of May
at seven o'clock in the evening
at St. Paul's Church
New York
Reception to follow at the Plaza Hotel
RSVP

June 2, 1984

Dear Mr. and Mrs. Hanson,
Thank you for the lovely mantel clock. Cole appropriated it at once for his study and it's perfect there.
  We plan to be in Washington shortly before Thanksgiving. I hope you'll join us for dinner. I look forward to seeing you both again and having an opportunity to get to know you better.

Sincerely,
Marsha Tarcher

To:Cole Tarcher
    First Guarantee Trust
    30 Wall Street

New York, N.Y.
December 2, 1984

Dear Cole,

Brendan and I regret that we couldn't have dinner with you and Marsha while you were in our area. Everything was still crazy after the Reagan-Bush reelection, we had some staff members quit at the senator's office and, well, you know how wild it can get. It was a hectic time for Brendan, too. He's trying to wrap up a lawsuit before he accepts a partnership in his father's firm in Manhattan.

Just thinking about finding a house and moving overwhelms me. And it's going to be wrenching to leave the senator. I've enjoyed this job more than anything I've ever done. I don't know what I'll do with myself in Manhattan or Connecticut or wherever we land.

We're going to Kansas for the holidays where we'll be juggling our time between Jack and Mom, and Dad and Helen. There are some things we just don't outgrow, aren't there?

Therefore I'm sending your astrology booklet early. You Scorpios are slated for some bumps in 1985. For one thing, the stars say you're going to work yourself toward exhaustion. But that isn't new, is it? Not for someone who wants to be a millionaire before age thirty. You have one more year, cowboy—will you make it?

Bad news on the baby front... still nothing. The disappointment gets harder and harder to bear. If I'm not pregnant by this time next year, we've agreed to seek fertility counseling. I wouldn't have believed it would be this difficult to get pregnant. But patience isn't my long suit. I want a baby tomorrow. Today. It seems that everywhere I go I see women with babies. Does it seem that way to you? I know I'll get pregnant eventually, I just wish it would happen now.

Merry Christmas, dear friend. I hope 1985 brings you and Marsha all good things.

Bailey

P.S. I sent this card to your office because I don't know if you and Marsha have moved into your new home yet.

To:Mr. and Mrs. Brendan Hanson
   11 Amsterdam Place
   Stamford, Connecticut

The Tarchers Announce a Dividend!
with the arrival
of Stephan and Shawn Tarcher
born September 4, 1985

September 10, 1985

Dear Cole,
Congratulations. I'm so happy for you and Marsha!

Bailey

Chapter Six

New Year's Eve, 1986

Bailey stepped out of Brendan's Mercedes, pushed her hands into the pockets of her camel hair coat and inhaled deeply.

The night was cold and cloudy to the north, the air sharp with the promise of fresh snow. In the exclusive new subdivision where their host and hostess lived, the homes were spaced widely apart and the glow of city lights didn't dim the canopy of stars about to be overwhelmed by the approaching cloud bank. Snow in the east reminded Bailey of Christmas card scenes, serene and lovely, not like a wind-blown Kansas blizzard.

"This is one of the things I love most about the East, nights like this," she murmured, taking Brendan's arm as he came around the Mercedes. They walked past the cars lining a circle drive, then followed a path of flickering luminarias leading to wide double doors decorated with holly wreaths. "Cold and crisp and you can almost smell the coming snow."

"Next year let's agree to spend New Year's Eve at home, can we do that? You know how New Year parties are. Everyone drinks too much, laughs too loudly and kisses everyone else's wife. No one gets any business done. We always stay too late and the next day we can hardly get out of bed."

Bailey paused beneath the porch lights and glanced at the fog condensing on the bottom of Brendan's glasses. "This wasn't my idea, remember? The Gordons are *your* clients. *You* are the one who made the decision to accept their invitation." Her voice was sharper than she had intended, a fault that seemed to happen more and more frequently of late.

"Which *you* agreed to because Cole and Marsha Tarcher are going to be here as Steve Gordon is also one of Cole's clients."

Bailey passed a hand over her forehead. Inside the house a live band performed oldies but goodies, the steady beat leaking past brick and glass. She heard the sound of laughter and loud conversation.

"Look, Brendan, we've both been under a lot of strain. I know it's unsettling to change firms . . . and there was the hassle of moving and finding the right house. Plus I've been at loose ends . . ." She didn't mention the real cause of the tension between them, the greatest strain of all—their failure to conceive a child. "Can we agree to put the aggravations aside for tonight? Let's just relax, enjoy ourselves and have a good time."

"Come on, Bailey. Can you honestly say you've ever had a really great time at a New Year's Eve party?" he asked, frowning at her. "Can you remember even one New Year's Eve that lived up to expectations?"

Immediately Bailey's mind flashed back six years to her senior year at Radcliffe, the year her New Year's Eve date had been her roommate's fiancé, a pity date. In spite of the peculiar circumstances, it had been a terrific evening. But that was years ago in another lifetime, when she and Cole were young and too idealistic to guess that New Year's Eve—and life—wasn't supposed to live up to expectations.

"I can think of one or two terrific New Years," she said softly. Then she patted her pockets and snapped open her purse. "Oh, dear. Did I remember to bring Cole's astrology booklet?"

A puff of vapor blew out before Brendan's lips, and he shook his head. "Don't you think this annual exchange of astrology booklets is just a little bit ridiculous?"

Bailey looked up at him. "I didn't know you objected."

"I don't object. I just think it's silly and childish. Don't you?" He jabbed the doorbell.

"Probably," she said stiffly. "But Cole and I have been exchanging astrology booklets for six years. It's a silly custom, but I enjoy it." It struck her that almost any topic could be escalated into an argument, especially recently.

"It seems out of character for both of you, if you want to know what I—"

"Hi!" Kelly Gordon pulled open the door in a swirl of crimson taffeta and beamed at them. "Come in, come in! Brrr, it's getting cold out here." Chattering with the exuberance of a hostess determined to set the tone for an upbeat party, Kelly Gordon pulled them inside and gestured for a maid to take their coats. "Brendy, you sourpuss, smile! It's New Year's Eve! Bailey, don't you look fabulous! That color makes your eyes glow like sapphires. Come in, come in, I'm sure you know everyone. There's nibble food scattered everywhere—we'll have supper about one o'clock—and there's a bar in practically every other room. Enjoy!" She winked at Bailey and grinned. "You two were the last. Now that everyone's here the fun and games can begin!"

"That woman exhausts me just to listen to her," Brendan grumbled. "Talk, talk, talk. Cheery, cheery, cheery."

After pasting a smile on her lips, Bailey drew a breath and paused a moment before she hurled herself into the crush of revelers. Absently she watched the wife of one of Brendan's partners flirting with a senator she recognized, but her mind was focused on Brendan. He didn't used to gripe and complain so often. When had that started? Was it a habit that had developed so slowly she failed to notice? Or was it one more piece of fallout from the shock of being unable to conceive?

Kelly Gordon swooped down on them again. Shaking her head, she clicked her tongue, then gave them both a little push. "This won't do, the two of you hanging in the foyer like wallflowers. Get in there and enjoy yourselves!" She waggled a playful finger under Brendan's nose. "And circulate! The rule for tonight is: no husbands and wives huddled in a corner together. Mingle! Mingle, mingle, mingle."

"How does Steve Gordon stand her?" Brendan muttered, staring after Kelly Gordon as she whirled through the living room dispensing cheer and instructions. "I'll bet she even talks in her sleep."

"She's just nervous, waiting to see if her party will get off the ground." Someone pushed a glass of champagne into Bailey's hand, and she tasted it than gazed around her with a determined expression. Tonight she absolutely was not going to think about any problems. Both she and Brendan needed a break from the problems.

The Gordons's home was large and spacious, designed for entertaining large groups. A twelve-foot Christmas tree dominated the space between a stone fireplace and a bank of windows overlooking the new Stone Violet golf course. A cloud of balloons floated near the two-story ceiling. More clusters of balloons bobbed above the staircase railing and wherever space would allow. A gilt streamer proclaimed Happy New Year from above the mantelpiece. The family room had been cleared for dancing, and a very young-looking band enthusiastically banged out toe-tapping songs that had been popular when Bailey was a toddler.

The next time Kelly Gordon flitted past, Bailey turned from the group she had joined and caught Kelly's hand.

"Relax, it's a wonderful party. Everyone's having a great time."

Kelly's eyes sparkled with pleasure, and she glanced at the diamond-studded face of her wristwatch. "It's about to get better. Just wait." Then she spun away to check on the catering service.

Bailey smiled after her, then jumped as she heard the voice she had unconsciously been waiting to hear. A tiny thrill chased down her spine, and her spirits lifted as if she'd swallowed a tonic.

"Hi, Kansas. I've been looking all over for you."

"Hi there, cowboy."

As they always did when they hadn't seen each other for a while, she and Cole stood in silence for a moment, holding hands and eagerly studying each other's faces, looking for subtle changes they believed no one else could see.

Cole's dark hair was shorter; Bailey's hair was styled in short permed ringlets that framed her face like a halo. He wore a mustache this year; she was trying a new matte makeup and glitter eye shadow. Neither had gained weight. Both were slightly tanned from winter vacations in summer sites. Both looked as if they were making an effort to have a good time.

"A mustache is good on you. I like it," Bailey decided, smiling. She resisted a crazy urge to lift her hand and touch his upper lip, but she wondered if the mustache was as soft and silky as it looked or if it would be coarse to the touch. Frowning slightly, she made herself shift her concentration to his expression, and decided she would save any questions about his look of distraction for later. As for her own expression and the tiny lines of anxiety, she hoped he wouldn't ask. "It gives you a sort of roguish air. What's next? An eye patch?"

He grinned. "I was right, you know."

"About what?"

"About you. You become more beautiful with every year. By the time you're seventy, men will be jumping out of windows when you pass by, dying for a glimpse of you."

She laughed, the rich husky sound as provocative as ever. "It's good to see you, cowboy. You're great for my ego." They continued to study each other a moment longer, then Bailey released his hands, suddenly feeling self-conscious. It occurred to her that it had been a long time since Brendan had looked at her the way Cole was looking at her now, as if she were the most fascinating woman in the world. She touched her fingertips to her throat and glanced around the room. "Where's Marsha?"

"She's here somewhere," Cole said, not looking away from her. "Brendan?"

"As far from the music as he can get, and probably counting the hours until we can go home."

"Brendan always was a fun guy."

Bailey narrowed her eyes. "Watch it, cowboy. Remember the rules." Then she leaned forward and eagerness lighted her eyes. "Cole, tell me about the twins! I want to know everything. How much do they weigh now? Are they wonderful? Of course they are! Do they look alike? Well, one is a boy and one is a girl, but do they resemble each other? Do they take after the Haversham side or the Tarcher side? Do they—"

Smiling, Cole held up a hand. "Whoa. You're starting to sound like Kelly Gordon. Stevie and Shawn are a few days shy of four months old and already they're a handful." Pride warmed his dark eyes. "They're as fat as the bonus I'm expecting, little butterballs. And yes, they resemble each other. At least at this point. Dark hair, what there is of it, and blue eyes, though everyone tells us their eye color will probably change."

Envy bit into Bailey's mind, poured acid into her stomach. It wasn't the first time this kind of thing had happened, leaving her feeling ashamed of herself. "You and

Marsha must be so happy." The remark came out sounding wistful and jealous, which she had not intended. She made a confused motion with her hands and embarrassment tinted her cheeks.

"I suppose we are."

The peculiar undertone roughening his voice caused Bailey to look up quickly. At once it was clear he had not noticed anything amiss in her tone. He was gazing across the crowded room, turning his drink in his hands, a slight frown pulling at his brow. After a second he turned and smiled down at her.

"I'm sure Marsha sent a note, but thanks again for the playpens you and Brendan sent. We're going to need them sooner than we thought." An appreciative glance swept her figure, then settled on her eyes. "You look terrific, Bailey," he said softly. "I always thought your eyes resembled aquamarines. Tonight they remind me of sapphires."

Tilting her head, Bailey studied his face. The sexy new mustache suited him, although she wasn't sure it fit Wall Street. With the mustache Cole looked more the weathered cowboy than ever. The lines at his eyes and down his cheeks were deepening into handsomely intriguing character lines. But his expression sounded a tiny alarm in the back of her mind.

"You look tired," she observed, still examining his face. "And distracted. Cole, is everything all right?"

"The truth?" Raising his drink, he drained the glass before speaking again. "Marsha and I had an argument during the drive up here. It was a whopper. I guess I'm still irritated."

Bailey nodded in understanding. "So did Brendan and I. Only ours probably wasn't as serious an argument since we didn't have as far to drive."

"Which reminds me, how are you liking the country? I think Connecticut agrees with you. You look wonderful." Bending near enough to inhale the intoxicating scent of her perfume, he murmured, "Did you realize you're wearing a Save The Ozone Layer button on that smashing dress?"

"Of course I realize," she said, tossing her head with a smile. "And I've got a Just Say No button on my coat." Using the button as a pretext, she edged backward from him. It confused her to recognize that even after all this time, Cole's nearness could still send her nervous system into a tailspin. She wondered if she would ever get used to the shock of feeling a powerful tug of attraction each time they met. "I'm a committed citizen, remember?" She raised a teasing eyebrow. "Some of us are still trying to save the world the rest of you are buying and selling."

He grinned. "That's one of the wonderful things about you that I hope will never change." He accepted glasses of champagne from a passing waiter and guided her closer to the Christmas tree where they could talk without shouting. "How are you, Kansas? Really."

"Fine," she said, lowering her head over the champagne.

"Come on now, don't give me a glib answer. We've been friends too long. Am I imagining it, or is some of the old fire missing from those killer eyes? What's going on with the Hansons?"

Bailey scanned the groups clustered around the room, settling on a circle that included Brendan and Marsha Tarcher. Marsha wore a black Halston that moved like spun gossamer around her lush figure and was wonderful with her auburn hair. Bright lipstick defined her pouty mouth, and Bailey decided Marsha Tarcher had the longest eyelashes she had ever seen.

"Marsha doesn't seem to have gained a pound. She's very beautiful," Bailey murmured, watching Marsha's slim fingers brush Brendan's sleeve. Brendan touched his tie and smoothed his sandy hair, pleased by the attention.

"Yes, she is."

Did Bailey imagine it, or did Cole's expression darken when he gazed at his wife? Did he object to her obvious flirting? Or was he still thinking about their argument?

"I can't help wondering," Bailey said sweetly, "does Marsha dye her hair?"

Cole burst out laughing. "Not that I know of. But speaking of hair...do I detect a bit less on old Brendan's distinguished head?"

"Nasty," Bailey commented, shaking her newly permed curls. "Brendan is very sensitive about his hair. He swears it isn't thinning."

"I'd be sensitive, too, if my scalp was starting to show."

They grinned at each other, feeling the familiar chemistry.

"This kind of sniping," Bailey warned, smiling, "is—"

"Against the rules," Cole finished, laughing. "God, it's good to see you. Which reminds me. I brought you something."

"My astrology booklet," Bailey guessed. "I didn't forget yours, either." She wondered if the day would ever come when she could stand beside Cole Tarcher without feeling a nervous flutter in her stomach, without remembering the taste of his kiss.

"I peeked at yours, Kansas. You Geminis are going to be bursting with creativity in 1986."

Immediately her expression changed and she bowed her head beneath an onslaught of sudden pain. There was only one kind of creativity she cared about. "I hope so," she whispered. "Oh, Cole, you don't know how much I envy you and Marsha. Twins. You're twice blessed, while I—"

Sympathy deepened the frown lines between Cole's eyes and he pressed her hand. "Have you seen anyone yet? There are several excellent doctors in Manhattan."

"Not yet." Bailey blinked at the sudden moisture welling in her eyes. When it came to this subject, her emotions were raw and quivering. "Consulting a specialist seems like an admission of failure." She looked around for a spot to set her empty glass. "But Brendan agrees it's probably time we did." For six months Bailey had been plotting, graphing, taking her temperature; turning lovemaking into a chore performed on demand instead of a pleasure. The pleasure was long gone. "It's just that we've been so busy with the move and getting settled..." She spread her hands, knowing she was making excuses. "Maybe next month."

"Bailey—"

But Kelly Gordon swept through the rooms, clapping her hands and calling for everyone's attention. Her eyes sparkled with anticipation, and she looked as if she was about to announce a momentous event.

"Maybe Martians have invaded Stamford," Bailey whispered.

"Attention, everyone!" Kelly called, leveling a mock frown at Bailey. "I heard that, Bailey Hanson." Gradually a hush ensued. "I have a surprise for you, the pièce de résistance. We're going to have a treasure hunt!"

Cole groaned at Bailey's side. "I hate party games."

"So does Brendan," Bailey murmured, sneaking a peek in his direction. Brendan cast her a glance from across the room that pleaded for rescue. His gaze begged her to drop in a swoon and pretend she was overcome by a mortal disease that required leaving for home immediately.

"Most of all I hate having anything in common with Brendan, but in this instance I applaud his sensibility," Cole muttered.

"Oh, come on, how bad can it be?" Bailey smiled. "Be a good sport," she said, mouthing the words in Brendan's direction.

Kelly Gordon fizzed and bubbled in the center of the room. "Even now limos are pulling up outside. Won't this be fun?" She pushed a pair of designer reading glasses up her nose and consulted a glittery notebook. "We'll have twelve teams of four. Each team has a car. Now pay attention as I read the list of teams.''

"Why can't I be on the same team as my wife?" someone groaned as the first teams were read out.

"We're mixing it up tonight, so no one has an advantage," Kelly said brightly. She wiggled a finger at the protester. "Now don't be dull, Martin."

Bailey and Cole slid a look of secret pleasure toward each other as their names were called. They were on the same team.

"Okay, now here are the rules," Kelly Gordon said, passing out lists of items to the team leaders. Cole held his list as if it was poisonous. So did Brendan. "The first team who returns with all the items on their list wins. All the teams have to be back here by a quarter to twelve in time to celebrate the new year." She gave everyone a wide cheerful smile and raised her champagne glass. "May the best team win! Get going, guys!"

Everyone drifted forward and jammed up in the foyer, collecting coats, grousing in a good-natured way about the treasure hunt and issuing challenges to the competing teams. There were loud groans as the team leaders scanned the lists of what they had to find and bring back to the Gordons' house.

"A Nancy Drew novel!" Brendan swore, appearing at Bailey's side as she pulled on her coat and scarf. "Now where in the hell are we going to find a Nancy Drew novel at eight o'clock at night?" He scowled at her. "I hate this. Can't you pretend to get sick or something?"

"Sorry, pal," Bailey said, lifting on tiptoe to kiss his cheek. "Your clients, your idea, remember?" She winked at Cole who was waiting beside the door talking to Marsha. "As it happens, I know how to lay my hands on a Nancy Drew novel. And we're going to get it before your team does. Take that." In a lower voice, she added, "Please, Brendan. Relax. Try to have a good time."

"Next year, we're staying home," Brendan said, staring at her with obvious irritation. "Just you and me. A nice quiet evening. No crowds, no loud music, just us, a magnum of champagne, and no idiotic party games."

"Bye." Groping for a smile, Bailey wiggled her fingers at him and followed Cole and her other two team members outside. A line of limos curved around the circle drive, chuffing exhaust vapor into the frosty night air. Chauffeurs held the doors; waiters wearing earmuffs passed down the line of limos serving drinks and dispensing champagne.

Chad Dexter, one of Bailey's team members, grinned at the line of limos. "Nice touch. If we have to do this, this is definitely the way to do it." He accepted a Scotch and water from a waiter and helped Karen Lesserman slide into the limo. When they were all tucked inside, Chad toasted Cole. "Okay, team leader, what items do we have to scrounge up?"

"You won't believe it," Cole muttered, holding the list near an interior light. "Would you believe a washboard, a Nancy Drew novel—Brendan wasn't kidding—and a toucan feather?"

"A toucan feather? You're joking!" Karen Lesserman rolled her eyes above a dark mink collar.

"How about an airline ticket stub, a chrysanthemum and a white mouse?"

"A white mouse?" Karen shuddered. "I don't believe any of this. Tell me you're making it up!"

Bailey leaned over Cole's arm to peer at the list. "A policeman's badge? Does that mean a real policeman's badge?"

Karen Lesserman took the list. "Oh, my God, look at this one. A handwritten New Year's greeting from the mayor of Stamford!" She fell back against the plush gray upholstery. "I'm not liking this."

"Okay," Cole said, as the limo edged along the circle drive. He released a sigh of resignation. "Let's get organized."

"Where to?" the limo driver called over his shoulder.

"Give us a minute, buddy," Chad said. "Okay, coach, what item do we chase after first?"

"We're a democratic team," Cole said with a smile for Bailey. "Everyone has a say. But for starters, does anyone know where the mayor is right now?"

"I might know," Bailey admitted. She was acutely aware of Cole's thigh pressed against hers. "I saw an article in the newspaper announcing Mayor Wagner would be stopping in at a fund-raiser at the Stamford Sheridan. But I don't know what time."

"It's worth a try." Cole's expression indicated that he, too, was aware of Bailey's warmth and closeness. Leaning forward, he instructed the chauffeur to take them to the Stamford Sheridan.

"Hell, why not?" Chad asked. "My question is, which of us crashes the mayor's party and demands his honor's autograph?"

Laughing and arguing options, they discussed various strategies, and arrived at the Sheridan in what seemed mere minutes. Bailey and Karen Lesserman slid out of the limo and eyed a stream of party goers flowing into the Sheridan.

"All right, Bailey and I accept this one, but you guys owe us!" Karen called into the limo.

"Hey, we'd do it, but we aren't as pretty as you two. You have a better chance of crashing the mayor's party than we do," Chad laughed. "Good luck."

For an instant Bailey's gaze met Cole's and held. She didn't object to party games the way he and Brendan did. But she wasn't in the mood for games tonight. She sensed Cole felt the same, that he was trying as hard as she was to sound upbeat for the sake of Chad and Karen. Then Karen was tugging her toward the doors of the Sheridan, and they allowed themselves to be swept inside along with a flow of brightly gowned party goers.

Actually, obtaining the mayor's handwritten greeting wasn't as difficult as they had supposed. Mayor Wagner was standing just inside the doors of a private ballroom as if to make it easy for treasure hunters like themselves, and he didn't seem surprised by their request.

"Kelly Gordon set this up with you, didn't she?" Karen demanded after they had thanked him profusely for signing the back of their list.

Mayor Wagner's eyes twinkled. "Could be. Happy New Year, ladies!"

"I wish we'd figured this out earlier," Karen said, laughing. "I was a nervous wreck coming in here. I haven't crashed a party since college."

When they returned to the waiting limo, Cole was standing outside. Bending, he opened the door for Karen, then leaned inside, blocking Bailey's access. "If we're going to play, let's play to win," he said, tearing their list of items in two. "Here, you guys take this half, Bailey and I will take the other half. When we've got our items, we'll catch a cab and meet up with you at the Gordon house about eleven-thirty."

"I don't know..." Chad said doubtfully. "Kelly didn't say anything about splitting the teams."

"Remember the old adage about rules being made to be broken," Cole said. "Our best chance to win is to split up." He shut the door and waved. After a moment the limousine pulled away from the Sheridan and he turned to Bailey.

"Is this a good idea?" she asked quietly, gazing up at him, realizing he had created an opportunity for them to be alone.

"I wanted to be with you," Cole said simply. "It's been a long time since you and I had the chance to be alone and talk without someone hanging over our shoulder."

The same sense of danger that Bailey had experienced the first time she met him flickered now. She didn't know how she felt about being alone with him. The idea made her feel peculiar and fluttery inside. And guilty. At the same time it felt wonderfully liberating to do something impulsive and spontaneous. She couldn't remember the last time she had said to hell with the rules and did what felt good at the moment. And it did feel good to be alone with Cole and have a chance to really talk.

"Look, if you honestly want to play this stupid game, we will. Or we could go inside, have a drink and do some serious catching up. I want to know what's really going on with you."

Biting her lip in indecision, Bailey gazed up at him. They had seen each other sporadically over the past couple of years, but not in situations where they could speak frankly. The last time they had talked, really talked, had been the night they ran into each other at Times Square.

"You've got a deal," she said finally, turning toward the door of the Sheridan.

"Good." Cole led her into the lobby, which was dominated by a soaring Christmas tree, then turned left toward the bar. The hour was still early and the bar almost deserted.

Cole chose a table near a window and helped Bailey off with her coat, his fingers brushing the nape of her neck. She bit off a small involuntary gasp, then sat across from him, halfway wishing she hadn't agreed to this. She had forgotten what being alone with Cole Tarcher did to her nervous system.

"I'll have a Scotch and water and the lady will have a daiquiri," Cole said to the waiter who appeared with a bowl of mixed nuts. He handed the waiter his half of the treasure hunt list, ignoring Bailey's disapproval. "There is a huge tip for you if you can lay your hands on any of these items."

"That's cheating," Bailey protested, trying not to laugh. Cole hadn't changed. He was still charmingly incorrigible.

The waiter ran a finger down the list, then lifted a speculative gaze. "How huge a tip?"

"Very huge."

"Very huge, huh? Well, let's see. We've got another hour before it starts to get crazy..." The waiter walked toward the bar. "A washboard should be fairly easy." He looked up at the barman. "Hey, Zack. Do you still have that policeman's badge? A guy over here will pay huge money for it..."

Bailey's grin widened. "Cheating is going to cost you a small fortune. Plus, I don't think this is what Kelly Gordon had in mind."

"Delegation, the key to success." After their drinks arrived, Cole's expression sobered. "Now tell me about this baby business. How deep does the problem cut?"

Bailey turned to gaze out the steamy window. "Deep," she said quietly. "It's all I think about." She paused to taste her daiquiri, then met his eyes. "Brendan is thirty-three, and an only child. This is going to sound old-fashioned, but he wants a son, an heir if you will. To be honest, I think Brendan feels the ticking of the biological clock more than I do. Although I'm starting to feel it, too." She passed a hand over her forehead. "Mr. and Mrs. Hanson are driving us crazy wanting to know when we're going to start a family. Sometimes I feel like screaming: Don't you think we're trying? Brendan's father wants to be assured the Hanson line will continue."

"An heir to the throne, so to speak?"

"So to speak." She moved her daiquiri glass in wet circles. "But that's only part of the strain. I want babies, too, you know that, Cole. I always have. Hell, if I'd known it was this hard to get pregnant, I'd have screwed around in college a whole lot more." When Cole didn't laugh, she blushed. "Sorry. Bad joke."

Reaching across the table, Cole squeezed her hand. "Is that what you and Brendan were arguing about tonight?"

"Yes and no." Bailey returned the pressure of his hand, then gazed out the window again. Half a dozen fat wet flakes scudded past the panes. "Getting pregnant wasn't what we were arguing about, but yes, that was the subtext. It's always the hidden agenda, no matter what we're talking about. It's probably fair to say our failure to conceive is the underlying cause of all the arguments. And there have been a lot recently." She sighed. "We didn't used to argue at all. Now it seems all we do is snipe at each other. I know Brendan's turning his disappointment and frustration into working longer and longer hours. But I can't stop resenting it. And he thinks I'm spending all my time moping around the house—and maybe I am. I don't know what to do with myself. I keep thinking: What if I can't have children? What if it never happens?"

"I'm sorry, Bailey."

"We had it all planned. We would move back to the New York area, I'd quit work and get pregnant." She spread her hands in a gesture of frustration. "That was supposed to be the next stage of our lives. Nothing to it, right? Except I stopped taking the pill a long time ago and I'm still not pregnant." When she looked at Cole, her eyes were a deep navy color, filled with pain and deepening distress. "The worst of it—the very worst of it—is..." she swallowed and bit her lip. "I keep thinking Brendan is blaming me, that he thinks the problem is my fault. And I guess he's thinking that I blame him. Maybe that's why we've delayed seeing an infertility counselor. We're both afraid the other is right, that it's our fault. Stupid, isn't it? We're worrying about who's to blame instead of focusing on the real problem."

"I don't know what to say. Except I'm sorry."

"So am I. You can't imagine the strain all this is putting on our marriage." Waving a hand in apology, she opened her purse, then raised a tissue to her eyes. "I'm sorry. I get weepy-eyed just thinking about the possibility of not having children."

She hadn't exaggerated the strain between herself and Brendan. Lately it seemed that every small aggravation exploded into anger and hurt feelings. She knew Brendan was experiencing a number of frustrations settling into his father's firm; and he knew Bailey felt as if she were rattling around their new big home, feeling at loose ends, brooding about nurseries and layettes, missing her job and feeling unsure about what to do with herself.

But recognizing the tensions didn't disarm them. Bailey griped about the long hours Brendan was working; he complained she was listless and not as supportive as she should have been. A chasm had opened between them and seemed to be widening. It was increasingly difficult to recall the areas of compatibility they had taken such pleasure in three years ago. As to their sex life, it had deteriorated to those times dictated by the charts and the thermometer—and then, Bailey thought with a grimace, it was nothing to write home about. They made love with grim purpose, neither relaxed, neither taking particular pleasure from the event. Too much was at stake. The residue of too many arguments simmered between them.

Bailey didn't mention the sex problems to Cole, but she and Cole were enough in tune that she identified the look in his dark eyes and understood he had guessed some of the things she wasn't saying. A dusting of pink tinted her cheeks.

"This is so strange," she said softly, rubbing her temples. "How did you and I get to be such intimate friends?" Her smile didn't quite reach her eyes. "You and I don't talk, really talk, for a couple of years. Then we do, and I find myself pouring everything out. I tell you things I don't tell my best friends. With them I make it sound like I'm not worried about getting pregnant, like it's no big thing. I deliberately give the impression that Brendan and I are handling the disappointment and that we're not panicked. Maybe it's pride, I don't know, but I pretend that it isn't killing me inside when one of my friends gets pregnant and I'm still not. That it hurts inside every time I see a woman carrying an infant. But with you..."

"I can't answer that, Kansas. Except to say I'm glad we have that kind of friendship." His warm dark eyes caressed her face. "Maybe it's history. You and I go back a few years now. Or maybe it's love. I really care about you, and I think you know and trust that. I believe you care about me. You and I have never had time for pretense. We've always been in a situation where we have to compress years into an evening. We don't have the luxury of leisure. We don't have time for nuance or subtlety, no time for anything except honesty." He pressed both of her hands. "Frankly, I wouldn't have it any other way."

Bailey nodded, looking at their clasped hands. His solid warmth traveled up her arms and pushed at the chill that had frozen her as she confided her failure to become pregnant. Suddenly she wondered if the waiter thought they were lovers. And she wondered for one crazy moment what would have happened if she had agreed three years ago when Cole asked her to give them a chance together.

The thought shocked her to her toes.

That kind of speculation wasn't fair to anyone, especially not to Brendan. An unconscious sigh lifted her shoulders and bewilderment clouded her gaze. She and Brendan were drifting apart, floating in a sea of unspoken blame and frustration. And she didn't know how to halt the process or what to do about it.

"Oh, Cole," she whispered. "It's such a hard time right now. Remember when I worried that the perfect life didn't exist?" Fresh tears brimmed in her eyes, embarrassing her.

He pushed a snowy handkerchief into her fingers. "Hey, it's not over yet. Come on, Kansas, give me one of those smiles that lights up the room. You're not exactly over the hill. What are you? Twenty-eight? Your biological clock hasn't run down yet. The infertility specialist is going to give Brendan a pill and bingo! More babies than you know what to do with."

Smiling, she blotted her lashes. "Now you're doing it—assigning blame. What makes you so sure the problem is Brendan's fault?"

"Hey, if I ever saw a guy who looks like he has a low sperm count, it's old Brendan."

Bailey stared at him, then burst into laughter. "Idiot! You can't tell by looking at someone."

"In Brendan's case you can," he insisted cheerfully. "The minute I met Brendan I said to myself, now there is a guy with sluggish sperm. I tried to warn you, but you wouldn't listen. Oh, no. You were swept off your feet by that boyish smile and Mayflower pedigree and didn't want to hear about no-account sperm."

"I never dreamed I'd be laughing about this!" Bailey shook her head over the fresh daiquiri that appeared in front of her. "Oh, Cole, you're exactly what I needed tonight. I do love you."

"I wish you had realized that three years ago," he said softly.

Chapter Seven

Bailey bit her lips and turned to look out the window. The snow had thickened. Large fat flakes floated in front of the headlights of passing cars, collected on the bill of the bell captain's cap as he opened the doors for arriving cars and cabs.

So Cole wondered too, she thought. But what-if was a dangerous game. Turning back to him she raised a bright smile and ignored his comment.

"Tell me about you and Marsha. I confided what Brendan and I were arguing about, now it's your turn. Why were you two fighting?" She was ashamed to admit it gave her a tiny bit of pleasure to know that Cole and Marsha were in the midst of an argument, and it surprised her that she occasionally felt so possessive toward Cole.

"We were arguing about horses," Cole said after a minute. He smoothed a finger over his mustache, a gesture that was developing into a habit. He directed a thin smile at Bailey. "Other people's arguments sound silly, don't they?"

Bailey gave him a sympathetic shrug that briefly molded pleats of sapphire silk over her breasts. "Sometimes people don't argue about what's really bothering them . . ."

"Marsha breeds show horses on a farm she inherited from her grandfather, in the Berkshires," Cole explained.

After a moment of silence, he glanced up again. "Hillendale Estates isn't a farm like people from Wyoming or Kansas would recognize. It's a farm like those featured in *Town and Country*."

"Why is Hillendale a problem?" Bailey inquired softly. "I thought you loved horses." She had never seen Cole ride, but she often visualized him on horseback. The rugged image suited him.

"I do." He pushed a hand through his dark hair. "But Marsha's horses are as different from the horses I grew up with as a put is from a call. I grew up with saddle horses, range horses, workhorses. Show horses are another thing entirely. Hell, Marsha's pampered horses have never seen a cow and never will. They're trained to walk just so, trot just so, carry their tail and neck just so. You don't ride that kind of horse solely for pleasure, Bailey." He spread his hands. "That's not entirely true, but it isn't pleasure the way I think of it. Marsha's prize horse, an Arabian, has never been ridden outside a show ring. Can you believe that?" He stared at her. "That horse has a wall filled with ribbons, but he's never been ridden outside a ring." Shaking his head, he jabbed a finger at the ice in his glass.

"This sounds a little silly, but were you and Marsha arguing about the purpose of a horse?"

"We disagree about training, about how and where to ride horses, about how much time to devote to this interest, and about everything else." He drained his drink and signaled the waiter for another round. "I can't think of a subject we do agree on."

When he glanced at Bailey he found she was studying him with those large intelligent eyes that seemed to see everything.

"Okay, cowboy, what's the underlying problem here?"

For an instant, he didn't think about her words, he just listened to how she said them. She had the most marvelous low husky voice, a smoky Lauren Bacall voice. If they didn't see each other again for ten years, Cole believed he would still recognize Bailey in an instance just by hearing her say hello.

"If you're worrying about saying something disloyal," she said, leaning forward with an earnest expression, "nothing you say will be repeated. But if this conversation makes you uneasy—"

Reaching across the table, he took her hand and turned it in his palm. Her nails were shorter than Marsha's, painted a light rosy color. The warmth of her hand touched him in a profound manner that he couldn't have explained. All at once he wished he could take her in his arms and just hold her, wished their lives had turned toward each other instead of in different directions.

"Marsha is obsessed by her horses," he said finally, running a finger over Bailey's smooth thumbnail. He drew a breath. "She didn't want children."

In fact, Marsha had wanted to terminate the pregnancy, which had been unplanned, but Cole, shocked, had refused. They had battled the issue for three months before Marsha sullenly resigned herself to being pregnant. But she had never accepted it. Through the following months and the actual delivery, she hadn't missed an opportunity to let Cole know her ungainly figure and eventual labor pain were his fault.

When he realized his grip had tightened painfully on Bailey's fingers, he released her hand and reached for his drink.

"Sometimes I think Marsha cares more about her damned horses than she cares about the twins. That's what we were fighting about."

"Oh, Cole, that can't be true." Genuine pain constricted her features. "You must be mistaken!"

He looked at her. "I wish I were. But it sure as hell looks as if she prefers her horses."

From the very beginning Marsha had shown little or no interest in the twins. The doctors explained that some women required a period of adjustment. The doctors assured him that given a little time and understanding, Marsha would emerge from her numbing postpartum indifference and would fall in love with her children.

But four months had passed and so far there was no sign of that happening. Marsha had resumed her life and her social schedule as if the twins didn't exist. She spent as much time in the Berkshires at Hillendale as she had before the twins were born. She looked in on them in the morning and—when Cole reminded her—again before she retired. The rest of the time she was content to leave the twins in the care of the nanny and the nursemaid as if they had no real connection to her or her life.

As for Cole, prior to Marsha's unexpected pregnancy he hadn't thought much about children one way or another. Like most men he assumed he would one day be a father, but he felt no particular eagerness to hasten the day. Nor had he felt much involvement during Marsha's pregnancy.

Then, minutes after their birth he had held his son and daughter in his arms. He had gazed into their tiny red faces and felt himself overwhelmed with awe and amazement. A wave of instant love washed through him and poured into a bottomless reservoir. Tears of joy and love spilled down his cheeks.

The twins astonished him. They enchanted him. Everything about them fascinated him from their tiny perfect toes and toenails to the downy fuzz capping their heads. He never tired of standing above their crib just looking at them, marveling that he had played a role in the miracle of their creation.

"It's just so unbelievable," he said to Bailey, smiling. "They're two helpless tiny creatures who are going to grow up into people." A flush of embarrassment tinted his throat. "I'm sounding like an idiot, aren't I?"

"No." Tears glistened in her eyes. "You sound wonderful. You're going to make a terrific father, cowboy."

"I hope so. I know I'm going to try like hell. Look, is this conversation upsetting you?"

"It's just so hard to believe," she said in a strangled voice, "that Marsha can have children but doesn't want them. It isn't fair!" Turning her face away, she waited a minute until she could speak without obvious anger. "I'm sorry, Cole," she said finally. "I'm an emotional mess."

Dropping his gaze, he looked into his drink glass. "The odd thing is, I understand my own father better now than I ever did before. I look at the twins and dream a father's dreams. I want so much for them. I want to lay the world at their feet." He raised his head. "My world."

Bailey nodded. "I think I see where this is leading."

He turned to look at the falling snow. "I thought I understood how disappointing it was for Dad when I decided to leave the ranch. But I didn't have a clue." He gazed at the snowflakes melting down the windowpanes without seeing them. "I guess all parents have hopes and expectations for their children. Maybe all parents want their children to want what they want, to value what they value. When I walked away from the Tarcher Ranch, Dad must have believed I was rejecting him, too, and everything he valued, everything he is as a man. None of that is true."

"Have you told him that?" Bailey asked softly.

Startled, Cole stared at her. He shifted uncomfortably and touched his mustache. "Well, no. Men don't— It's difficult to..." Shaking his head, he let the words trail.

"Listen to me, cowboy," Bailey said, reaching across the table to grasp his hands. "I'm one of your oldest friends and I love you, so I can say things other people might not. You're being an idiot." She gazed into his eyes. "Take a weekend and fly home to Wyoming. Tell your father everything you just told me."

"Come on, Bailey. I—"

"No, listen to me. Your father has already had one stroke. Another might kill him. If that happened, you'd spend the rest of your life regretting that you didn't make things right with him. Go home, Cole. Tell your father that you love him. Help him understand that your dream isn't the same as his, but that doesn't mean you don't respect and love him. Let him know that you admire what he's accomplished in his life even though his life isn't what you've chosen for yourself. Do it. Do it soon."

He pushed his hands through his hair. "You make it sound so simple."

"It is."

She was wrong about that, but she was right about everything else. In a painful flash of insight, Cole realized it had been years since he had embraced his father and spoken those three words that were so easy to say—and so damned hard.

But those three words might sweep away the bewilderment and the hurtful silences that had opened between himself and his father. His father, who had undoubtedly stood over his crib and dreamed dreams as Cole did now. To his embarrassment, a lump formed in his throat.

"Let's get out of here," he said gruffly.

When he stood to help Bailey on with her coat, he noticed with surprise that the bar had filled and was now crowded with noise and people. Cigarette smoke thickened the air. A foursome in the back had linked arms and were singing Auld Lang Syne. When Cole glanced at his watch, he realized an hour had passed in the blink of an eye. It was always that way when he was with Bailey, there was never enough time.

At the door, Bailey tugged his arm. "We're forgetting our waiter. A huge tip, remember?"

"The stupid list," Cole groaned. His shoulders dropped in a gesture of exaggerated resistance. When he straightened and rubbed his hand over his mustache and chin, he caught the scent of Bailey's perfume on his fingers. For a moment he gazed down at her and their eyes held and he wondered how different his life would have been if Bailey were the mother of his twins.

"Stop thinking that," she ordered as if she had read his mind. When his eyebrows lifted in a guilty expression, she grinned and tapped a finger on his chest. "We are not going to duck out just because you hate party games. We can at least inquire and discover if our waiter located anything on the list."

She turned and pushed back toward the bar, and Cole followed, glad she couldn't see his expression.

The waiter was watching for them. With a flourish of his hand, he indicated an impressive pile of assorted items covering the far end of the back bar. "Voilà!"

Bailey stared. "Good God!" Moving around the countertop, she poked through the items, then laughed. "Where on earth did you dig up a black, size 38D bra?" She cast a twinkling glance at Cole. "And we thought this was going to be difficult."

"I believe you used the word 'huge,' sir," the waiter murmured, grinning proudly and thrusting out his hand.

Cole laughed and shook his head as he withdrew his wallet. "You earned it, buddy. Is there anything you *didn't* find?"

The waiter counted, then tucked away the wad of bills with a pleased smile. "I didn't locate a toucan feather. Also, I had a guy working on the white mouse...maybe you heard the screams in the storage room? All we could find was a gray mouse but he disappeared." A shrug accompanied the waiter's smile.

"You even managed shopping bags so we could carry this stuff." Bailey gave him an admiring gaze. "You're wasting your talents working here. You should be a magician."

After wishing the waiter a Happy New Year, they left the bar, crossed through the lobby, then pushed outside, pausing to inhale the damp cold air. Bailey turned up the collar of her coat and Cole adjusted his scarf.

"Any idea where we might find a toucan feather?" Cole asked, gazing down at the snowflakes collecting in the little curls that covered Bailey's head. She was so heartachingly beautiful.

"Let's walk awhile. Maybe inspiration will strike."

"Walk? Are you sure?" He eyed a short line of cabs.

"When was the last time you walked in a lovely wet New England snow?" she asked, taking his arm. Cole suspected she was really asking the question of herself.

He fell into step beside her, enjoying the possessive warmth of her hand on his arm, watching her swing the shopping bag in her free hand. They were so good together, so easy and natural. Why hadn't they realized it before life got so complicated?

"I'm getting the impression that you don't do many spur-of-the-moment things," he said, keeping his voice light. "That doesn't sound like a Gemini to me."

She smiled at the snow collecting on the sidewalk. "You bring out the impulsiveness in me." The look she gave him was almost flirtatious. "I'm not sure that's a good thing. Generally I'm happy enough with life being routine."

"Routine? I must have missed that rule."

"You would," she said, laughing. They ran across the street, then slowed on the other side, holding hands. Turning, Bailey faced backward, making Cole face backward too, watching the footsteps they made in the fresh snow. "See? I can be spontaneous and silly. Haven't you always wanted to do this?"

"Bailey, let's be serious a minute. As serious as people can be who are walking backward." They smiled at each other, and she still had the kind of smile that could make a man forget what he was talking about. He halted and just stared at her for a minute.

"Oh, Cole," she said softly. "Don't look at me like that."

"Sometimes you take my breath away," he whispered, lifting his gloved fingertips to her face.

She pressed his palm against her cheek, then stepped back. A sudden film of moisture glistened in her eyes before she dashed it away, then straightened her shoulders and gave herself a shake. "What were you about to say?" she asked in an unsteady voice.

He drew a breath. "What are you going to do next? Are you going to look for a job? Take up writing again? Or are you just going to sit in your big new house marking days off the calendar, waiting to get pregnant?"

"You sound like Brendan," she said in a warning tone, dropping her head. "I don't need that, cowboy."

"Maybe you do." They faced forward again but this time she ignored his hand and thrust her glove into her coat pocket. "You gave me some good advice, now I'm going to give you some." He overlooked her groan. "If I understand what you said, Kansas, you're floundering. So why don't you get your buns in gear and find a job? Wouldn't that be better than sitting around stalled, watching the calendar? A challenging job would give you something to think about besides babies."

She stopped and faced him through the falling snow. "Don't you think that's occurred to me?" Her flashing eyes narrowed. She tapped the Just Say No button on her lapel. "I still want to make a difference in the world, and wearing a dumb button isn't enough. I miss Washington like you wouldn't believe! At least there I was doing something! Now all I'm doing is what I've always done, waiting for my real life to start. And I hate it." She kicked at the snow, then walked forward, her head bent.

Cole caught up to her, matching her angry stride. "So why don't you change your situation?"

"Brendan doesn't understand that I'm going crazy at home." Bailey shoved her gloved fingers through her hair, scattering slushy droplets. "He wants me to *do* something, but that something doesn't include taking a job. Brendan has a fuzzy idea that wives should be content to shop, lunch, play bridge, join half a dozen social clubs, plan entertainments and tinker with a few hobbies. That's what he wants me to do. I wish I could, damn it, but I can't. I want, I don't know, I want something more. At least until we start a family."

Because he felt a need to touch her, Cole cupped her elbow and helped her cross the street before she remembered she didn't want help and jerked away from his hand, glaring at him.

"That doesn't sound so unreasonable," he said, ignoring her irritation.

"I don't want to play bridge or make craft projects out of egg cartons." She spread her gloves in a wide gesture, nearly spilling the items from the shopping bag she carried. "I want to save the kids starving in Biafra, I want to stop drug abuse, I want to clean up our environment." Stopping on the pavement, she lowered her head and her shoulders sagged. "I'm so frustrated I could scream."

"Leaving Washington, D.C., was tough on you, wasn't it?" he asked softly, touching her cheek again. "Have you told Brendan how you feel?"

She waved a hand, let it fall. "Brendan shares my concerns, but he doesn't feel the same need to get involved. For him it's enough to send a check. I've tried to explain that staying home isn't an answer for me, not right now. All I do is focus on getting pregnant and feel sorry for myself."

"Maybe—"

"Look, I don't want to be unfair." She gazed up at him with those magnificent eyes. Light from a nearby street lamp filtered through the falling snow and highlighted her cheekbones. "Brendan doesn't understand what I'm feeling, but he tries. He's entitled to his opinion just as I'm entitled to mine. He's had a working wife, and it was pretty hectic. Now he'd like a stay-at-home wife and a more predictable routine. That's how we planned it. That's what I wanted, too. Except..."

They fell into step again, walking in silence. Cole couldn't help making comparisons. Brendan Hanson wanted the kind of wife Cole had. Brendan would have understood Marsha, whereas Cole did not. Cole's ambitions were so clear-cut and focused that he couldn't understand Marsha's lack of goals. It seemed to him that Marsha whirled through life like a butterfly floating from one pleasure to another, with nothing more serious on her mind than the next dress-fitting or the next show ribbon. Marsha's life would have made sense to Brendan Hanson.

In contrast, Cole understood Bailey. Her goals were not directed financially or toward career advancement, but they were no less defined or compelling. There were issues and conditions outside herself about which she felt passionately. Bailey Meade Hanson would never be content to while away her days as one of the ladies who lunched.

"You know," he said slowly, glancing at her, "You may be one of those women who will want to continue working even after you have children."

"Superwoman." Finally she smiled again. Then laughed. "The same awful thought has occurred to me. Brendan would have a fit." She let him take her hand again as a gesture of peacemaking. "Look, thanks for trying to help, but there really isn't a solution. Even if I were willing to wrestle Brendan to the mat on this issue, there aren't too many classified ads reading: Potentially pregnant do-gooders wanted."

He grinned at her. "Let's think about that. We'll come back to it." Lines of honking cars jammed the streets, radios blared from windows open despite the snow and cold. Cole remembered walking from the Boston Symphony Hall to Tante Maison's, six years ago. It had been snowing then, too. But the world had been younger and less complicated then.

"You know," Bailey said, "I've been thinking—"

"Oh, no," he groaned, slapping his forehead. "I hate women who think. The minute they say: 'I've been thinking...' you know something awful is coming."

"You're a real comic, cowboy." She poked him in the ribs with her elbow. "I'm trying to be serious." Drawing a breath, she began again. "I've been thinking...maybe Marsha is resisting her role as a mother because she thinks she has to surrender her role as a woman. Maybe she feels it has to be either-or. I'm not saying this very well, but does that make sense?" She gazed up at him wiping snow from her lashes. "This is hard to say, but have you thought about romancing Marsha? Letting her know she's still attractive to you? That you still see her as a beautiful woman and not just as the twins' mother?"

"I thought I was being attentive, but I suppose I could step up the heat, so to speak." They stared at each other, then Bailey wet her lips and stepped out ahead of him. "Men like romance, too," he said to the back of her head. The halo of curls had tightened into a cap of corkscrew ringlets. "What about you? Have you considered a few intimate dinners with no underlying agenda? An evening where you forget about trying to get pregnant and just enjoy each other? When you wear something slinky and exciting like black stockings and a lacy garter belt?"

An image of Bailey attired as he'd suggested swept his mind and he felt his stomach tighten. He imagined her standing in a doorway wearing something black and filmy, a glimpse of long leg showing, a lock of hair falling over one eye. And that husky voice murmuring his name.

But it would be Brendan's name she called. Jealousy bit hard and deep, and he suffered a sense of loss. Whether or not Cole had the right to desire her, he did. He always had.

But he would never see her in actuality as he saw her in his imagination. It was never going to happen. That opportunity was lost to them.

She halted and faced him, her face pale in the snowy light of passing headlights. And suddenly Cole comprehended that Bailey was upsetting herself with thoughts of him and Marsha together the same way as he was tormenting himself with images of her and Brendan.

"Oh, Cole, do you...do you ever wonder what might have happened if—" She bit off the blurted words and her cheeks flushed with color. A horrified look clouded her eyes, and she bit her lips and tried to spin away from him. "I'm sorry."

Cole caught her arm. "Of course I think about it. Do you?"

She stared at his mouth, his eyes. "God forgive me— yes." She covered her face with her glove. "Yes," she whispered again.

"Bailey, it's all right. We—"

She dropped her glove and stared up at him with a helpless expression. "No, Cole, it isn't all right. Fantasizing about you is a betrayal." Anger and frustration clouded her bright eyes. "Sometimes I wish we'd gone to bed that first night and gotten it out of our systems! Then you would have gone your way and I would have gone mine. And we could run into each other without—" she lifted her hands and shook her head "—without wondering!"

"I can't get you out of my mind," he whispered.

She gave him another helpless look, almost angry. "I know," she said softly. "Do you think it's any different for me?" Then she made a chopping motion with her hand. "We can't talk about this anymore. Please." Turning away, she dashed for the curb and lifted her arm to hail a passing cab. The cab slipped on the snow and slid to a stop in front of them. "Come on, cowboy," she called, beckoning him forward without looking at him. "It's time we finished off our list and returned to the party."

Inside the cab, Bailey made a production of studying the list and comparing it to the items in their shopping bags, then she asked his opinion as to where they might find an embroidered pillowcase and a kiwi.

"Bailey—"

She raised a glove. "Don't say anything more. Please, Cole."

She was right. If their friendship was to continue, they had to obey the rules they had agreed to. That meant some topics were taboo. Cole nodded, and they focused on subjects other than their marriages and their feelings for each other as the cab dashed around town in pursuit of the items remaining on their list.

"You'll be thirty this year," Bailey said, smiling as Cole returned to the cab, swearing, and looking in disgust at a kiwi he had finally located in a Dumpster behind a grocery store. The cabdriver chuckled and rolled his eyes. "You wanted to be a millionaire by the time you were thirty. Are you going to make it?" She sounded interested, but her tone maintained a distance.

He wrapped the kiwi in his handkerchief and placed it carefully in Bailey's shopping bag. "Remind me never to go to another party without first checking to see if the hostess plans any stupid games."

"That's one of the things I like about you, you're such a good sport," she teased, grinning at him.

"I'm doing it, aren't I?" He settled back against the cab's cracked vinyl upholstery and dropped his arm around her. The scent of her perfume rose in his nostrils. "I probably won't make millionaire this year, although it could happen . . . but next year for certain."

"Congratulations." Disappointment pushed at the warmth in her eyes. "I wish I was as close to achieving my goals as you are. But aside from getting pregnant, I don't have any."

"You know, I've been thinking..."

"Oh, no. Now I understand what you said earlier. I have an idea something awful is coming."

"I'll ignore that. Listen, you enjoyed D.C. so much, and you need hills to climb..."

She rolled her eyes. "So *you* say. I've never said that. You're the one who's always throwing hills in my path."

"Why don't you run for Congress?"

She started forward and spun to stare at him. "This again? Me? Run for Congress?"

"Why not? You'd be terrific. Aldridge is retiring this year, you wouldn't have an entrenched incumbent running against you. And what better place to change the world and make a difference than in D.C.? You said that yourself."

"Have you lost your mind? You're the risk taker, not me." Bailey blinked, then stared again. "I don't want to run for Congress."

"You can't change the world without taking risks, Kansas."

"Get serious, Cole. I hate it when you say things like this." Anger flushed her face. "You of all people should know I don't have big ambitions. But you say things like this, then I feel like some kind of loser if I don't agree, the lowest kind of coward. You aren't being fair."

"And you aren't being honest with yourself, Bailey."

"What the hell is that supposed to mean?"

He lifted the lapel of her coat. "Just say no," he read off the button on her lapel. "Are you telling me that ending drug abuse isn't a large ambition?" He tapped her chest and the button on her dress beneath her coat. "Or fixing the ozone layer? That isn't a big ambition? The hell it's not. You've *always* had big ambitions, Bailey Meade Hanson. Changing the world is no small thing. That's about the biggest ambition you could have!"

Shock darkened her stare.

"So do it. Go back to Washington and kick some butt. Only this time do it as a Congresswoman, not as a staffer."

"Good God," she whispered. The direction of her thoughts altered abruptly as the truth dawned. "All these years...I really thought I was a small thinker. I *believed* it." She shook her head and gave him a wobbly grin. "I never looked at this squarely. Of course I have big ambitions. Big scary ambitions. Good Lord. Why didn't you point this out before?"

Cole spread his gloves and looked at the ceiling of the cab. "Lord, please help this poor deaf girl. She can't hear and she's a little dumb, but her heart's in the right place."

"Cole, do you really— No. This is crazy." But she couldn't help thinking about it. Suddenly Bailey's mind was ablaze with possibilities. Cole was right. Ames Aldridge had already announced his intention to retire. And she knew everyone on the Hill, she had connections. It wouldn't be like starting cold. Maybe...

"No, this won't work," she said slowly. "*If* I decided to do this crazy thing, and *if* I actually won the election, I'd have to live in Washington."

Cole studied her in the glare of passing headlights. One dark eyebrow lifted. "You could commute, it's not that far and Brendan can afford it. You could get a small place in D.C. for those times you had to stay over."

Bailey bit her lower lip, her thoughts flying at the speed of light. Suddenly she was seeing herself and the world from a very different perspective. She felt fluttery inside, frightened by the thought of waging a political campaign but also strangely exhilarated. "You know," she said slowly, her voice huskier than usual, "I might be good in government. And I'd love it."

"You'd be terrific. You're a natural."

"But what if I get pregnant? I couldn't just quit, I'd have a responsibility to the people who voted for me."

He shrugged. "A representative's term is two years. The worst that could happen is that you juggle your schedule for two years, then retire. Or, you might find you can be a mommy *and* a congresswoman and excel at both."

A fire kindled in her eyes and blazed. Then a cloud dimmed her excitement and she shook her head. "What am I thinking? Brendan will never agree to this, not in a million years."

"Why not? He loves you, doesn't he? Of course he'll support you. I would."

But Brendan wasn't Cole, Bailey thought, turning her face to the window. Brendan would be flabbergasted by this idea. Not for one moment would he understand or approve. He would be bewildered by her wanting to take on a killer schedule and being willing to work hard and commute instead of relaxing into the leisurely role of being Brendan Hanson's wife.

But suddenly, overwhelmingly, she wanted to do it. It was as if Cole had put into words something she had been unable to articulate or quite bring to the surface. With a few simple words, he had opened her eyes to the truth. She did have ambitions, huge ambitions, so huge she had been afraid to really look at them. She closed her eyes and pressed the heels of her palms against her cheekbones.

"You're a bad influence on me, cowboy. You've just complicated my life in about a thousand ways." A mixture of gratitude and irritation flickered in her gaze.

"Then you'll run for Aldridge's seat?" he said, grinning.

"I'll think about it."

"You're more of a risk taker than you admit, Kansas. And I never did understand that delusion about modest goals and small ambitions."

She pushed up her coat sleeve to glance at her wristwatch, suddenly eager to return to the Gordons' and talk to Brendan. "Oh my God! Look at the time! It's eleven-thirty."

Leaning forward, Cole tapped the cabbie's shoulder. "Step on it, will you, pal? We need to be at this address before midnight."

But this time the promise of a large tip didn't work magic. Near the turn off into the Stone Violet subdivision, the cab slid into a traffic snarl that none of the participants seemed in any hurry to untangle.

The cabbie shrugged and looked over his shoulder. "Sorry, folks, we aren't going to make it by midnight. Might as well relax." Winking, he lifted a bottle of champagne and a stack of plastic cups. "Will you join me in a wee one?"

Bailey and Cole looked at each other, then at the traffic snarled outside. People had climbed out of their cars and were laughing and dancing in the snow. A few wore paper hats, and colored streamers hung off their coats.

"Might as well," Cole said after a moment. "Looks like we're stuck here."

The cabbie poured champagne into the plastic cups and snapped on his radio. The announcer in Times Square began the countdown, and his voice blared from half a dozen car radios. Then everyone was leaning on their horns and shouting. Bells pealed in the distance. The people dancing in the snow linked arms and sang along with the radios, singing Auld Lang Syne.

"Happy New Year!" the cabbie shouted, pounding his horn.

Cole and Bailey touched the rims of their glasses and drank their champagne, then Cole framed Bailey's face between his hands.

"Happy New Year, Congresswoman. This is going to be your best year ever. Who knows? First Congress, then Madam President." He grinned into her eyes.

"You're impossible. One thing at a time, cowboy. I haven't even agreed to run yet." As always, there were no limits with Cole Tarcher. Madam President. Bailey laughed out loud. "Happy New Year, my dear friend."

Her gaze dropped to his lips and her mouth suddenly dried. Her heartbeat accelerated as Cole's arms closed around her, and he kissed her tenderly, as if she were a fragile creature made of glass. Whatever passion he felt, he carefully held it in check.

And inexplicably, Bailey felt like weeping. Tears glittered like diamonds on her thick lashes. Raising a hand, she touched trembling fingertips to his cheek. "Oh, Cole," she whispered.

"I know," he murmured in a hoarse voice, holding her close. He stroked her snow-damp hair.

"Sometimes life is so unfair!"

"Don't you worry. Everything is going to work out fine." Still holding her, he kissed her temple. "You're going to have it all, just like we planned way back when."

The cab moved forward then, slowly winding through the honking horns and celebrating couples. Bailey eased out of Cole's arms and snapped open her compact. Hurriedly she repaired her lipstick and eye makeup, shoved at her hair.

"This has been a nice night," she said softly, "but strange." She found Cole's astrology booklet in her purse and pushed it into his hands. "You Scorpios are going to have an exceptionally prosperous year. You'll pass the million mark, no doubt about it."

Cole glanced at his watch—five minutes after midnight—before he peered through the windshield at the Gordon house. Then he took Bailey's hands in his, knowing they wouldn't have another chance for a private word.

"Look, Bailey, don't let Brendan talk you out of doing whatever you want to do. And don't let the risk scare you. Sometimes you have to put yourself on the line and take a chance for something you believe in. Win or lose, at least you'll know you tried.''

"And you're going to go to Wyoming and talk to your father, right? You promised, Cole.''

"I will. And Bailey, thanks.''

She squeezed his hands, then looked toward the Gordons's door. "I have a feeling you and I are in trouble.''

She was right. Kelly Gordon almost fell on them when they staggered inside, carrying their shopping bags of items.

"We were worried sick!'' Kelly cried, peering into their faces. Her hands fluttered over the shopping bags. "Oh dear, you might have won, but you're too late. Martin Scarborough's team won. You had to be back by 11:45.''

Bailey looked over Kelly's crimson taffeta shoulder and met Brendan's cold gaze. Marsha Tarcher stood beside him. She looked furious.

"We got stuck in a colossal traffic jam,'' Bailey explained. She sounded guilty and suspected she looked guilty. Bending, she poked through the shopping bags. "Did anyone find a toucan feather?''

Cole touched her shoulder. "Goodbye, Kansas. Stop playing it safe and make a grab for the gold ring. You're ready and you'll be a terrific congresswoman. I'll be watching.''

"Don't put off the trip to Wyoming. Go this month.''

Brendan stepped up beside her. He glared at Cole, then looked down at Bailey. "Where the hell were you? Everybody was worried to death!''

"Happy New Year to you, too,'' she said, lifting on tiptoe to kiss him. He didn't kiss her back. From the corner of her eye, she watched Marsha turn her back to Cole and storm into the living room. Cole followed her.

"I'm sorry we worried you,'' Bailey said, taking Brendan's arm. "We couldn't anticipate the traffic snarl. There wasn't anything we could do.'' Still tight-lipped, Brendan reached to help her off with her coat, but Bailey shook her head. "Let's go home." The excitement returned to her eyes, and she felt it bubbling inside. "There's something I want to talk to you about."

"What is it?" The words were cautious, but he looked a little happier, knowing they were leaving.

"I'll explain in the car." Throwing her arms around his neck, she smiled up at him. "Oh, Brendan, this is going to be a wonderful year!" She smoothed his thinning hair, then dropped her fingertips to his lips. "I do love you."

Right now she loved everyone. After weeks of feeling at loose ends, she felt herself knitting together again. For the first time in months the future looked bright again, and filled with promise. Cole was right. Sometimes risks could be exhilarating.

When she and Brendan went in search of Kelly and Steve Gordon to say their goodbyes and thank-yous, Bailey spotted Cole standing beside the Christmas tree, frowning at Marsha who was waving her hands and speaking in a furious undertone.

For an instant their eyes met, and Bailey winked and gave him a surreptitious thumbs-up sign. His expression didn't change, but he gave her a tiny almost imperceptible nod of encouragement.

Already she missed Cole's enthusiasm and support. She slid a glance toward Brendan, and for a moment her resolve wavered. She knew she was facing a battle. Brendan wasn't going to be easily persuaded that Bailey should make a bid for Representative Aldridge's congressional seat.

At the door, she looked back over her shoulder and caught Cole's eye. Marsha had vanished, and he was standing alone beside the Christmas tree.

"Do it," he mouthed, and returned the thumbs-up sign she had given him a few minutes earlier.

By the time she and Brendan pulled the Mercedes into their garage, she had explained what she wanted to do.

Brendan cut the motor, then turned on the seat to stare at her. "Are you *crazy?* How much champagne did you drink tonight?"

Bailey kept a smile pasted on her lips. It was going to be a hard-won battle indeed. She looked at her husband and wondered how it was possible that the very qualities that had caused her to fall in love with him were the same qualities she now found it so difficult to live with.

Chapter Eight

Brendan,
I have a meeting at Democratic Headquarters—your dinner is in the oven. Dr. Frye phoned this morning; we'll talk about it when I get home. Basically he said you passed your sperm analysis with flying colors. Looks like I'm the culprit—my fault, my problem. Dr. Frye thinks it's too soon to think about extraordinary measures but he wants to explain laparoscopy, which is the next probable step. Meanwhile we should just keep trying.

I love you.
Bailey.

P.S. The air-conditioning is on the blink. Do you have time to phone a repairman?

Bailey,
How can we try when you're never home? This bid for a congressional seat is turning out just as I feared it would. We never see each other anymore. If it wasn't for refrigerator notes, we wouldn't communicate at all.

P.S. My secretary phoned a repairman. He'll try to get here tomorrow afternoon.

Mr. Tarcher:
Your wife phoned. She's riding in the Connecticut Arabian show and says she forgot about the interviews this afternoon. Can you do them? If not, call the New Nanny Agency and cancel.

Marsha,
Should you happen to notice a large cheerful woman with an English accent now living in our house, she is Mrs. Peppercorn, our new nanny. I hired her to look after the two babies also living in our house, whom you may have noticed when you were passing through. I wonder if you realize that we have six photographs and one painting of your Arabian but only one photograph of our children in our house? Must we go to the Van Halders on Saturday?

Mrs. Hanson—your husband called to cancel lunch. He has to be in court. Also, Mr. Larrabee phoned. He says you have a three-percent lead in the polls. He's talking to local cable about setting up a debate between you, Frank Blevens and that teacher who just entered the race. Your housekeeper called. The washing machine broke and flooded the laundry room and part of the kitchen. Dr. Frye also called. He wants to schedule your surgery and needs to clear a date.

Dearest Marsha, Happy Birthday. I know it's been a tough and confusing year. But we're bright people and we care about each other. We can work things out and make the necessary adjustments, can't we? If you don't like the bracelet, Tiffany's will exchange it.

                                                     Love, Cole.

August 15, 1986
Gladys, please call Dr. Frye and cancel my surgery. Tell him I'll call later today to apologize and explain in person. Just tell him how frantic this campaign is and that I've decided

to delay surgery until after the election.

Mrs. Hanson

September 24, 1986
Dear Cole,
I can't believe it's almost autumn. It seems like only yesterday that you were here in Wyoming and we were sitting around the kitchen table, talking. Can't believe it was nine months ago.

You know Dad, he never says much, but your visit meant the world to him. Whatever you two said to each other that day in the barn, it made a huge difference. He no longer looks hurt or uptight when your name comes up. Whatever you said, Cole, I'm glad you said it and glad you and Dad have made peace.

Harlan and I have thought a lot about your proposal and we talked it over with the folks as you suggested. Dad's stubborn. He won't change his will—says he's leaving the ranch to you and me in equal shares. (Mom will take the house in town if anything happens to Dad.) So, I guess Harlan and I will accept your offer and buy out your share when the time comes. We can't imagine living anywhere but here on the ranch or living any other life.

Actually Dad seems pleased with this arrangement. I think he was worried the ranch would be split up and sold off to strangers after he was gone. In his heart I suspect he wishes you would come home and make your life here. But I think he's finally accepted that's not going to happen. At least he knows how much Harlan and I love the place and I think he's comfortable about how things are working out.

Jimmy has chicken pox and it looks like Greta will be next. John is in the school band this year. And I'm pregnant again. Harlan says it's going to take a lot of little ranchers to run this place. Mom and Dad are fine. We all miss you.

Love, Beth

Mrs. Bailey Hanson
11 Amsterdam Pl.
Stamford, Conn.
October 14, 1986

Dear Bailey,
I was in Hartford last week and caught your debate on TV.
You put those uptight sticks in the dirt, Kansas. That jerk,
Frank something or other, looked like he'd never heard of
the water issue. And the ex-teacher was just hopeless. Every
time you spoke he looked like he was thinking: Why didn't
I say that? You're a shoe-in!

I've seen a lot of Brendan lately. I'm sure he told you
we're working together on the Pie Rite deal. He's proud of
you, Bailey. Sometimes he brags about you through grit-
ted teeth, but he's bragging. I'm proud of you, too.

Cole

Hartford Courant, November 8, 1986
By Craig Martin, elections desk. The battle for Represen-
tative Ames Aldridge's seat ended in a landslide victory for
Bailey Hanson. Following a spirited campaign, Hanson, a
first-time candidate, defeated her closest opponent, Frank
Blevens, by a wide margin. At her victory celebration at
Democratic Headquarters, Hanson said, ''The district was
ready for a change and...''

November 8, 1986
Representative Bailey Hanson
Democratic Headquarters
WAS THERE EVER ANY DOUBT STOP CONGRATULATIONS
STOP
Mr. and Mrs. Cole Tarcher

Wall Street Journal, June 6, 1987
Associated Press. Rutherford Delaney, vice president of

Mangan and Mangan, announced that Cole Tarcher has accepted an appointment as head of Mangan and Mangan's aggressive new Mergers and Acquisitions Department. Tarcher was previously First Guarantee Trust's principal rainmaker in Corporate Finance. When asked to comment why he left First Guarantee Trust, Tarcher said . . .

Representative Bailey Hanson
1414 Wayne St, Suite 101
Washington, D.C.
June 30, 1987

Dear Bailey,
Thanks for your card. The move wasn't as sudden as it appeared. I've been looking to make a change for about a year. New challenges, new opportunities—you know the drill. Marsha says it's male mid-life crisis. Maybe she's right. She says I have all the signs: restlessness, irritability, boredom.

You're going to think this is odd—or maybe you won't—but recently I've been thinking about the Tarcher Ranch. Before you start looking smug and thinking "I told you so," let me assure you that I don't regret agreeing to sell my interest to my sister and her husband. But sometimes I think about the life-style and experience a wave of nostalgia. Manhattan is no place to raise kids. And I was kidding myself to think finance was an easier profession than ranching. I must be getting old, I'm starting to sound like my Dad.

I'm glad everything went well with your operation. Brendan sounds hopeful and optimistic. Call me the minute there's good news.

I haven't seen you in two years, do you realize that? I'm seeing far too much of old what's-his-name and not nearly enough of you. Marsha and I are planning to be in Aspen

for the holidays. Brendan says you two may be there, too.
Try to make it, Kansas. It's been too long . . .

                                                            Cole

Chapter Nine

New Year's Eve, 1988

The sky was clear and icy blue, the air so sharp and cold Bailey felt as if she were breathing needles. Behind her, pine garlands draped Victorian street lamps, and thousands of tiny Christmas lights wound through the trees running down the center of Aspen's outdoor mall. Although it was early, the lights blinked and twinkled, adding an air of festivity to the afternoon.

Tilting her head, Bailey cast a glance toward the snow-capped peaks glistening in the winter sun and tried to imagine Aspen in the summer. She couldn't. This was a winter town. A town fashioned for snowy lanes and jingling horse-drawn sleighs, for soaring condos and skiers zipping down powdered slopes.

Smiling, she turned back to the window of an outrageously expensive children's shop. The display featured mink caps and mink-trimmed parkas for toddlers. The smile faded from Bailey's lips, and a shudder of distaste passed down her spine. She didn't like the idea of fur coats for anyone.

"For the kid who has everything," a deep voice said directly behind her.

A familiar thrill tingled through Bailey's body before she spun on her boot heels with a delighted smile. "Cole!"

"Hi, Kansas. I've been looking all over this town for you."

She wanted to give him a hug but he carried the twins, three years old now, and both hands were occupied holding them on his shoulders. Rising on tiptoe, Bailey touched her cold pink cheek to his, inhaling his after-shave, then she stepped back to admire the twins. They were beautiful active toddlers, bright-eyed and curious. Stevie stretched a mitten toward an icicle dripping from the shop roof, Shawn pressed her forehead against Cole's cap and peeked down at Bailey.

"They're wonderful," Bailey enthused, smiling, wriggling her fingers at Shawn, who giggled and hid her face against Cole's cap before she peeked at Bailey again. "I can't decide who they look like." But her heart insisted they looked like him, like Cole.

"They look like imps." Cole grinned. "And old dad needs a break. We're on our way to a place that has an indoor playground and the best ice cream you ever tasted. Will you join us?"

"For ice cream?" she asked incredulously, her voice melting to vapor in the cold air. She returned his grin with affection. "I was just thinking this is a perfect day for ice cream."

"Where's Brendan?" Cole fell into step beside her, and Bailey noticed several people smiling at them, mistaking them for a family. It made her feel funny inside. One of the twins waved at everyone they passed, the other made a grab for the ball on Bailey's stocking cap before she laughed and ducked aside.

"Brendan's skiing. And Marsha?"

"Shopping. She's around here someplace." The vitality drained from his voice, and he answered in a hard expressionless tone. Bailey glanced up quickly, but said nothing.

Inside the ice cream parlor, she and Cole peeled off the twins' parkas and snow pants and grinned as the children raced through the tables toward the indoor swings and hanging ropes.

"Now it's your turn," Cole said, reaching to help Bailey out of her parka. After dropping her coat over the back of a chair, he pulled the chair out for her. When she remained standing, waiting for him to look at her, he glanced up at her wide radiant smile. Then his gaze dropped to the maternity sweater draping her swollen figure. "Bailey!"

"It's true," she said, laughing at his expression. She had waited a long time for this moment. "Finally."

Before she could protest, he rushed around the table, caught her in his arms and swung her in a circle, grinning in delight. Several families at other tables smiled at them. When he set her on her feet, Bailey laughed, then turned slowly in front of him proudly showing off her new rounded shape.

As always she experienced a thrill and a sudden weakness from his touch. But after all these years, and especially now that she was pregnant, she could cope with the exhilaration of his presence. Their continuing attraction for each other added spice and zest to their friendship. But Bailey was confident neither of them would jeopardize that friendship by taking it beyond an occasional touch, an occasional word.

Cole helped her into her chair as if she were a piece of porcelain. "You didn't say a thing! Why didn't you call me?"

They gave their order to a waiter dressed in a clown suit before Bailey answered. "I wanted to but—this is going to sound silly—I was afraid I might jinx things if I told anyone too soon. We've waited so long and gone through so much..."

"And Brendan is delighted? Of course he is. He's got his heir to the throne. God, you look beautiful!"

Bailey's eyes glowed with a light from within. "Oh, Cole, this is such a good period for me. Brendan and I haven't been this close or this happy in years. It's like all the problems and all the tensions have just melted away.'' That wasn't quite true, but it was close. She spread her hands, groping for words. "It's fabulous! A dream come true. I'm almost afraid to believe this has really, finally happened and we're going to have a baby! But we are! And it's...it's wonderful!''

He studied the glow illuminating her face before his smile returned. "I'm happy for you, Kansas, really glad. I know how long you've wanted this. One thing is certain—pregnancy agrees with you. You look more beautiful than I've ever seen you.'' A hint of wistfulness repeated the look in his dark eyes.

Bailey laughed and waved her hand in a gesture of denial, but in truth she felt beautiful. And that was strange because she was wearing less makeup than she ordinarily did, her figure was distorted, and she wore her hair wrapped into a careless ponytail. Yet she felt she had never looked better in her life. Her skin glowed with health, her hair was thick and glossy, and her eyes sparkled with happiness.

"You look great, too, cowboy.'' Cole never appeared to gain a pound. He was as broad-shouldered and as lean in the waist as he had been when she met him in college. And as handsome. From the corner of her eyes, Bailey noticed several young mothers discreetly giving Cole the once-over. "What happened to the mustache?''

"It went down the sink about a year ago. Something you would know if you weren't neglecting your friends.'' Beneath the tease was a serious note. "I thought we agreed not to lose touch.''

"I'm sorry I had to cancel lunch last month, but you wouldn't believe how hectic my schedule is. I'm trying to get caught up before the baby's due, and it's just—''

"Last month?'' His dark eyebrows lifted. "Try three months ago.''

"You're kidding!" She stared at the amusement growing in his brown eyes. "Well, I guess that proves my point about my schedule. It's crazy. The days just zip past. It's like working in a whirlwind."

As she talked about Washington, D.C., and how busy her life was, Bailey examined Cole for changes. She noticed a streak of silver winging back from his temples, which shocked her at first before she decided she liked it. The lines between his eyes and framing his mouth had deepened a bit as if he frowned more than she remembered him doing. And she thought he looked tired.

"It's been a tough year, hasn't it?" she asked softly.

The amusement faded abruptly from his smile. "Now there's an understatement if I ever heard one." They sat facing the indoor playground, watching the twins. "For starters, moving to Mangan and Mangan was a mistake," he said finally, bluntly.

"At the time you made the move, you couldn't have anticipated the insider trading scandal or guessed that one of Mangan and Mangan's people would turn out to be a key figure in the trading ring."

"I didn't predict the October crash, either—but it happened." Lifting a hand, Cole raked his fingers through his hair. "I'm dealing with the results of several appallingly bad guesses, bad choices. And I'm not alone. Everyone on the Street is trying to cope with the fallout."

"Oh, Cole, I don't know what to say."

He shrugged, his eyes fixed on the playground and the twins. "There isn't anything to say. I didn't get hurt too badly on a personal level, and I'm damned grateful for that. But the firm will be a long time digging out from under. Clients sense these things. Many are hemorrhaging out the door. So are a significant number of key employees."

In silence they watched the children playing on the swings and ropes and in the sandboxes. Circus music played overhead, and a small carousel did a brisk business near the soda fountain. The clown waiter served coffee and asked if he should hold the twins' cones for a little longer. Cole nodded.

"When is the baby due?" Cole inquired, turning the conversation back to her.

Briefly Bailey closed her eyes, responding to the deep timbre of his voice. Always, always she was haunted by the might-have-beens, even when she didn't want to think about them. Whenever she saw Cole, the what-ifs appeared.

What if this baby had been his? What if Shawn and Stevie had been theirs? What if...

"The baby's due the middle of May. It's a girl." Her gaze followed Shawn toward the sandbox.

Reaching across the table, Cole took her hand. "You look exactly the way I knew you would...radiant, beautiful."

The look in his eyes told Bailey he was comparing her to his memories of Marsha's unwanted pregnancy, that for a moment, he was pretending Bailey belonged to him. She pressed his hand and drew a breath. "We're trying to decide between Jeanette Meade Hanson or Emily Meade Hanson. What do you think?"

"I like the name Shawn." A smile nudged at the soberness that had overtaken his expression.

"That name is already taken." Bailey laughed. Recently it seemed everything made her laugh or smile. She couldn't remember being this happy before. There were moments when she stopped whatever she was doing and just smiled into space, enjoying the exhilaration of sheer happiness, marveling that she could feel like this, that her real life had finally, finally begun.

Leaning over her coffee cup, her husky voice vibrating with excitement and pleasure, she tried to explain how happy she was.

"Seeing you again is the icing on the cake," she added softly, smiling at him with affection. "Right now there isn't another thing in this world I could ask for."

Cole's gaze caressed her face, her mouth. "I never thought I'd envy Brendan, but right now I do," he said quietly. Then he cleared his throat and asked, "Will you run for Congress again? This is an election year."

Bailey looked surprised. "Not a chance, cowboy. I'll finish out my term, but I won't run for reelection. I want to be home to see the first smile, the first step, the first everything. I've waited too long for this baby. I don't want to miss a thing."

He nodded but didn't say anything.

"Serving in Congress has a downside, too. It's as frustrating as it is exciting. Believe me, it's tough sledding for the new kids on the Hill. Without a little seniority, we might as well be invisible. It takes years before a new congressperson can be effective."

"Congress*person?*" he asked, grinning.

She ignored him. "Plus, commuting has never really been satisfactory. I don't think Brendan has ever reconciled himself to how much time I have to spend in Washington. He's been a good sport about it," she said loyally, and not altogether truthfully. "But I don't think either of us will be sorry to see my term end. It's been a fabulous experience and I wouldn't have missed it for the world, but Washington was always a substitute for the real dream."

"Mmm."

"Damn it, Cole. Don't give me that knowing look. I ran, I won, and I've done a good job during the time I've been on the Hill. At least as good as I could as a junior representative whom no one listens to. Now it's someone else's turn to carry the torch. So why am I getting the feeling that I've disappointed you?"

"I'm sorry, I didn't mean to give you that impression."

"But?"

"No buts. If you're picking up some tension it has nothing to do with your decision to be a full-time mommy. You're right, Bailey. You've waited a long time for this baby, and you should enjoy every minute of the experience. Knowing you, I think there'll come a time when you'll want to resume a career." When Bailey rolled her eyes and made a face, he smiled. "You'll know when and if the time comes." His gaze steadied on her eyes. "The truth is, Kansas, maybe I'm envious." Her hair was drawn back in a shining dark ponytail, but a strand had pulled loose and lay on her cheek. Cole restrained an urge to brush back the strand.

"Envious?"

Abruptly he shifted in his chair and looked toward the twins. Shawn was playing happily in the sandbox. Stevie, more active, was trying to soar higher in a swing pushed by the playground supervisor.

"I think Marsha is having an affair," Cole said quietly. So far he'd resisted similar temptations, but sometimes he asked himself why. He honestly didn't believe Marsha cared anymore what he did. He wasn't sure that he cared anymore what she did.

Shock darkened Bailey's eyes, and her voice sank to a husky register. "Oh, Cole! I'm so sorry."

"If it wasn't for Stevie and Shawn, we'd probably divorce. Actually the jury's still out on that one. I'm not sure parents do children any favors by holding together an unhappy marriage."

Genuine distress pinched Bailey's features. She leaned forward and spoke in a low voice. "Isn't there anything you can do? Counseling maybe?"

"We've tried counseling." A humorless smile thinned his lips. "Counseling led to some interesting fights but not much else."

"Where do things stand now?"

"Everything's on hold until after the holidays. Then we'll talk. I don't expect much to come out of it. I can't give Marsha the constant attention she needs, she can't be the wife and mother I'd like her to be. Neither of us thinks we're asking too much, but apparently we are." He shrugged, then pushed to his feet. "Time to dust off the kids and get them a cone before this place runs out of strawberry ice cream."

While the kids happily devoured dripping pink ice cream cones, wriggling in their seats and chattering to each other, Bailey and Cole engaged in a mild debate, arguing the pros and cons of regulating the Wall Street markets.

But Bailey kept thinking about the disintegration of Cole's marriage. The news upset her more than she would have guessed. And another onslaught of what-ifs troubled her thoughts. For a moment she gazed at Cole over Stevie's head, thinking he was the most handsome man she had ever seen and one of the most exciting. Their eyes met and held, then she quickly said something perfectly idiotic about the recent insider trading scandals.

"As usual, we don't agree," Cole said, smiling and wiping ice cream from Stevie's cheeks and chin while Bailey cleaned up Shawn.

"Have we ever agreed on anything?" Bailey asked lightly.

The minute the kids climbed down from their chairs, they streaked back to the swings and ropes.

Cole touched her hand. "You and I agree on a lot of things, the important things. The basics. Most important, we respect each other as individuals. We may not agree on specific issues—"

Bailey laughed. "We *never* agree on specific issues."

"But we respect each other's right to have differing opinions. There's never anything personal in our arguments. You don't attack me to get at my ideas."

Slowly Bailey nodded. His last statement was a telling one. Suddenly she had a glimpse into his arguments with Marsha.

"But we do have fundamental differences, Cole." She drew a breath. "You can deny it all you like, but in your heart you really don't understand why I don't plan to run for another term in Congress. You think I can be a Congresswoman *and* a super mother. Maybe I could be. It's also possible that I'd end up doing a half-baked job on both fronts. I don't want to take that risk. At least not right now. You, on the other hand, you're willing to stick your neck out, willing to pile on the risks. But me, I need to know where the stop signs are. I like to know my parameters."

"Tell me something," he said, studying her face. "Ever since I met you, you've been wearing lapel buttons protesting something or making a statement about something. So where is this year's button?"

She didn't answer immediately. "Congresswomen don't wear protest buttons."

"Why is that?"

"Isn't it obvious? It wouldn't be politic to shout one's position so intractably. A compromise may be necessary down the line." She watched Cole's dark eyebrows rise and form into commas, and she wished she didn't care so much what he thought of her. "I know," she said irritably. "That doesn't sound honest. But that's how the game is played on the Hill."

"No offense, Kansas, but this kind of compromise doesn't sound like you." He studied the color lingering in her cheeks. "Maybe I'm starting to understand a little better why you're willing to leave politics."

Bailey cast a brooding glance toward the twins happily chatting with a clown. Stevie pushed at the clown's nose.

"You want the truth? Washington frustrates hell out of me. I've assisted on a couple of bills I'm proud of, but nothing moves fast in D.C. except gossip. Most likely some special-interest group will shoot down my bills or dilute them to the point they're weak and unrecognizable. There are times when I've caught myself wondering if I'd be more effective applying pressure from the outside. I'm not being as effective as I'd like on the inside, that's for sure.''

It occurred to Bailey that even though she and Brendan were in a happy period, Brendan didn't listen to her as intently as Cole did. He didn't look at her with eyes that made love to her mouth and hair and throat. She swallowed and dropped her gaze.

"It sounds like this pregnancy happened at a good time," Cole said after a minute. He had taken her hand again and absently turned her wedding ring on her finger.

"You were right about the future. I haven't ruled out resuming a career down the line when Jeanette or Emily starts school... but I doubt I'll return to politics." Biting her lip, she gave him an uncertain look, then plunged ahead. "Would you think I was nuts if I told you I've been thinking about publishing again?" She hadn't mentioned this to Brendan yet.

"Not at all. That was your original dream, wasn't it?"

"I might have guessed you would be supportive," she said softly. "An environmental magazine has asked me to do an article for them. I told them I would if they weren't in any hurry."

"I'll always support you, don't you know that yet? I love you. I care about you." They stared at each other, then Bailey bit her lip and looked away. She heard Cole draw a breath. "I take it you won't do this article until after your term ends?"

"Someone should skewer this administration's failure to perform on their environmental promises. But it would be suicide to do any skewering while I'm still in office." She met his eyes. "Never mind that. All we've done is talk about me, and I'd rather talk about you. You're my best friend, cowboy, and I want you to be as happy as I am. But you're not."

The longer Bailey spent in his company, the more she realized how restless he was. Even when he relaxed, the frown lines remained between his eyes. And she was aware of the deep weariness he thought he was concealing. It broke her heart.

Cole signaled for more coffee and waited until the clown had departed before he answered.

"It's no single problem, Bailey, it's everything—personal and professional. Marsha and I can't seem to agree on anything. I'd like to buy a home outside Manhattan— Marsha wants to keep the Park Avenue apartment. I'd even move to Hillendale to get the kids out of the city. But Hillendale is Marsha's, her place. She likes having it as a private getaway, but not as a permanent residence. That's one example, there are a hundred others. Everything seems up in the air right now. It's like that charged feeling you get immediately before a storm."

"A lot has happened this year…"

"Whatever is going on with me started a long time ago," he said in a moody voice. "Changing firms is only a symptom. I've been questioning just about everything for some time now."

"Like what?"

"Can't you guess?" he asked quietly.

Briefly she closed her eyes. "Please, Cole. We can't—"

"I know." He glanced at her swollen stomach. "A different example then—there isn't much I like about Marsha's breeding operation, but more and more I find myself drawn to Hillendale. Not to the tony show scene, but to the clean air, the space, the good earthy smells, the hint of a different—and slower—type of life."

After a moment Bailey broke the silence that had opened between them. "Talking about horses makes me think of your father. How is he?"

"Dad had another stroke in September."

"I'm sorry," Bailey said quietly. "That must be a worry."

He gazed at her. "Thank God I took your advice and put things right with him. It's one of the best things I ever did."

"Any regrets about selling your interest to your sister and her husband?" Bailey asked.

Cole spread his hands and a shrug adjusted his sweater. "Honestly? I'm not sure anymore. I don't regret choosing Wall Street over ranching, that was the right decision at the time. And I've been successful beyond my dreams. I'm approaching that line that separates wealth from merely rich. I expect to be invited to be a partner in the firm in the next two or three years. But what have I really achieved? What legacy will I pass on to them?" He nodded toward the twins who were chasing each other through a brightly colored hollow cube.

"What kind of legacy would you like to pass along?"

"I don't know," he answered, frowning. "Maybe something they can poke and feel and touch. Something real. Something more substantial and solid than a portfolio of gilt-edged paper."

"Like the Tarcher Ranch?" Bailey inquired in a low voice.

Cole stared at her. "I've asked myself that question a dozen times, as you always knew I would. And in the end the answer is no. Beth and Harlan are ranchers, I'm not. I'd feel isolated, overworked, and eventually resentful. No, not the Tarcher Ranch. But possibly something on a smaller scale."

Bailey studied his face, wishing she could touch him and comfort him somehow. "Are you talking about a major career change, cowboy? How would Marsha feel about that?"

As if on cue, Marsha Tarcher swept into the ice-cream parlor, bringing a blast of frigid air into the large overheated room. Pausing, she adjusted the packages in her arms and scanned the tables until she spotted Bailey and Cole. Then she moved toward them, frowning, wearing a stylishly expensive ski outfit beneath a silky fox fur with matching hat. Diamond studs sparkled in her earlobes as she wound through the scattered tables.

"Well, if it isn't Mrs. Hanson," she said to Bailey, her gaze cool and indifferent. If she noticed Bailey was pregnant, she chose not to mention it. And she waved aside the chair Cole offered her. "We have to get back to the condo. We're due at the Wilks's by eight."

"It's only four o'clock," Cole commented. "The kids are having a wonderful time working off some energy... you have time for coffee."

Marsha looked around the room, found the indoor playground, then waved a hand. "I'd prefer to leave now, Cole. I want a long bath and a manicure, and I have to do something with this hair. I don't want to be hurried."

"Would that be Senator Wilks's party?" Bailey asked, embarrassed and a little irritated at being so roundly ignored. "Brendan and I are invited, too."

Marsha's perfectly penciled eyebrows arched. "I'm not at all surprised. New Year just wouldn't be New Year without Cole's dear friends the Hansons, now would it? I can't imagine how we'd celebrate without you." She stared at Bailey. "And of course there's the all-important astrology book exchange. How would the two of you plan your year if you missed exchanging horoscopes?"

The acid in Marsha's tone was unmistakable. Bailey bit her tongue and fell silent, sipping her coffee while Cole called to the twins. Marsha made a showy fuss of collecting their parkas and caps and mittens, but they ran past her to Cole, insisting that he and only he help them on with their coats and caps.

A flush of heat tinted Marsha's cheeks, and she clenched her teeth and angrily reached for her packages. She threw

Cole a look that seemed to say: See what happens when I try to get close to them?

"Are you coming?" Cole asked, pressing Bailey's shoulder.

"Not yet." She found a smile and leveled it up at all of them, wiggling her fingers at Stevie and Shawn who were again perched on Cole's wide shoulders. She kept her voice light and tried to include Marsha in her smile. "I think I'll stay awhile, finish my coffee, then stop in at the boutique next door."

"We'll see you later," Cole promised. Marsha said nothing. The twins waved, then they were gone.

Bailey looked after them and shook her head. They were such a good-looking family. But the tension between Cole and Marsha was obvious and uncomfortable to witness. With all her heart Bailey wished Cole could be as happy as she was now.

Brendan found her an hour later, still sitting in the ice-cream parlor, observing and enjoying the children with a dreamy expression. When he asked what on earth she was doing, Bailey rose from the wire-backed chair and wrapped her arms around his waist, smiling up at him.

"Have I told you how happy I am? We're so lucky!"

"Seriously, Bailey," he said, embarrassed that she was hugging him in public, "if I hadn't glanced in the windows and happened to notice, I'd never have thought to look in here for you."

She told him about running into Cole and how they had brought the twins here for cones. Something in Brendan's eyes retreated. "The Tarchers are in Aspen?"

"You knew that—you've just forgotten. Oh, Brendan, you should see the twins. They're three now and so cute. I wish I had half their energy."

"You're tired because you're doing too much," he said as he helped her into her parka. "I've said it before and I suspect I'll say it again—you should resign your seat in Congress. Stay home and take care of yourself.''

It was an ongoing argument. Brendan had never approved of her commuting. He especially objected now. But Bailey resisted rising to the bait.

''Maybe I will,'' she said, surprising them both. ''But not just yet.'' Taking his arm, she followed him outside, drawing the cold sharp air deeply into her lungs. With darkness as a backdrop, the twinkling lights turned the snowy mall into a fairyland. For a moment Bailey saw the brightly colored lights and the looping garlands through the eyes of a child and thought it magical. There were going to be so many wonderful experiences ahead.

Without thinking about what she was doing, she scanned the crowds thronging the brick street, unconsciously seeking two small figures astride a set of broad shoulders.

Gently Brendan urged her forward. ''I don't mean to rush you, but we're due at the Wilks's at eight. And we'll want dinner sent up first...''

Bailey pushed her mittened hands into the pockets of her parka and dropped her head, frowning. She was remembering Marsha Tarcher's acid voice and pinched mouth. She suspected the last thing the Tarcher marriage needed was the presence of someone Marsha Tarcher obviously resented. Marsha had never understood Bailey and Cole's friendship.

Sometimes Bailey wasn't sure she did, either. If someone had told her ten years ago that her best friend would turn out to be a man who was not her husband, she would have vigorously denied the possibility. Yet that's how it had turned out.

Weeks or even months could elapse between the times she and Cole were in contact, yet when they did speak it was as if no time had passed at all, it was as if they had seen each other only yesterday. They shared a level of trust and caring that Bailey shared with few other people. She knew without doubt that if she ever needed someone, really needed someone, Cole would be there for her. And if he needed help, she would be there for him.

It seemed the least she could do for her best friend was stay home from the Wilks's party.

Chapter Ten

Bailey stood in her bathrobe before the floor-to-ceiling windows that overlooked the valley. In the distance, she could glimpse the festive lights of Aspen, twinkling like small beacons through the light snow that had begun to fall. The flakes were not fat and wet like a New England snow, but tiny, almost pelletlike, as powdery as sugar crystals.

Behind her, a cheery fire popped in the living room fireplace, and the lilting strains of Vivaldi filled the condominium. She could hear Brendan in the bedroom, humming to the music as he dressed for the Wilks's party.

When she realized she was lost in thoughts of Cole, she gave herself a small shake, then poured a Scotch and water for Brendan and more juice for herself and carried them into the bedroom.

"Thanks." Brendan swept a look over her robe before he tasted his drink and then leaned to the mirror to swear at his tie. "Shouldn't you be getting dressed?" he asked. "It's a quarter after seven."

"Would it upset you if I didn't go to the Wilks's party?"

"We don't have to go if you'd rather not," he said after a moment.

"I didn't mean for both of us to send regrets. I think you'd enjoy going. Several of your clients will be there, a lot of politicians, a few wheeler-dealers and a sprinkling of celebrities. Irene Wilk said Robert Wagner and Jill St. John will be there. Maybe Dustin Hoffman.'' She smiled. ''There won't be any disco music or party games. I think you'll have a good time. Certainly I don't want you to miss a nice evening on my account.''

Concern tightened his brow. ''Are you ill?''

She touched his cheeks. ''I just don't feel up to a room full of people and making conversation. What I'd really like is to be alone for a little while. Just me and little Whoozit and some dream time.''

Brendan studied her, tugged by indecision. ''What would you do?''

''Read. Watch a little TV.'' She shrugged. ''Maybe I'll go downstairs and sit in the hot tub. Don't worry about me, I'll be fine. You can't guess what a luxury it is just to enjoy the quiet.'' She gave him a little push toward the door. ''Go. Have a good time and don't worry about me. I need a little private time.''

''You're sure?''

''Absolutely!''

Making a show of indecision, he pushed his arms into his topcoat. ''I'll return in time for New Year.''

''Don't be silly. Stay at the party and kiss Jill St. John when the big ball drops.''

After Brendan left, Bailey almost regretted her decision. She thought of the Scorpio astrology booklet in her purse and was sorry she wouldn't be able to give it to Cole in person. She would mail it instead. On the other hand, she felt almost certain that Cole and Marsha would have a calmer evening if she was not there. Marsha's sarcasm in the ice-cream parlor had made her dislike obvious. It wouldn't reassure her to watch Cole dance attendance on Bailey all evening, as he surely would.

Relaxing on the condo's polished cotton sofa, Bailey watched television for a while, feeling a slight depression over the year-end review. She snapped off the TV set and decided to treat herself to a soak in the hot tub downstairs. She guessed she would have it all to herself. And she told herself that was exactly what she preferred. Really.

COLE DIDN'T REALIZE he'd been watching his wristwatch and the Wilks's front door until Brendan appeared in the senator's posh living room without Bailey. When he could politely do so, Cole left the group chatting beside a twenty-four-foot Christmas tree and made his way across the crowded room to Brendan.

"Where's our little mother?" he asked after they shook hands. "Bailey isn't ill, is she?"

"Nothing like that," Brendan said, glancing around the room to see who was present. "You know how unpredictable pregnant women are. At the last minute Bailey decided she preferred an evening alone. She insisted I attend the party without her."

Surprise lifted Cole's eyebrows. As far as he knew, Bailey had always enjoyed New Year parties. She was the one who usually wanted to make an all-nighter of the evening and watch the sun rise on a new year. Plus—and this was admittedly egotistical—he had assumed that because he was here, Bailey would be, too. They didn't have many opportunities to enjoy each other's company in person, and he looked forward to such occasions. He had supposed Bailey did, too. Moreover, the Wilks's party had furnished an opportunity to exchange the astrology booklets and laugh over them in person. It was a silly thing, but the tradition had become important to him over the years.

While he and Brendan discussed the Pie Rite deal, Cole pondered Bailey's absence, wondering if he had said something to annoy her when they were in the ice-cream parlor. It wasn't until nearly an hour later when Marsha returned to his side that he glimpsed the most probable reason for Bailey's discretion.

"I notice your horoscope buddy didn't make it to the party," Marsha commented. Sarcasm pinched her smile and she looked up at him with cold eyes. "Usually we know whose husband she's zeroed in on for New Year's Eve. This year we'll just have to wonder." Her gaze found Brendan. "Certainly it won't be her own. But that's not unusual, is it?"

Cole frowned down at her shining auburn hair. "That's not fair, Marsha. Bailey doesn't deserve remarks like that."

"How charming. Do you jump to my defense as quickly as you jump to defend Bailey Hanson, your dear, dear friend?"

Cole's fingers tightened around his drink and he bit his tongue. The last thing he wanted was another argument. "Didn't we agree to a truce? I seem to recall we said there would be no fighting or hurtful remarks during the holidays."

"That was before I realized the Hansons followed us to Aspen."

"Followed us? Whatever gave you that idea?" He looked at her in surprise. "They own a condominium here. They both ski. Months ago Brendan mentioned that he and Bailey planned to spend the holidays in Aspen. They didn't follow us."

"I see. Then we followed them."

"Marsha, it was *you* who decided to spend the holidays in Aspen. No one followed anyone."

"How naive do you think I am?" Her beautiful face twisted into something decidedly unbeautiful. "Brendan may be too dumb to see what's happening right under his nose, but I'm not!"

He frowned. "What the hell is that supposed to mean?"

"It means I know you and Bailey are having an affair. It's been going on for years!"

The accusation stunned him into speechlessness.

"That's ridiculous," he said finally, staring down at her. "Bailey and I are old friends, that's all. That's all we've ever been. Is it so hard to believe that a man and a woman can be friends?"

"As a matter of fact, yes!"

"Well you're wrong!"

"No, I'm not. You've been in love with Bailey Hanson for as long as I've known you. I was always second choice!"

"Marsha, listen to me." Reaching for her, he framed her shoulders between his hands and looked intently into her face. "Bailey and I are good friends and I hope we always will be. But there's no affair going on between us, nor has there ever been. I married you because I loved you and because I thought we could build a life together. Somewhere along the line we've grown apart, but our problems have nothing whatsoever to do with Bailey Hanson or with any other woman for that matter. As for being second choice, that's utterly ridiculous. I'm willing to do whatever it takes to make our marriage work."

"Are you really?" she asked, throwing the words like a dagger. "Well, I'm not the fool you obviously think I am. You're not going to cover up the truth with a few smooth words." Her chin rose beneath flashing eyes. "Maybe you aren't the only one who's having an affair. What do you think about that?"

Genuine pain tensed his muscles. What she said hurt. Even though he'd suspected as much, it hurt to hear his fears confirmed.

"I think we need to talk," he said in a low raw voice.

"It's too late for talk," she said between her teeth. Angry tears sprang into her eyes. "I'm tired of 'trying.' I'm tired of being made a fool of! I'm tired of you always being so damned reasonable. I'm tired of talking, talking, talking! I've just told you that I'm having an affair. Don't you care?"

"Of course I care! Don't you think it hurts?"

Wrenching out from under his hands, she jerked away from him. Then she hurled her drink in his face.

In the first frozen instant, all Cole felt was shock. In the past Marsha had confined her temper to private moments. Never before had she created a public scene. It shocked him that she had lost control to this extent.

Scotch and water dripped down his face. An ice cube had caught in his cummerbund. Several people fell silent and stared at him, then quickly looked away as he stiffly fumbled for his handkerchief.

"Oh God, Cole." Marsha stared at him, then glanced at the people standing nearby. "I'm sorry. I didn't mean... you know how I get, I just..." Stepping forward and biting her lips, she brushed at his jacket and shirtfront, her fingers shaking.

He understood her well enough to know her contrition was as genuine as her fury had been. As always, her abrupt emotional swings exhausted and confused him. This time he could add embarrassment and anger. But when he finally brought himself to meet her eyes, he discovered his anger had dissipated to pity.

"Sometimes I feel sorry for you," he said in a quiet voice that only she could hear. "You've led a Cinderella life. You've had everything you ever wanted. You're beautiful, bright, and charming when you want to be. Yet for some reason you can't accept that anyone could really love you. So you drive away the people who genuinely care. You punish them for daring to love you."

"I know," she said wildly. "I know I do that. And I don't know why. It's just...wait, Cole. I *said* I was sorry!"

He paused and looked back at her over his shoulder. "Sometimes sorry isn't enough." He met her eyes. "I'm tired, too. I'm tired of the accusations, tired of all the effort having to come from me. I'm tired of watching you throw up one wall after another, then daring me to knock them down and love you in spite of them. I'm worn out with it.''

She followed him to the foyer and waited beside him as the butler fetched his topcoat. Fresh anger and justification mounted in her eyes and hardened her expression. Cole watched it happen with a feeling of helplessness and frustration.

''Don't you dare walk out of here, Cole Tarcher.'' She spoke between her teeth. ''You started this fight!''

''I'd like to return to the condo and talk about this, Marsha. I think we should explore whether there's anything in our marriage worth salvaging. Are you coming with me or not?''

She glared at him. ''You can storm off if you want to, but I refuse to let you spoil *my* evening!'' Turning on her heels, she strode back into the crowded room, leaving a trace of her perfume lingering in the foyer.

Cole stared after her. Then he accepted his topcoat from the butler and stepped out into the clean cold night air.

THERE WAS NO CLOCK in the hot-tub room, just steam and ferns and tall dark windows, so Bailey didn't know if it was close to midnight or if the new year was still an hour or so distant. Maybe there would be fireworks at the magic hour. If so, she would see them, she hoped, gazing through the haze of steam floating over the hot tub. The city lights sparkled through the snow drifting past the windows.

This was the first time she had ever spent New Year's Eve alone, and it felt a little strange. Despite a sudden pang of loneliness, choosing to spend New Year's Eve alone seemed a very adult thing to do. Rather like a rite of passage into genuine maturity. Or something like that. Bailey smiled at the thought and considered getting out of the hot tub, but the water was warm and comfortable, and she felt too lazy to move.

The hallway door opened. "Aha. Here you are. I found you!"

"Cole?" She sat up in surprise and stared at him, suddenly aware that her hair had gone limp in the steam and a few strands dripped toward the water. And she wasn't wearing any makeup. There was no doubt about it; she didn't look her best. Cole, on the other hand, wore black tie and formal attire and looked as if he had just stepped off the pages of *GQ*. "What on earth are you doing here?"

"Did you really think I was going to let you spend New Year's Eve alone?" Grinning, he raised a bottle of Tattinger's champagne and two fluted glasses. "Not on your life."

"You're crazy!" she said, laughing and suddenly feeling foolish over how she had been trying to persuade herself that she wasn't feeling lonely and forgotten. It was so good to see him and know he had sought her out.

"A couple of glasses of champagne won't hurt you," he said, bending to drop a kiss on the top of her damp head before he pushed aside her empty juice glass, then twisted the wire off the neck of the Tattinger's. The cork shot up and bounced against the ceiling before it dropped into the hot tub and splashed water across Bailey's breast. Cole gave her a sheepish grin. "I know it's totally unsophisticated to let a champagne cork pop like that, but I've always wanted to do it."

"Me too," she admitted, laughing.

"Are you wearing any clothes under all those bubbles? Or are you one of those jaded creatures who goes hot tubbing in the nude?"

"This is me, remember? Uptight prude from Kansas? Of course I'm wearing a swimsuit. If anyone comes in here and starts talking nude, I'm outta here. Even if I was sophisticated enough to ignore nudity, which I'm not, I'm too self-conscious to appear in the buff, and especially when I look like a pear. Last but not least, I am a gen-u-ine United

States congressperson, and most of us don't go cavorting around in the nude.''

"Just checking." He spread his hands. "Hey, D.C. is a wild place, especially these days. It's reassuring to know you haven't been corrupted." After filling their champagne glasses, he shrugged out of his coat and tugged off his tie, then began to remove the studs from his cuffs and shirtfront.

When he opened his belt and started to unzip his pants, Bailey pushed up in the water and stared. "Cole, what are you *doing?*"

"I'm going to join you, of course." He stepped out of his pants and stood in front of her in a pair of bikini briefs and knee-high black socks, which he bent to peel off. "New Year wouldn't be New Year without you, Kansas. If you're spending it in a hot tub, then so am I. If seeing my briefs embarrasses you, then don't look."

After throwing his socks aside, he straightened and laughed at her shocked expression, then he stepped into the hot tub and took a seat facing her. "Do you realize I've spent more New Years' Eves with you than with anyone else? The New Years' Eves without you don't seem real. It's like they don't count unless you're there."

Bailey was still seeing visions of his hard athletic body, mostly nude. His body was hard and muscular, his stomach flat and taut. He was as sexy and exciting as she had always secretly imagined he would be.

"I didn't know you had hair on your chest," she blurted. A rush of embarrassment turned her cheeks pink, but she couldn't stop staring at him. The humidity was making the hair curl on his head and on his chest. He looked gorgeous and sexy as hell, like a model in an ad for hot tubs.

"And I didn't know you had that sexy mole on your shoulder." His feet found hers beneath the water and they sat sole to sole, bracing each other and smiling.

When the moment became awkward, Bailey cleared her throat and spoke, mostly to take her thoughts off the fact that he was sitting across from her in his underwear. She told herself his bikini briefs were no different than a swimming suit, but somehow they were. It occurred to her that she might not have been entirely comfortable even if he were wearing a swimming suit.

There was no evidence of middle-aged spread, no lumps or bumps on Cole's body. The years of tennis every other morning had kept his body lean and athletic. She thought he jogged, too. Whatever he did, he had kept his body as toned and tight and gorgeous as it had been in college.

"Okay, cowboy, what are you really doing here?" Bailey inspected the swell of muscle rippling down his shoulders, mesmerized by the sight before she quickly averted her eyes.

"I had to deliver your astrology booklet, didn't I?"

Bailey glanced at her tote bag, which she had dropped on the tiles beside a potted fern. His astrology booklet was inside. "I have yours with me," she said, suddenly wondering why she had thought to tuck it inside her bag. Turning back to him, she examined his face. "Cole, let's be serious a minute. You really shouldn't be here. Marsha will be furious when she learns where you are." She suspected Brendan wouldn't be too thrilled about this, either.

"Believe me, Marsha could care less where I am right now," Cole answered in a flat tone.

"Did you have an argument?"

"When don't we argue?" He continued speaking in a strained, flat tone. Tilting his head, Cole studied her across the bubbles, and Bailey self-consciously lifted her hand to push at the wet strands of hair falling out of her ponytail. She wished she had thought to dab on a little lipstick at least. Despite the heat of the water, she could feel the warmth of his feet pressing against hers. "Tell me if I've figured this out. You didn't go to the Wilks's party because you didn't want to upset Marsha—is that right?''

"I wanted some time alone, and—''

"Come on, Kansas. We've always tried to be honest with each other.''

She drew a breath and let her arms float on top of the water. "Okay, maybe I figured Marsha would have a better time at the party if you and I weren't in a corner catching up and laughing over horoscopes. It doesn't take a genius to know I'm not one of Marsha's favorite people.''

"That's what I figured.'' He turned brooding eyes to the steamy windows, then back to her. "I'm sorry, Bailey. Marsha and I caused you to miss a nice party.''

"It was my choice, cowboy,'' she said lightly. "No one is to blame here. And I don't mind missing the party. Unless—'' her blue eyes twinkled like sapphires "—unless you tell me Dustin Hoffman was there. Then maybe I'll start feeling sorry for myself.''

"Hoffman wasn't there, but Robert Wagner was.''

She watched him as he talked, taking pleasure in his rugged good looks, in the fact, guilty as it made her feel, that he had chosen to leave the Wilks's party and spend New Year's Eve with her. As Bailey sipped the icy champagne, then rolled the glass across her hot cheek, she thought about urging him to return to the party and to Marsha, then rejected the idea. Cole was an adult. He knew he was doing something Marsha would find hard to forgive. Maybe that was part of the reason why he was here.

"What's going to happen to your marriage?'' she asked quietly.

"The truth? I don't know.'' Twisting, he found the Tattinger's on the tiles behind him, then leaned across the bubbling water to refill Bailey's glass. "I'm not sure I care anymore.''

"Don't you love her?''

Cole hesitated before he answered. "I think we loved each other once. Or maybe we just wanted to love each other. In any case, our marriage has been over for a long time. I'm not sure it ever really got off the ground. Now we're just coasting on habit, punishing each other for old slights we don't even remember."

"I'm sorry." The news upset her more than she had expected it would.

A shrug raised his broad muscled shoulders. "Marsha is a nice person and I'm a nice person. But we can't seem to make a marriage work. Somewhere out there is a man who will appreciate Marsha's good qualities and who will make her happy. She deserves the chance to find him. And maybe there's someone out there for me."

Bailey met his steady gaze and it seemed they looked at each other for a very long time.

"The timing is always wrong for you and me, isn't it?" Cole said finally, speaking softly. When he saw that his question disturbed her, he waved a hand in apology, then leaned forward and asked her consent to place his hand on her stomach. Feeling flustered by the abrupt change of topic, Bailey nodded permission. And she smothered a gasp when Cole's electric touch settled gently over her stomach.

"I guess it's too soon to feel movement," he said after a moment. His head lifted and his mouth was only inches from her own. He met her eyes, then dropped his gaze to her lips.

As she couldn't speak, couldn't breathe, Bailey nodded.

"Some men think pregnant women are wildly sexy."

"Are you one of them?" she whispered, feeling dizzy.

"Actually, no." He grinned at her, then slid back onto his seat across from her and reached for his champagne glass. "I think pregnant women are beautiful and they bring out in me a caveman urge to protect them, but no, I don't think I've ever thought of pregnant women as particularly sexy."

She stared at him, then a burst of laughter broke from her lips. "You always surprise me." Then her smile faded. "Some people are meant to be friends instead of lovers," she said softly. She didn't think there was any regret in her tone. She hoped there wasn't.

"Wrong, Kansas. Some people are meant to be lovers, but fate screws it up."

She knew what he was saying. And with her usual directness, she went to the heart of it. "You and me—it just wasn't meant to be, Cole," she said in a whisper.

"At least I know you're happy. That helps."

"I am happy." Beneath the water, her hands gently cupped her stomach. "This is my one and only chance to have a child." It was important that he understand that. "Immediately after the birth, I have to have a hysterectomy. There won't be any more pregnancies, no more children."

She didn't know exactly what she was trying to tell him, only that somehow it tied into what they had been saying to each other.

Leaning forward, Cole found her hands beneath the water and gazed into her eyes. "Look, Bailey, I care about you. I always have. The last thing I'd ever want to do is cause you any kind of problem. I know you and Brendan have had some trouble during the last couple of years, but I realize things are better now. Even if that wasn't the case, I know how you feel about divorce. What I want you to understand is that my problems with Marsha have nothing to do with my friendship for you. And I'm not going to turn up on your doorstep, footloose and fancy-free, talking about might-have-beens or could-be's. I'm not going to be a problem for you. I think you and I would have been fantastic together, but fate never gave us a chance. I accept that."

"Do you?" she asked, searching his eyes.

"Yes."

"Maybe you and Marsha will work things out."

"I doubt it. But stranger things have happened."

For the first time in their relationship an uncomfortable silence opened between them. Inexplicable tears brimmed in Bailey's eyes, and she turned her face toward the tiny pellets of snow hissing against the windows.

"Well, Congresswoman," Cole said finally, his voice hearty and injected with cheerfulness, "are you ready to argue to the death about excessive government regulation versus the free enterprise system? Frankly, what you people on the Hill are proposing for Wall Street is a sucko deal."

"Oh, yeah?" she said, mustering a smile. "Haven't you seen *Wall Street?* The truth is exposed. Now we know all about you wheeler-dealer types. Suspicions confirmed."

"The best argument you can muster is a movie?"

"Pretty lame, huh? Actually, I'm in no mood for arguing tonight. Something about impending motherhood saps the will to fight." Her smile softened with affection. "Especially I don't want to fight with you. Not tonight." She had a suspicion he'd already wearied of battle before he arrived.

"I can't believe my ears." Cole grinned at her, deliberately keeping the mood light. "Are there no inflammatory issues I can incite you with?"

"Nope. I'm unincitable tonight." A dreamy expression softened her gaze. "I'd rather hear about when the twins got their first teeth. I've gone mushy."

"This baby is really important to you, isn't it?"

"It's everything." Tears of emotion welled in her eyes, embarrassing her. "I waited so long, Cole. We endured all those demeaning tests, then I had the operation to enable me to conceive... And there won't be another..."

Fireworks exploded against the black snowy sky, and Bailey broke off speaking with a cry of delight. As bells pealed and noisemakers erupted in the distance, Cole jumped out of the hot tub to turn off the overhead lights. When he returned, Bailey moved to sit next to him, their bodies touching beneath the water. His arm lightly encircled her shoulders. Because neither wished to disturb a delicate balance, they both pretended it was not erotic or unusual to be sitting together almost naked.

They watched the fireworks display, the bursts of colored light flickering over their faces and reflecting in the bubbles spread before them.

"Happy New Year, little mother," Cole said in a gruff voice. Turning to face her, he touched his champagne glass to hers. "You'll let me know immediately that you and the newest little do-gooder are fine, won't you?"

"Happy New Year. I'll let you know about the baby."

Then, after he brushed the strands of wet hair back from her cheeks, Cole kissed her. He kissed her tenderly, gently, a long deliberate kiss between two people who were more than friends but less than lovers. A kiss that spoke of love and regret, of bittersweet emotions that could never be fully expressed. Despite their intentions, it was a kiss that tasted of lost opportunity, hinted at a future that might have been.

When their lips parted, Bailey stared at him through a shine of tears, seeing his face in the flare of the fireworks. She had been a fool to believe that because she was pregnant, because her marriage was better now than it had been in a long time, that she would be indifferent to Cole Tarcher's kiss. She wasn't and she never had been. His kiss thrilled her as no other ever had.

"Cole, if you need to talk...call me," she whispered, swallowing hard. For no discernable reason, she felt a great wave of sadness.

"I really care about you, Kansas," he said before he let his arms fall away from her. "I'm glad everything is working out for you and that you're happy. You deserve the best."

"I care about you, too, cowboy." Quickly, so he wouldn't see, she dashed the tears from her eyes as he climbed out of the hot tub and toweled off. "Don't forget to take your astrology booklet," she reminded him, averting her gaze from the gleam of his skin, from the taut muscles and tendons.

Cole flipped on the lights after he was dressed, breaking the spell between them. Bending, he retrieved the astrology book from her tote bag and placed her booklet inside it. Then he riffled through the pages before casting her a look of mock despair and rolling his eyes. "Not good, Kansas. It says right here in black and white that I should just sit out 1988. Did you see the advice for January?" He pretended to read. "January is going to be so dismal that Scorpios should stay in bed the whole month. Sleep until March at which time life will become merely awful instead of appalling."

Bailey smiled up at him. "Thank you for being here, Cole."

He stood at the edge of the hot tub, dressed now in black tie and cummerbund, looking wonderfully, impossibly handsome, like a fairy-tale prince. It was unimaginable to suppose there was a woman anywhere who wouldn't be proud to share his life. Bailey thought of Marsha and felt heartsick that things had gone so terribly wrong between them.

Cole's expression suggested he wanted to say a hundred things to her. But all he said was, "Thank you for another very special New Year's Eve, Kansas. The new year is easier to face when it begins with you."

By the time Brendan arrived a few minutes later, Cole had gone. And Bailey was quietly weeping.

Chapter Eleven

Western Union for: Cole Tarcher
February 15, 1988

LOST THE BABY STOP CAN'T HAVE MORE STOP AM DEVAS-
TATED STOP AM GOING AWAY FOR A WHILE STOP I WANT TO
DIE STOP BAILEY

Mr. Tarcher,
Mr. Hanson phoned while you were in the strategy ses-
sion. He asked me to convey his appreciation for the cards
and flowers, and thanked you for your concern but said
Mrs. Hanson is not accepting or returning telephone calls
right now. She's in seclusion and resting.

Representative Bailey Hanson—private correspondence
1414 Wayne St., Suite 101
Washington, D.C.
April 5, 1988

Okay, Kansas, it's been almost two months without a word
from you. It's time to get in touch with your friends. I'm
worried sick about you. I've left a dozen phone messages
at your office and at your house. If you don't want to talk,

that's fine. I understand. But drop me a card, a note, something to reassure me that you're all right.

I deeply regret your loss, Bailey, and I'm thinking about you.

Cole

Cole Tarcher
c/o Mangan and Mangan
15 Wall Street
New York, New York
April 10, 1988

Dear Cole,
Forgive me for not answering your calls or notes. I'm grateful for your concern, but I'm still among the walking wounded and don't feel up to talking. It's been so hard. Some days I fool myself into thinking I'm coping, then I see an infant on TV or in the grocery store and I simply fall apart. Brendan tries to be understanding, but he's hurting, too.

She was so real to me, Cole. I could see her in my mind wearing her christening gown. Wearing a Brownie uniform. Wearing her first prom dress. Her wedding gown. Now she's gone and none of it will ever happen. I loved her so much.

Bailey

Brendan,
I returned the puppy to the pet store and asked them to credit your American Express account. I know you meant well, but when I found the puppy and your note, there was a moment when I came close to hating you. How dare you think that a pet will make everything all right, that a puppy can replace our child!

I'm taking the commuter to D.C., and I plan to stay in the apartment for a few weeks. I think we need a break from each other. I wish we could comfort each other, but we don't seem able to. Instead, we're just adding to each other's pain.

Bailey

September 11, 1988
Cole,

I'm going to Hillendale for the weekend. When I return on Monday, I want you moved out of the apartment. I think you'll agree we should have done this after we returned from Aspen.

I phoned Jack this morning and instructed him to begin working out a divorce agreement. You can keep the twins. I'll take them for the summer and a week at Christmas. I'll keep Hillendale, of course, and the apartment. I think we can work this out where no one is hurt too badly financially.

I know it's cowardly to end a marriage in a note instead of face-to-face, but you can be very persuasive and I didn't want to be talked out of it again. Cole, we've tried. We've made a dozen fresh starts and none of them worked. At this point we're just beating a dead horse. You probably won't believe this, but I'm sorry it didn't work out.

Marsha

Mr. Cole Tarcher
c/o Mangan and Mangan
August 1, 1988

I just hung up from talking to you and I'm so angry I can hardly think straight. Who are you to decide six months is long enough to grieve? I know you didn't say that, but that's sure as hell what you meant. But you don't know a damned thing about what I'm going through.

Losing the baby is the biggest part of it, but that isn't all. Another large part is the years of waiting and hoping and praying; it's subjecting myself and Brendan to all those tests, then the operation, and through it all the hope and the terrible fear that I'd never be able to conceive. Then finally the indescribable joy of becoming pregnant at last followed by hours and days and weeks of planning and dreaming. Then the miscarriage and the hysterectomy and the knowledge that all the dreams are lost and will never come again.

I'm struggling to cope with the loss of my only baby. And with the loss of a lifelong image of myself as a mother and as a woman. Now I'm an empty shell who looks like a woman but who isn't a woman. Can you understand that? Hell, no you can't! So spare me, and don't try. Biology is destiny, remember? But now I have no destiny because my biology was altered by the hysterectomy. I no longer have a purpose in life.

So don't you dare hint that I should pick myself up and get on with my life. You're supposed to be my friend and support me. You're supposed to be on my side, damn it. I need your sympathy not a lecture, no matter how well-meant.

Don't phone, Cole, I mean it. I'm too angry to speak to you. I won't accept your call.

                                                          Bailey

Representative Bailey Hanson—private correspondence
August 4, 1988

Dearest Bailey,
It's *because* I'm your friend and because I love you that I'm telling you the time for sympathy is past. It's time to accept what you can't change and step into life again. Or are you planning to hide out in your office or your apartment forever?

I'm enough of a friend to tell you that all that baloney about biology and you being nothing more than a scooped out shell is so much self-pitying crap. If what you say were true, then a woman's value would depend solely upon possessing a womb. Is that what you're claiming? No womb—no reason to exist? Time to find the nearest cliff and jump off of it.

Well, that's crap. Look, Bailey, I'm not discounting your pain or the terrible loss you've suffered. I remember sitting in Pam's apartment that first New Year's Eve and watching your eyes shine and your face come alive when you talked about the children you wanted to have. I do know what having a family meant to you. And whether you believe it or not, I *do* have a good feel for the loss you've endured. But nothing can change what's happened. No matter how loud you scream at fate, you can't go back and make things turn out differently.

Right now, you're standing at a crossroads. Which road you choose is going to affect the rest of your life.

If you define yourself solely in terms of what you aren't and can't be—a mother—then you choose a path of sorrow, pain and regret. You'll spend your life stuck in the past, wallowing in self-pity and enduring agony every time you see an infant. The suffering will become a daily part of you and will never ease. You won't be much good to yourself or anyone else.

But if you define yourself as a woman, a woman who has experienced pain, but a bright, vivacious, valuable member of the human community, then you choose a path toward the future. You have a lot to give, Bailey, both privately and in the public domain, and your gifts don't rely on having a womb. Brendan needs you; your constituents need you. Your family and friends need you. You can have a happy fulfilling life despite your loss. Granted, it won't be as complete without children—all the pockets won't be filled. But your life can be rich and satisfying nonetheless. If you make it happen.

So what's it going to be, Kansas?

If I had to put money on it, I'd bet you'll choose the future. You'll dust yourself off, shake off the poor-me's, and put your butt on the campaign trail. I'd bet that you'll patch things up with Brendan and start thinking about someone besides yourself. I'd put my money on it that you'll phone the Democratic Headquarters and tell them to set up some debates and start printing reelection posters. Or maybe you'll start phoning publishers and solicit bids for a political exposé. Whatever you do, I'm betting that you'll pull yourself together and you'll do it soon. The mourning period is past; it's time to step forward and reenter life.

I'm wagering the family fortune that you're stronger than you think you are, that you aren't going to allow this devastating event to define the rest of your life. Don't let me down, Kansas; I hate to lose money.

With deepest affection,
Cole

Mr. Tarcher,
Mrs. Hanson phoned from Washington, D.C. She said to tell you that you are a manipulating, low-down, hit-below-the-belt, insensitive, insulting and arrogant, hard-nosed Wyoming hick. You possess too little sympathy and too much honesty. And she thanks God that she has a friend like you. She says since you kept your money, you can send a campaign donation to Democratic Headquarters. She said you'll know what that means.

Mr. Hanson,
Your wife phoned and asked that you meet the five o'clock commuter flight from D.C. She's coming home. She wants you to cancel your last appointment and make dinner reservations at Bagatelle's.

Hartford Courant, November 8, 1988
By Craig Martin, elections desk. Incumbent Bailey Han-

son easily won reelection in yesterday's balloting. At her victory celebration held at the Sheridan Hotel, Hanson stated . . .

Mr. Cole Tarcher
34 E. 69th St., Apt. 5C
New York, New York
December 19, 1988

Dear Friend,
It's been a rough year for everyone, hasn't it? So many changes. I've checked our horoscopes for 1989 and, thank God, things are due to get better. (If you tell anyone that I'm depending on astrology for optimism, I'll deny it!)

As for me, the pain will always be present but it's manageable now. I'm busy, reasonably content, and this term I have a few colleagues more junior than I am to lord it over. Still, I'm not sure politics is what I want to do with the rest of my life. But I've put that decision on hold.

Given your circumstances, it seems too Pollyanna-ish to wish you a merry Christmas. I hope you're going home to Wyoming to spend the holidays with your family. Will the twins be with you for Christmas?

I'll miss you when the big ball drops, cowboy, and I'll be thinking about you. Good friends know when to cry with you and when to deliver a kick in the pants. I owe you a lot. Brendan sends his best.

Bailey

Rawlins Gazette, February 28, 1989
Obituary. William Henry Tarcher, age 61, died yesterday following a brief hospitalization for heart problems . . .

Mrs. Hanson,
Your husband phoned. He won't be on the six o'clock flight. He said to tell you he's sorry, but he can't fly down

for the embassy reception. He has a brief he has to review.

Mr. Hanson,
Your wife phoned. She said to tell you that she's stuck in
D.C., for the weekend. Budget meetings.

Mrs. Hanson,
Mr. Hanson phoned to say you might as well stay in D.C.,
as he's buried at the office and will have to work through
the weekend.

Mr. Hanson,
Your wife phoned to say she's home from the European
junket, but needs to stay in D.C., for a few days and put
together her findings report.

I knew I forgot something... Your birthday. I'm sorry. Why
didn't you remind me? I hope these earrings will help you
forgive my oversight. Does it occur to you that our secretaries are communicating more than we are? Let's talk
about it next weekend.

Brendan

New York Post, Sept. 18, 1989
By Mata Hari. Talk about fireworks! The explosive divorce is finally final, dahlings, and you know who your favorite spy is talking about. Socialite Marsha Tarcher née
Haversham celebrated D day by throwing a posh bash at
Trump Tower for three hundred of her closest friends.
Overheard: "Marsha Tarcher doesn't have friends, just
acquaintances." Now girls, let's sheath those claws! The
auburn-haired hostess was wearing a smashing new Un-
garo to absolutely die for! Rumor has it that Marsha's ex,
the scrumptious Wall Street legend, Cole Tarcher, was invited but didn't show. Get ready, dahlings, Gotham's dish-

iest bachelor is back in circulation, handsomer and richer than ever! Marsha's loss is definitely going to be some lucky girl's gain. Rebound, anyone?

Chapter Twelve

New Year's Eve, 1990

The Kempinski Hotel was almost new by European standards, charmingly ancient from Bailey's American perspective. Her suite was furnished with a motley collection of genuine antiques and rather hideous postwar pieces that miraculously blended into a harmonious whole. Best of all, in Bailey's opinion, her parlor window offered a view of Berlin's crowded main thoroughfare, Kurfürstendamm, and she could glimpse the landmark spire of the Kaiser Wilhelm Church whose ongoing renovations were nearly complete.

This was an enormously exciting time to be in Berlin. And Bailey was grateful the committee had selected her as a member of the fact-finding junket. On November 10, the Berlin Wall had come down, forever altering the face of Europe. No one knew exactly what would happen next or what other changes were coming. But the promise of further momentous events charged the city with feverish expectation.

Though it was cold outside and still early, Kurfürstendamm was packed with revelers wearing paper hats, blowing noisemakers, and throwing colored streamers at the electric trams that traveled the center of the boulevard. The television news reported that East Berliners were pouring into West Berlin by the tens of thousands, determined to celebrate the new year on freedom's soil.

Bailey didn't doubt it. East German Trabants clogged the traffic lanes, and the sidewalks were awash beneath a tide of people. The shops and boutiques along the Kurfürstendamm were offering twenty-four-hour service, struggling to cope with the continuing onslaught of astonished East Berliners. Sidewalk cafés overflowed and spilled into the streets where customers who could not hope for a table were served standing. No one minded. A delirious and joyous frivolity had seized the city. Strangers embraced and laughed with each other. Reunited families danced and sang in the streets. And hope had never soared as high as on this very special New Year's Eve.

A jarring summons from the telephone on her bedside table roused Bailey from her joyful observation of the scene below her windows. Lifting her long skirt, she hurried to answer.

"Your limousine is waiting, Frau Hanson."

"Thank you." Time had gotten away from her; she hadn't realized it was so late.

Bending to the mirror, she smoothed an errant strand of hair, tucking it into a chignon, then dabbed her favorite perfume, Halston, behind her diamond earrings and between her breasts. Stepping back, she examined herself with a critical eye. Was the floor-length emerald satin too form-fitting? The satin gleamed over her breasts and the top of her hips before it swirled into a gentle flare.

"It will have to do," she muttered, catching up her purse and a floor-length wool cape.

The elevator was crowded, but nothing like the mass of people jammed into the lobby. After fixing her bearings, Bailey drew a breath and inched toward the outer doors.

"Excuse me. May I get through, please? Excuse me." She progressed a few feet before she was stopped again, buffeted by shoulders and elbows, by too many people crowded into too small a space.

"Good God. I'd know that voice anywhere! Bailey?"

She couldn't believe her eyes. "Cole?" She blinked at him in astonishment. They had been practically thrown together and now stood almost toe-to-toe, steadying each other by the elbows, staring in disbelief. "I don't believe this. What are you doing in Berlin?"

"It's a long story. Why are you here?"

"I'm on a fact-finding junket. Which in this case, I suspect, means our committee wants to witness the excitement for ourselves and share in it."

A wave of humanity surged around the island they had created in the center of the hotel lobby, reminding Bailey of the night in Times Square a hundred years ago. The acknowledgement in Cole's dark eyes told her he, too, recalled that night. Smiling, he gestured to a quieter area near a planter overflowing with scarlet poinsettias, then, when she nodded, he led her forward.

While they negotiated a tortuous path toward the poinsettias, Bailey studied Cole from the corner of her eyes, shocked by his appearance. In fact, she thought it likely that she might have passed without recognizing him if they hadn't bumped squarely into each other.

In the two years since she had seen him last, Cole's hair had turned a rich salt-and-pepper color. That didn't shock her; in fact, his thick silvery hair was strikingly attractive. But she had never seen him looking so disheveled before. He needed a haircut and a shave. It looked as if he had pulled his fingers through his hair several times without smoothing it down afterward. And at least a day's stubble darkened his chin and cheeks.

Equally as startling was his clothing. His topcoat was a Burberry, but it was as wrinkled as if he had slept in it. His tie was askew and the tops of his shoes were scuffed and muddy.

But it was his expression that worried Bailey most. Cole's eyes lacked their usual spark and vitality, and a deep line ran between his eyebrows. Beneath his unshaven face, he was pale and he looked utterly exhausted.

"Did you just arrive?" Bailey asked when they could speak without shouting. Was he suffering jet lag?

For a moment Cole didn't answer. He stood in front of her, drinking in her face as if he were observing a vision he couldn't quite believe. Then a shine of moisture clouded his eyes and he enfolded her in a bone-crushing embrace.

"God, Kansas, I've never been more glad to see anyone in my life!" He continued to hold her tightly even when Bailey would have gently eased away.

When he finally released her, she grasped his arms and peered anxiously into his face. "Cole, what on earth's wrong? What's happened?"

"Marsha is dying. She's here in Berlin, in the Memorial Hospital."

Bailey's hands flew to her lips. "Oh my God. Cole, I . . . I'm so sorry. But what happened? Why is Marsha in Berlin? And . . . dying? I just—"

He covered his eyes, then pulled his hand down over the stubble. "She went to Paris for Christmas. Apparently she and her friends decided Berlin was shaping up as Europe's most festive site for the holidays so they changed their plans, chartered a plane and flew here."

"The plane crashed?" Horror darkened Bailey's eyes.

"It was one of those stupid inexplicable things. The plane crashed in a field, and everyone walked away with only a few cuts and bruises. Except Marsha." The exhaustion deepened around his mouth and eyes. "One of her friends phoned me, and I came. She's been unconscious since it happened. The doctors don't think she'll make it."

Stunned, Bailey sat down hard on the rim of the planter. "Good God." When Cole dropped beside her, she took his hand and held it in her lap. Finally she swallowed the lump rising in her throat and turned to look at him. "Cole, what are you doing now?"

He rubbed his eyes with his fingers. "I'm practically living at the hospital."

"No, I mean now, this minute."

His shoulders dropped and he rubbed the back of his neck. "I've been here two days. I should go to my room and get some rest before I fall over. But I can't sleep. I was planning to go for a walk and find something to eat when I ran in to you."

"I have a limo waiting outside to take me to a party at the American embassy. Cole, come with me. I need an escort and I suspect you need to be with people. You need something to take your mind off this tragedy if only for a little while."

Cole raised his head and peered around the lobby. For the first time he appeared to realize Bailey was by herself. "Where's Brendan?"

Bailey stiffened slightly and lowered her head. "He's in Manhattan. He's not in Berlin, if that's what you mean."

"You're spending New Year's Eve alone?"

"Yes." Biting her lip, Bailey brushed a hand across her cape, then she rose to her feet, drew a breath and held out a hand. "Come on, cowboy, let's go to the embassy party. We'll have a nice dinner, a few drinks, and we'll talk. You can relax. If you prefer, we can leave early."

"A party..." he said doubtfully, casting a look at the throngs of people moving through the lobby. All of Berlin was a party.

"I won't take no for an answer." Tucking her arm through his, Bailey stepped forward, sensing his reluctance. At the door, she glanced up at him and spoke in a firm voice. "Cole, I'm not going to let you be alone right now."

Inside the limousine, he sank back against the plush upholstery with an unconscious sigh, then he rubbed his eyes again and reached for Bailey's hand. "I can't believe this is happening. It isn't possible. I try, but I can't make my mind accept that Marsha could be dying."

"Have you seen her often since the divorce?" Bailey asked, shifting on the seat to face him.

He stroked her hand, turning it between his own, absently running his finger over her wedding rings. He did this without seeming to be aware of what he was doing.

"We saw each other occasionally. Not often." Closing his eyes, he let his head drop back on the upholstery. "Oddly, when we did see each other there was none of the old animosity, none of the old tension. Occasionally a flash of bitterness surfaced, but for the most part the times we were together were congenial. Shortly before Marsha left for Paris, we met for dinner to discuss the holiday arrangements for Stevie and Shawn." A spasm of pain tightened his mouth. "And it was a pleasant evening. It was almost like before we were married. Marsha was charming and funny. She talked about Hillendale and her horses, but we didn't argue. She wasn't trying to make a point and neither was I. She seemed genuinely interested in what I was doing. I didn't have the feeling she was just being polite. We even talked about the kids without fighting."

Bailey sat quietly, letting him remember without interruption. Cole recalled how he and Marsha had met, spoke about their courtship and the final deterioration of their marriage. He told Bailey that Marsha had seemed calmer the last time he saw her, and he'd been pleased by that. He remarked that her attitude had softened toward the twins. Recently she had met some new friends whom she enjoyed. And she had hinted there might be a new man in her life.

"How did you feel about that?" Bailey inquired softly.

"Happy for her." After a moment he turned to the window, not seeing what lay outside. "She's only thirty-three years old. She has a whole life in front of her. She's too damned young to die!"

"I'm so sorry, Cole." The words were utterly inadequate, so completely bereft of any real comfort. But Bailey couldn't think of anything else to say. Frustrated, she peered through the limo windows as the driver approached the American embassy. Here, too, throngs of people crowded the sidewalks. Many were dancing and waving wine bottles, holding chunks of the Wall like trophies.

Cole lifted his gaze to the flags snapping in the breeze above the embassy entrance. Then he looked at the revelers celebrating in the street.

"Look, Bailey." Turning on the seat, he stroked his fingers down her cheek. "Thanks for trying to help, but I'm in a lousy mood for a party. I wouldn't be good company for anyone. Plus I'm not dressed properly, I need a shave, and... I'd only embarrass you."

"You could never embarrass me, cowboy, you know that."

"You go to the party. It's New Year's Eve, you should enjoy yourself and have a good time. I'll take a rain check, okay? We could plan to meet for breakfast or lunch tomorrow."

Bailey covered his hand with her own and pressed it to her cheek. "Can you really imagine that any party would be more important than you are?" Easing away from him, she leaned to the open door and spoke to the chauffeur standing beside it. "We've changed our minds," she said. "Please take us to the Memorial Hospital."

"Bailey—"

"That's where you want to be, isn't it?"

Cole looked at her for a long moment, and the unexpected vulnerability overwhelming his expression broke her heart. "Thank you," he said in a low voice.

They didn't speak as the limo swept past the embassy and spun along the Spree River toward the hospital. Finally

Cole broke the silence as if it were important to him that
Bailey understand.

"The marriage was basically indifferent, the divorce bitter...but once Marsha and I meant something to each
other. She's the mother of my children. Can you understand what I'm feeling, Bailey? I never wished her ill. I
don't want her to die. And certainly not like this, in a
strange country with no one to be with her. Her so-called
friends went home." He struck the door with his fist.
"Right now I wish I did love her. She deserves to be with
someone who loves her now."

"You do love her, Cole," Bailey objected quietly, stroking his hand. "Maybe it isn't the kind of love that could
sustain a marriage, but if you didn't feel something strong
and positive, you wouldn't have come all this distance to be
with her now."

He stared out the limo window. "We said some terrible
things to each other. I keep remembering how we hurt each
other."

"Even in the best marriages, people occasionally say
terrible things to each other. It's unfortunate, but it happens. Cole, listen to me. You did everything you could. You
have nothing to blame yourself for." He gave her a startled look as if she had read his mind.

"Maybe if I'd tried a little harder..."

"Then there would have been no divorce and Marsha
wouldn't have come to Europe and there wouldn't have
been a plane crash—is that it?"

He raked his fingers through his hair. "Or maybe—"

"Or maybe you would have been with her and maybe
you could have done something to prevent the crash or save
her?" Bailey shook her head and gently pressed his hands
between her own. "Not too long ago a very wise man told
me that I could scream at fate until I was hoarse, but I
couldn't turn back the clock and make things come out
differently. Neither can you, my dearest Cole. All you can

do is accept whatever happens and deal with it the best way you can.''

''I keep asking myself—why did this happen? And why to Marsha?''

Cole's pain reflected in Bailey's expression. She looked down at their entwined hands. ''There's no answer to that question,'' she said. ''You'll only drive yourself crazy if you try to understand the why of it.''

When they reached the hospital they went directly to the intensive care unit on the sixth floor. Cole led Bailey to a garishly lighted waiting room that was littered with crumpled magazines, paper cups and overflowing ashtrays.

''Do you mind waiting?''

''Not at all. Stay with Marsha as long as you like.''

At the door he turned to face her. ''Thank you, Bailey. I won't forget this.''

''I owe you one.'' She met his eyes. ''You were there for me.''

Cole thought she looked as out of place in the shabby waiting room as a spring rose in winter frost. Her fresh elegance contrasted sharply with the tired dreariness of the gray walls and sad-looking clutter. Behind him, Cole sensed the night nurses straining forward to glimpse her, and he overheard them whispering, wondering who she was. Tonight Bailey looked like a film star.

Then he turned down a shadowed corridor, moving toward the double doors that led into a perpetual twilight. He moved quietly in the dim light until he reached Marsha's still form. One side of her face was bandaged, but otherwise she appeared to be sleeping. The lethal damage was hidden inside.

Trying not to make noise, he pulled a chair forward, then sat beside her. Carefully he took Marsha's hand between his and stroked her fingers, feeling his eyes fill. The last time she had been in a hospital was when the twins were born.

She had worn a satin bed jacket and a silly pink-and-blue ribbon in her hair.

"Hi, honey. It's me, Cole," he said, speaking quietly enough that he hoped he wouldn't disturb the other patients, but loudly enough that Marsha could hear, if that was possible. "I went out for a while, but I'm back now. I was thinking that you might be worried about the twins, and I don't want you to be. They're in Wyoming with my sister and her family. You remember Beth and Harlan, don't you?" He stared at her, willing an eyelash to flicker. "A few days ago Stevie watched a calf being born. And Shawn and Greta are inseparable. I wish you could have been with us when the calf was born. It was a miracle."

A totally inappropriate impulse to laugh warred with the lump in his throat. If Marsha had been able, he thought she would have laughed too at the idea of spending time in a barn on a working ranch. It was an incongruous image. It always had been. He used to tease her about taking her back West to live on a real ranch, and she had laughed and said, "Not on your life, buster."

"I'm sorry it didn't work out for us, Marsha. I wish it could have. I'm sorry for the pain we caused each other, for all the bitter words and all the petty hurts. You deserved better." He looked around the dim room. "You deserved a hell of a lot better than this."

Later, Dr. Freiberg drew him away from Marsha's bed. He was allowed to kiss her before they closed the curtains around her body.

WHEN COLE RETURNED to the waiting room, Bailey took one look at his ravaged expression and knew that Marsha was gone. Wordlessly she went to him and opened her arms. Cole clasped her tightly and buried his face against her hair. For several minutes they embraced in silence, holding on to each other.

When they finally moved apart, they dropped down on the sofa and Cole put his arm around her. Bailey rested her head on his shoulder. On the wall in front of them was a round clock that showed five minutes to twelve.

"I didn't realize I was gone so long," Cole said in a hoarse voice.

"It doesn't matter. I'm glad you were with her."

Silently they watched the hands of the clocks come together. The nurses manning the station across from the waiting room door didn't react. No sound disturbed the deep silence in the corridor; not a hint of the merrymaking outside penetrated the hospital's thick walls. The only noise was a dim rustle as someone quietly passed in the hallway.

Cole closed his eyes and pressed his lips to Bailey's forehead. "Happy New Year."

"Happy New Year." She kissed his cheek, then dropped her head back to his shoulder and watched the clock's minute hand jerk forward into 1990.

"We've spent a lot of New Year's Eves together, Kansas—"

"The first was ten years ago, remember?"

"But this one..." He shook his head and made a sound deep in his throat, then he stood and held out his hand. "Come on. Let's get the hell out of here."

The limo was still parked in front of the hospital, waiting for them. Bailey hadn't been sure it would be. They slid inside and Bailey instructed the driver to take them back to the Kempinski Hotel. After the glass partition slid up, she opened the latch of the bar and poured them each a strong Scotch and water. The liquor was smooth and hot and hit her empty stomach like a small explosion.

Cole rubbed a hand over his forehead, then gazed at her from drowning eyes. "I can't tell you how thankful I am that I found you in the lobby. You're probably the one person in the world who can understand what I'm feeling."

Bailey did understand because she knew what kind of man Cole Tarcher was. He was the kind of man who never spoke badly of his ex-wife. If there was blame to be leveled, he took it on himself. Marsha had been the mother of his children, and his loyalty to her ran deep. He may not have loved her, but he had cared about her and that caring had survived a bitter divorce. Moreover, he grieved for Marsha on the twins' behalf. He understood their loss was the greatest of all.

"What will I tell them?" Cole said staring at her. "How do I tell them that their mother is gone?"

Bailey's heart ached for him. Lifting his arm, she slid beneath it and rested her head on his shoulder. She slipped her hand around his waist and hoped her physical presence would offer comfort that words could not.

"Dearest Cole, when the time comes you'll find the right words," she murmured. Beneath her cheek, she felt his warmth, could hear the steady pulse of his heartbeat.

His arms closed around her and he buried his face in her fragrant hair. "I'm so glad you're here!"

After a moment Bailey eased back in his embrace and gently smoothed the silvery hair away from his face, murmuring soothing sounds deep in her throat. "I know it doesn't seem so now, but in time you'll—"

She bit off the words as he brought her hand to his lips and kissed her palm. His dark intense eyes met hers and locked. In those dark depths burned a raw hot passion swirled to the forefront by hours of excruciating tension. The breath left Bailey's body in a rush, leaving her weak and limp-boned as his lips moved against her palm, as his burning, hungry eyes caressed her face and throat.

The tension crackled and peaked in a taut electric moment of silence as they stared deeply into each other's eyes, breathing each other's breath, feeling the magnetic heat of each other's bodies. The night rushed past the darkened windows but inside, time hung suspended in one endless breathless moment.

"Bailey," he whispered, his eyes on her lips.

"Oh, Cole." She couldn't breathe, could hardly speak.

Then his mouth covered hers in a hard bruising kiss, almost punishing in its hunger and driving need. Bailey moaned and her arms circled his neck, her body strained against his. The passion they had suppressed for so many years exploded with volcanic force.

Her breasts crushed against his chest; her hips thrust forward to meet his in a fierce hot embrace. One of Cole's hands cupped her head, the other moved like fingers of fire over her waist, then up to cover her breast. A groan wrenched from her throat and she called his name again and again. Their hands flew to caress and explore; the urgency of need heated a rain of kisses, giving direction to stroking hands that enflamed and scalded.

"Bailey. Oh God, Bailey..." His voice was as thick and ragged as her own urgent whispers. "I need you so much!"

His mouth plundered hers and she surrendered willingly, eagerly. And it flew through her mind that they were strangers in a city gone mad where no one knew them or cared what they did. They were alone as never before and more vulnerable than ever they had been. And they needed each other with a passionate desperation that devoured resistance.

The realization excited and frightened her.

Chapter Thirteen

Neither of them heard the glass partition slide open, nor did they hear the chauffeur until he cleared his throat for the second time. Then they swiftly broke apart and Bailey felt a rush of embarrassment flame on her cheeks. As discreetly as possible—which wasn't very discreet at all—she hastily arranged her clothing and attempted to repair her falling chignon.

"This is about as close to the hotel as I can get, Mrs. Hanson," the chauffeur apologized, glancing at her in the rearview mirror.

Directly ahead was Kurfürstendamm. Like the side street they were stalled on, Kurfürstendamm was a scene of thick crowds and loud revelry. Bumper-to-bumper vehicles, some of them seemingly abandoned, clogged the thoroughfare. A few of the trams still managed to move, but they were papered with colored streamers, and people clung to the sides and hung out the windows. Shoulder-to-shoulder pedestrian traffic thronged the boulevard, and wherever a space opened, people danced into it, many wearing elaborate costumes that reminded Bailey of Mardi Gras.

"This will be fine, thank you," she said to the driver.

Outside the limo, Cole took her into his arms and kissed her forehead, then he smiled down at her flushed face. "You are spectacular, so beautiful. But you know that already." His fingers were tender on her cheek. "Are you all right?"

"I'm not sure," Bailey admitted, still trembling. Breathing deeply, she inhaled the cold air, hoping it would clear her head. She knew she needed time to think and time to calm her pounding heart. "Do you suppose it's at all possible for us to find something to eat? That Scotch went right to my head."

"I forgot. You didn't have any dinner."

"Neither did you." Bailey's heart was still racing, and she couldn't make herself meet his eyes. A series of aftershocks shivered down her body, and for the first time in years she felt awkward with Cole, unable to think of anything to say.

They fell into step, moving toward the bright lights of the Kurfürstendamm. And Cole must have felt as tongue-tied as she because several minutes elapsed before he said, "Let's see if we can persuade a headwaiter to find us a table somewhere."

At first it appeared impossible. The sidewalk cafés were jammed; people danced between the tables and waited in long lines. The situation was no more encouraging in the more formal restaurants; people pressed against the windows waiting to get inside. Finally Cole positioned Bailey beneath one of the many trees lining the Kurfürstendamm and instructed her not to move, then he vanished into the tide. By the time he reappeared, wearing a grim smile, Bailey had recovered her composure and could meet his eyes with an expression that was almost natural.

"I found a table," Cole said, taking her arm.

Briefly Bailey closed her eyes, then gave him a bright smile. "You're kidding. How much did this miracle cost?"

"You don't want to know."

When she saw the table he had arranged through cajolery and bribery, Bailey laughed until she had to wipe tears from her eyes. But the laughter was good; it cleared the tension between them.

Their table, complete with candle and party favors, was near the steam table inside the restaurant's kitchen, pushed against the wall as much out of the path of the hustle and bustle as possible. Still, the kitchen staff dashed past them, gesturing and shouting in German; waiters ran in and out the doors. But even with the clash and clatter of trays and pots, it was quieter here than anywhere else they had been in the past twenty minutes.

"So," Cole said, smiling at her after they had been served an excellent wine. "Here we are."

"Here we are," Bailey repeated softly.

"Bailey... we have to talk about what happened in the limo."

She ducked her head and bit her lip, plucked at her napkin. "Tonight was a terrible strain for both of us," she whispered, not looking at him. "We just... I wanted to comfort you and things... got out of hand."

He shook his head, watching her. "It was more than that and I think we both know it." Leaning forward, he tried to take her hand, but Bailey dropped her hands into her lap. "I've wanted you from the first moment I saw you, Bailey. Tonight—"

"Please, Cole." She interrupted with a quick gesture. Lifting her head, she gave him a pleading look. "Please don't misunderstand—I don't regret what happened between us. Maybe you're right, maybe it had to happen sooner or later, but please don't attach more importance to this incident than it merits."

He stared at her. "It wasn't important to you?" he asked quietly.

A look of helplessness stole over her expression. "That's not what I'm saying. I'm saying what happened was an isolated incident. It can't be anything else. We were swept up in an emotional moment, caught in something larger than our usual selves." She drew a deep shuddering breath, then spoke in a whisper that begged for understanding. "Cole, please. Let it drop. I'm still married . . . that hasn't changed."

He stared at her, then looked aside. Several uncomfortable minutes elapsed before he spoke again. "So. Tell me everything that's happened to you since I saw you last."

"Oh, Cole. You sound so stiff and distant." Bailey put down her fork. "Is this incident going to ruin our friendship?"

His reserve vanished in an instant and he reached for her hand. "Forgive me, Bailey. It's just that for a moment I hoped . . . No, nothing is going to ruin our friendship." His shoulders straightened and when he smiled, his smile was relaxed and genuine. "Okay, what happened, happened. It's behind us now. So talk to me, Kansas. What have you been up to?"

"Thank you," she whispered, meeting his eyes. Then she drew a deep breath and forced the memory of their wild kisses out of her mind. "I guess that old cliché about time being the great healer is true." She paused. "I think I've reached a dead end on several levels."

Cole leaned back in his chair. "What do you mean?"

Bailey watched the head chef arrange thin slices of sauerbraten across a platter. "I've reached that point where it's time to step back and take a hard look at things. Life didn't work out the way I thought it would, or hoped it would. It's time to examine the life I've got. Is this what I really want? Or am I just drifting, settling for what I have?"

Cole leaned forward, and this time she let him take her hand. "Is what you have so bad, Kansas?"

"Honestly?" She met his gaze. "I don't know anymore."

"Exactly what are we talking about?" He released her hand and leaned back as a waiter appeared with steaming entrées. "Brendan? Politics? Life in general?"

She tilted her head and gazed at the overhead pipes as if the answers might be hidden there. Finally she looked at Cole again, her face expressionless. "I think Brendan may be seeing someone else."

Cole put down his wineglass. "Bailey, I'm sorry."

"I'm as much to blame as anyone. I knew from the beginning that Brendan opposed my running for Congress. And I should have known it would be impossible to keep a marriage fresh when one partner essentially lives in D.C., and the other lives in Connecticut. Weekend marriages don't work. From the beginning Brendan wanted a traditional marriage—and I thought I did, too. Somehow we lost sight of that. Or maybe it's more honest to say that *I* lost sight of that."

"Do you regret serving in Congress?"

She turned the question in her mind, examining it carefully. "No," she said finally, "I don't. There have been frustrations, compromises, a lot of things I haven't liked. But all in all, the experience has been positive. I've had an inside look at how the system works, I've chipped away at it in my own fashion, and I've learned a lot about myself and my abilities. But I think I've reached the end of the line, Cole. That dead end I mentioned. The frustrations are starting to outweigh the satisfactions. The cost has been high."

He smiled at her. "You want to wear lapel buttons again."

Bailey smiled. "Something like that. Although I'm weary of politics, I'll always be interested in political issues. And this is certainly an exciting time for the world...."

"But?"

"But maybe it's time I stepped outside the system and discovered if the view is the same. I suspect it isn't. I also suspect I may like it better."

After the waiter removed their plates, Cole leaned to take her hand again. "I've been wondering about something.

Did I rush you into this second term, Kansas? Did I push you into something you weren't ready for or didn't really want to do?''

"Probably," she admitted. "But I needed that push, Cole. This time, though, the decision to run for reelection is all mine. And this time I'm better equipped to make that decision. I stumbled through the last campaign on automatic pilot. I don't want to do that again. Before I decide to run for reelection I first need to decide if I really want to be a career politician. If I had to make that decision right now, tonight, I'd say no."

"I see. So what do you want to do instead?"

She shrugged. "I don't know yet. Maybe I'll write The Great American Novel. Maybe I'll take a few refresher classes. Maybe I'll travel a little or open an antique store. Who knows? Or maybe I'll do nothing. Maybe I'll concentrate on being Brendan's wife and try to discover if the old Bailey Meade still exists."

Over coffee Cole asked her about Brendan. "And I want the truth, Kansas, not the glossy version."

"The truth." She looked at him and smiled at his mussed hair and thickening stubble. Then her smile faded. "It's pretty rocky right now," she admitted frankly. "Brendan has never said so—I'm not sure he even admits it to himself—but I sense that he blames me for losing the baby."

"That isn't fair."

"The minute we learned I was pregnant, Brendan wanted me to resign my seat in Congress. He thought my schedule was too demanding, and commuting was too exhausting. I agreed but I kept putting it off, telling myself I would resign next week or the week after that. As soon as I wrapped up this committee or finished reviewing that bill or concluded this series of meetings. I was healthy and I felt fine. I never dreamed that . . ."

"Do you blame yourself, Kansas?"

Sudden tears glistened behind her lashes. "Maybe. Sometimes, even though I know it's dumb. You don't have to tell me, I know what happened just...happened. It wasn't anyone's fault." When she could speak again, she said, "Brendan and I saw ourselves as the ideal all-American couple. When the 1.5 children—or however many it is—didn't work out, we fell apart." She spread her hands. "Maybe we blamed each other or ourselves. Maybe we had an image of ourselves that was all expectation and no substance. Who knows? Whatever happened, there isn't much to talk about anymore. We communicate through our secretaries and tell ourselves we're going to change that, but we don't seem able to. It isn't that we argue, we hardly talk at all. When we do talk it's with that terrible politeness that people use with strangers whom they don't wish to encourage."

"I'm sorry, Kansas." Cole studied her face, thinking she had matured into one of the most beautiful women he had ever seen. "Are you considering a divorce?"

A tiny involuntary shudder sent ribbons of candlelight glowing down Bailey's satin bodice. "I still have a knee-jerk opposition to the idea of divorce. No children would be involved in this case, but still..." When she glanced up, his face was expressionless. "I don't mean any reflection on you, Cole. You've always accepted divorce as a solution whereas I never did. I just can't bring myself to throw away my marriage. At least not yet. To me, marriage is supposed to be forever."

Suddenly Marsha was with them again, and they both fell silent.

"You know what I forgot?" Cole sat up straight and stared at her. "Your astrology book. Did you bring mine?"

She smiled. "Of course not, I mailed your booklet to Wyoming. I didn't know you'd be in Berlin."

"We've got to buy you one." Standing, he stepped aside as a waiter rushed by, then he held the back of her chair.

"It doesn't matter."

"Of course it matters. We're talking tradition here. Come on. All the stores are open. We're bound to find a bookstore."

Once outside, they drew deep breaths of the cold air, clasped hands, then hurled themselves into the melee. It was almost two o'clock, but the celebration showed no signs of diminishing. Street musicians crowded every corner, the shops continued to do a brisk business. The Kudamm was as crowded as if it were noonday.

Laughing, caught up in the noise and celebration, Bailey and Cole let themselves be swept forward by the crowds, breaking out of a snake dance only when Cole spotted a bookstore and interrupted the chain. They tumbled inside, breathless and still laughing.

"Aha. Just what we're looking for," Cole called triumphantly. He plucked a booklet from a wire display rack. "The only problem, it's written in German. Can you read German?"

Bailey laughed and pushed at the waves of dark hair falling past the collar of her cape. Her chignon had pulled loose long ago. "Not a word, cowboy."

"Fortunately for you, I can pick out a phrase or two." Riffling the pages, he picked one and jabbed a finger on a paragraph. "All right, here we go. According to the stars, 1990 is going to work out exactly as you want it to. And—" he held the page to his nose and pretended to concentrate "—and, yes, it says there's going to be a new romance in your life."

Bailey ducked her head. "Never mind romance, oh great Swami, what do the stars say about my marriage?" Too late she realized her comment revealed that she considered romance and marriage as separate entities. Until now, she hadn't realized she was making that distinction.

"What do you want it to say?" Cole asked in a gruff voice. When she looked up, he was watching her. Their eyes met and held.

"I don't know," she whispered. When he looked at her like that, nothing made sense anymore.

The door banged open and a man dressed in a harlequin costume jingled into the shop, his painted mouth grinning. He danced and spun around the book displays, then paused in front of Bailey, scanning her cape and satin gown and sparkling earrings before he bowed low and held out his arms. The people in the bookstore grinned and clapped their approval. Apparently it was an honor to be chosen by the harlequin.

"Thank you, but—"

Before Bailey fully understood what the harlequin intended, he had clasped her in his arms and waltzed her out the door of the bookshop. Spinning madly, they danced from one set of street musicians to the next, whirling down the block, turning and turning until Bailey was laughing uncontrollably and her head spun.

When the harlequin finally kissed her lips and released her, she recognized they had almost reached the Kempinski Hotel. And she feared she had lost Cole somewhere behind in the shouting, dancing melee.

Then suddenly he was standing in front of her, guiding her into his arms and continuing the mad waltz. They had always danced well together and people pressed backward to give them space. Bailey's cape billowed behind her and her hair floated around her laughing face. She thought it no wonder that people applauded them. Even disheveled and in need of a shave, Cole Tarcher was the handsomest man she had ever seen.

"Do you know how beautiful you are?" he whispered, gazing into her shining eyes. "You're like a star blazing in an empty sky. You blind me and take my breath away."

Directing her with expert skill, he twirled her out of the street, then across the sidewalk and into the shadows beside the hotel's entrance awning. And then he was kissing her, his hands urgent and hot on her waist, his mouth asking the question that had waited so long for an answer.

When his lips released her, Cole clasped her so tightly that she could feel his heart pounding wildly against her own. "I need you, Bailey."

"Oh God, Cole," she whispered against his neck. She knew what he was saying, what he was asking. In her heart she had always understood this moment was inevitable; they had been moving toward it for years. Earlier, when she had asked him in the restaurant to forget what happened in the limo, she had known neither of them could forget. What happened in the limo was only a beginning. "I want to, you must know that. But . . . I can't."

"I need you, Bailey. And I think you need me." His hoarse murmur sounded against her hair. "Tonight of all nights, I need to know that I'm alive, that you're alive, that whatever happens life does go on. I need to celebrate life tonight, and I want you with me. I saw your face in the hospital and I felt you tremble in the limo. I think you feel the same need for life and reassurance tonight as I do."

"Cole—"

"I love you, Bailey. I've always loved you. We've been deceiving ourselves that the only thing we felt for each other was friendship. It's always been more than that. From the moment we met, we've been moving toward tonight and this moment. Surely you feel that, too." Holding her slightly away from him, he gazed down at her with burning eyes. "Can you honestly tell me that you don't want me as badly as I want you?"

A great weakness overwhelmed her and she sagged against him, pressing her face against his neck, inhaling his warmth and a lingering trace of his after-shave. Yes, she wanted him. She wanted him with every fiber of her being;

she wanted him as a dying woman wants life. She wanted
Cole Tarcher with a passion she had denied for ten long
years. Blood pounded in her temples and her body trembled with her desire for him.

But she was still Bailey Meade Hanson, a woman who
had always stood for honesty and for doing the right thing.
She didn't believe in deception, didn't accept cheating. Not
for others, not for herself. Especially not for herself. She
was what she was. And she couldn't change that with a kiss.
No matter how earth-shattering that kiss had been.

Cole rested his chin on the top of her head and spoke in
a low ragged voice. "You told me it was over between you
and Brendan, that he was seeing someone else."

"I'm still married, Cole. The bonds are still there."

And she was still playing it safe, still unwilling to take the
one risk she wished above all else that she could take.
Without warning, she saw what would happen if she surrendered to their shared passion. She glimpsed a future she
couldn't predict, a confusing open-ended future swirling
with what-ifs and strange uncertain possibilities. The vision scattered her thoughts in alarm.

She didn't want additional complications in her life. On
the plane to Berlin, Bailey had taken a hard look at the
problems in her life and had decided that when she returned, she would finish out her term in Congress but she
would not seek reelection. She would devote all her ener-
gies to revitalizing her marriage. She owed herself and
Brendan one last try to be the kind of wife they had both
once believed she wanted to be. She no longer knew if this
was what she genuinely wanted or even if it was possible to
restore her marriage. But she knew she couldn't live with
herself if she didn't make one final honest attempt.

There was no possibility of reconciling that with what
was happening between herself and Cole. Already she had
betrayed Brendan and her own values. To go further was
unthinkable.

Tears glistened in her eyes. A hot lump formed in her throat and hurt. Gripping Cole's lapels, she rested her forehead against his chest. When she spoke, her voice was a ragged whisper and nothing had ever been as hard to say.

"I can't."

His fingers bruised into her arms as he held her away from him to stare into her drowning eyes. Then he kissed her, a fierce passionate kiss that set fire to her body as if she were nothing more than kindling awaiting his flame. Her knees collapsed and if he hadn't held her, she would have fallen.

"You're a fraud, Bailey," he said angrily, gripping her arms. "You'll take on the United States Congress for an issue you believe in, but you won't risk a damned thing for yourself!"

"Some risks have the potential to change lives forever," she whispered, not sure he heard her.

"Would that be so terrible?" he demanded. "Would it be so wrong to put right a mistake we made years ago? You and I should have been together from the beginning. Everyone saw it but us. Pam saw it—that's why she called off our engagement. Marsha saw it. I'm sure Brendan sees it. Why can't you see it, too?"

"Marsha?"

"Damn it, Bailey. You see everything so clearly, why are you so blind when it comes to seeing yourself? You're right about so many things, but you've never been right about Bailey. You've always seen yourself as so much less than you are. Long ago you clamped onto a square peg and said this is Bailey Meade, and ever since you've been trying to fit that peg into a round hole. Why can't you just be you? Why can't you for once do what *you* want to do instead of what you think you ought to do? Why can't you be selfish for once in your life?"

"Stop it, Cole," she ground out, staring at him. "You're going too far." He always had. That was the difference between them. She recognized a stop sign when she saw it; he didn't.

"Maybe I haven't gone far enough." He kissed her again, a hard passionate kiss that demanded surrender, that pressed her against rock-hard thighs and chest, that left her weak and breathless when he released her, shaking as if she stood in the aftermath of a hot tropical storm.

He stared into her eyes, seeing the desire she tried to deny. "You can't tell me you aren't feeling the same things I am."

A tear slipped down Bailey's cheek and she brushed at it with an angry gesture. "What do you want me to say? That I want you? That I'm shaking with desire? Yes, I want you! Do you want to hear that tonight I suddenly felt mortal and was terribly afraid of dying? Yes, I felt that! I feel it now." She stepped back from him. "And don't you think it's occurred to me that you and I could be together and no one would know? But, Cole—*I* would know. You would know. This one act based on need, desire and vulnerability would change our relationship forever."

"Change it? Or turn it toward what it should always have been?"

"Don't confront me with might-have-beens. Let's deal with what is. I'm married." She swept back a wave of hair that was falling over her forehead, then extended her hand to cut off his protest. "Right now my marriage is at the lowest ebb it's ever been, and that makes me the most vulnerable I've ever been."

"Bailey—"

"Cole, don't you see?" She spread her hands, begging for his understanding. "If I go to your room with you now, I'll never be sure if I went with you because what you say is true, or if I'm hitting out at Brendan, trying to repay him for having someone else in his life."

"Brendan has nothing to do with this, Bailey. This is just you and me, needing each other."

"I wish it was that simple, but it isn't. A lot is going on beneath the surface with both you and me. Please, Cole. Do you really want to risk ten years of friendship on an emotional impulse? Do you want to inject an ugliness into our relationship?"

He pushed his hands into the pockets of his topcoat and stood close but not touching her, staring at her. Gradually the desire in his eyes gave way to sadness.

"We've come full circle, Kansas," he said in a low voice. "It's the risk, isn't it? The possibility that we might disturb the status quo. The status quo may stink, it might not be good for anyone, but it's familiar and by God, let's not take a chance of upsetting it for something uncertain, even if the uncertainty might be less painful."

"Cole, don't."

They gazed at each other in silence, unaware of the noise and revelry that erupted around them.

"You win," Cole said finally, his soft tone filled with regret. "This is one area where I won't push you, Bailey. If you ever come to my bed, it has to be solely your decision." He drew a deep breath of the frosty air. "Thank you for being there tonight, Kansas. I appreciate it more than you will ever know."

Pain constricted Bailey's chest and she bit her lip hard. He needed her and she was letting him down. A feeling of helplessness darkened her eyes to navy.

"I'm sorry," she whispered. "I wish I . . . but I just . . ."

Gently Cole took her into his arms and held her with only a hint of his previous passion. "I'm the one who should apologize. I went too far. And I'm sorry."

"No, you only—"

But he wouldn't let her speak. "Let it go, Kansas. We've covered it." Taking her arm, he walked her to the steps leading into the hotel lobby. "Shall I see you to your room?"

"Where are you going?" Her voice stuck on the lump in her throat.

"I plan to find the nearest bar and then I plan to get very, very drunk. I'm going to raise a glass for Marsha, and for life, and for freedom, and for you and for me, and for all the screwed up people in this crazy world."

"Oh, Cole." Tears glistened in her eyes. Regret stung like acid. But if she ever once let herself admit that she might love him, might love him other than as a friend, she sensed she would be lost.

"Happy New Year, darling Bailey."

For a long moment he looked into her face, then he turned and walked into the crowd. Bailey watched him go, his hands in his pockets, his head down, and she thought she had never seen a lonelier person in her life. When she dashed the tears from her eyes and looked again, the crowd had swallowed him.

She went to her room, put on her robe and brushed out her hair. Sleep was hopeless. When her arm tired of brushing, she wandered to her parlor window and watched the people along the Kudamm, searching for a silvery head and slumped shoulders.

After an hour Bailey swore between her teeth, then dressed in slacks and a silk shirt and went in search of the Kempinski's night manager. Later she couldn't remember how she managed it, but she finagled Cole's room key from him. After letting herself into his room, she ordered up a pot of coffee, and settled down to wait.

Near dawn, she finally heard Cole, trying to fit his key into the lock. When she opened the door, he staggered inside, looking terrible. His cheeks were half-frozen and desperately in need of a shave; his eyes were raw and reddened. He smelled of liquor.

"Is'at you, Kansas?" he said, blinking at her.

Grimly Bailey dropped his arm over her shoulder and helped him toward the bed. "Stand still," she ordered. "Let's get those clothes off."

"She shouldn't have died," Cole murmured as she peeled off his shirt, then pushed his pants down over his hips. "It isn't fair. Not fair." Frowning, he shook his head, steadied himself by gripping Bailey's shoulder. "Don' know what I'm gonna tell Stevie and Shawn. Terrible, terrible." His voice caught.

When she had him undressed down to his Jockey shorts, Bailey gently pressed Cole down to the bed. Kneeling, she pulled off his shoes, then his socks.

Cole spoke to the ceiling. "At least she wasn't alone. If nothing else, at least someone was with her." After Bailey swung his legs up on the bed, she leaned over and drew up the sheets and blanket. He caught her hand and focused a puzzled look on her face. "Kansas? How'd you get in here?"

"You're a good man, Cole Tarcher." She sat on the edge of the bed and smoothed back his hair. "Try to sleep now."

He stared up at her as if she had appeared out of nowhere. "I always loved you, right from the beginning. Did I ever ask you to marry me? I must have."

"No." Smiling, hoping he wouldn't notice the glitter of tears in her eyes, Bailey tucked the sheets under his chin.

"I din? I'm an idiot. If I'd asked you, how would you've answered?"

"Dearest Cole, get some rest." A tear dropped from her chin and fell on his cheek. She brushed it away with her thumb, feeling the soft stubble beneath her finger.

He mumbled something, then fell instantly asleep.

Quietly Bailey sat in the chair beside his bed, still holding his hand and watching the sky lighten against the window shade. She didn't know how long she sat there, listening to him breathe, thinking about everything that had happened during the course of the long night. But when she finally thought to glance at her wristwatch, Bailey realized she had only an hour to shower and dress before she was due to meet Senator Albermaryl for brunch.

Bending over the bed, she gently kissed Cole's lips. "Happy New Year, cowboy," she whispered, blinking at sudden tears. "You're an emotional roller coaster ride, one of the most exciting and wonderful things that ever came into my life, and one of the scariest. You think I'm this strong shining creature who is capable of flying in the face of all the rules—but I'm not. I'm just a small-town girl who goes through life suspecting she's bitten off more than she can swallow."

She pressed a trembling palm to his cheek. "Don't you see, cowboy? You're the only person in my life who genuinely believes in me. I don't want to risk losing that. I don't want you to see that I'm eight parts bravado and two parts coward. It's too important to have one person in this world who thinks I'm wonderful." She brushed another tear off his face. "That's why you still scare me ten years later. Because I could love you so much and I'd end up disappointing you."

Gently she disengaged her hand from his and quietly stood, looking down at him through a shine of tears.

"Happy New Year, darling."

Chapter Fourteen

March 20, 1990

Brendan,
I wish you would try to see my point of view. I've privately announced that I won't run for reelection, but I can't re-sign my seat now. I have a responsibility to the people who elected me. I'm not saying I have no obligation to you, I wish you could see that. My concern for our marriage is the primary reason I've chosen not to stand for reelection. Please, can't you be patient just a little longer?

Bailey

Bailey,
After nearly four years of making do with a part-time wife, I'm running low on patience. Either you want to make a fresh commitment to me or you don't. Maybe we've reached the point where it's time to examine whether our marriage is worth saving. Think about it, Bailey. We'll talk this weekend.

Brendan

May 3, 1990

Dear Mother Hanson,
Thank you for your nice note. I appreciate your concern,

but I don't think there's anything you can do. You asked if
Brendan was at fault, and the answer is no. It's just one of
those things. Over the years Brendan and I moved in different directions, grew apart from each other. We're hoping this separation will give us an opportunity to think
things over and decide where we want to go from here.

Bailey

June 28, 1990
Mr. Tarcher,
The real-estate agent phoned from New Mexico. He said
he's found just the place you've been looking for, about
three miles outside of Santa Fe. Four-bedroom house, two
guest houses, a barn and stables on ten acres. The price is
just under a million. A steal, he says. (????) If you can meet
him in Santa Fe next week, he'll take you to the Fourth of
July barbecue then show you the property.

July 11, 1990

Dear Brendan,
I received your message on the answering machine. I'm
writing instead of phoning because speaking in person
would be too painful.

I don't know what to say about Nancy being pregnant.
You must know that your joy is equaled by my pain. Until
last month I didn't even know there was a Nancy; now she's
pregnant and you want to marry her. You hope I won't
stand in your way. You hope I'll be happy for you.

Maybe I can be happy for you someday. But right now
I'm angry and hurt. I'm jealous and resentful and a lot of
other ugly feelings that are difficult to deal with. If that
isn't the civilized response you said you expected from me,
I'm sorry.

But I won't throw obstacles in the way of a divorce. That's what you really want to know, isn't it? I've already spoken to Marvin Lithgow. Have your attorney phone him.

No, Brendan, I don't want to get together to discuss any of this. I suppose it's possible that we'll turn into one of those used-to-be-married couples who can be congenial and who make a point of keeping in touch. But I'm sure as hell not ready for that yet, and I'm not sure I ever will be.

Bailey

Hartford Courant, August 1, 1990
By Craig Martin, elections desk. Popular congresswoman Bailey Hanson announced yesterday what was privately rumored, that she will not stand for reelection in November. Hanson denied that her decision has anything to do with her impending divorce from respected Manhattan attorney, Brendan Hanson. When asked about her plans for the future, Hanson stated she intended to rest, travel, and write...

New York Post, August 3, 1990
By Mata Hari. To those in the know, dahlings, Representative Hanson's recent announcement of a forthcoming divorce comes as no surprise. Shuttling between D.C., and Gotham, and dressed in a stunning mauve Donna Karan, our favorite congresswoman had time to stonewall you know who. But we know better don't we, dahlings? One of the Hansons has been playing footsie with a certain red-headed interior decorator for over a year. Rumor has it this backstreet twosome will soon become a threesome. Tacky, anyone? We say it's high time the gorgeous congresswoman looked for a new candidate. And your favorite spy predicts Gotham's most eligible bachelors are even now lining up at her door.

Western Union to: Bailey Hanson
From: Cole Tarcher
August 6, 1990

WHY AREN'T YOU ANSWERING YOUR PHONES STOP AND
WHY DIDN'T YOU TELL ME ABOUT THE DIVORCE STOP WANT
TO SEE YOU STOP LET'S ELOPE STOP

Memo from the office of Representative Bailey Hanson
To: Cole Tarcher
September 1, 1990

I'm sorry I haven't gotten back to you before now, but my
office has been swamped with calls and letters. Plus, I'm
trying to wrap things up so the transition will be smooth
when I leave office.

It seems like everything is up in the air right now. So
many changes. I'm taking life a day at a time and trying not
to make any long-range commitments or decisions. Otherwise I'm holding up and doing fine.

As for the divorce, I'm angrier about being publicly hu-
miliated than I am about the divorce. If there's someone
out there who doesn't know about Brendan and Nancy, I
haven't met them. If I'd been honest with myself, I would
have seen the handwriting on the wall way back when.
Maybe I did and refused to recognize what I was seeing.
Whatever the case, when the moment of truth arrived I felt
as if I'd been blindsided and, worse, that I had let it happen.

Thanks for the flowers and notes, Cole. But I'm not
ready to resume a social life. The idea of throwing myself
into the dating scene absolutely horrifies me. Right now I'm
trying to cope with the idea of divorce, trying to deal with
feelings of failure and decide a direction for the future.
Once I get these items sorted out…well, let's play it by ear.

Thanks for caring,
Bailey

September 5, 1990

Mr. Tarcher,
Your real-estate agent in Santa Fe phoned to say your offer was accepted. He wants to schedule the closing for the first week in October. He'd like you to call back and confirm a date.

Wall Street Journal, October 14, 1990
By Robert Alred. Marshall Hearst Brownly, Chairman of the Board of Mangan and Mangan, today announced the early retirement of partner Cole Tarcher. "Cole's decision comes as a surprise," Brownly said. "He'll be keenly missed." Tarcher could not be reached for comment.

To: Bailey Hanson
c/o Mr. and Mrs. Wm. Meade
22 Smokey Hill Road
Oakley, Kansas
December 20, 1990

Bailey,
Where the hell are you? Your office says you've cleaned out your desk and gone. There's no answer at the apartment. I even phoned Brendan, for God's sake. He says you aren't in Kansas but suggested you might be receiving mail at this address. So I'm sending your 1991 astrology booklet and this letter into an apparent void.

I've been thinking about you often, Kansas. It seems to me that you and I have a lot to talk about. Apparently you don't agree or you would have returned my calls or written.

Does this have anything to do with last New Year's Eve in Berlin? If so, Bailey, let's talk. We've been friends too long to allow any misunderstandings to fester.

Have a wonderful holiday and get in touch, okay? Note new address.

Cole

Cole Tarcher
347 Lariat Loop Road
Santa Fe, New Mexico
January 14, 1991

Dear Cole,
Enclosed is your 1991 astrology booklet. I thought I mailed
it before Christmas, then found it on my desk when I returned from Mexico. Better late than never, I guess.

I spent the holidays relaxing on a beach in Cancun. The
holidays seemed strange without snow or cold, but it was a
good strangeness. And it was good to be alone, too. I used
to dread the possibility of being alone for the holidays, but
I discovered it isn't so awful. Does that mean I'm finally
growing up, cowboy?

As for Berlin, I think a lot was going on with both of us
that night. You said some things that were hard to hear.
Maybe I did, too, I can't remember. But you were right
about one thing, Cole, when you said I didn't know Bailey
very well. It's time I learned more. My resolution for 1991
is to take a hard look at me and try to discover if I'm really
that square peg you mentioned, and if so what can I do
about it?

Right now I don't know what I want to do with the rest
of my life. Sometimes that realization is exciting and
sometimes it's a little scary. After all, how many chances
does a person get to do it right?

When I've worked out some answers, you'll be the first
to know. In the meantime, and meaning no offense, friend,
I don't want anyone influencing me. That means you.

I hope your Santa Fe rancho is all you wanted it to be.

Don't worry about me. Maybe it will ease your mind to
know I'm wearing a lapel button as I write this, and loving
the freedom to do so. It's a photo of Saddam Hussein with

a red line drawn through it. Tomorrow we'll know if the world is going to war. Pray for peace, cowboy. The only time I've missed being in Congress was on Saturday when the Houses voted to support the President. I wish I could have been there to add my voice.

With affection,
Bailey

December 10, 1991

Dear Bailey,
I've respected your wishes by staying out of your life while you went in search of the real Bailey Meade Hanson. It's time for a progress report, don't you agree?

If you haven't found yourself in D.C., how about extending the search to New Mexico? I'm hosting a New Year's Eve party this year, and I'd like you to be here. You and I have a lot of catching up to do, so it'd be great if you'd plan to arrive the weekend before New Year's Eve and arrange your schedule to stay at least a week. Bring your jeans, Kansas. I have a beautiful little mare quarter horse you're going to fall in love with and will want to ride.

And yes, you'll have your own guest house. Shame on you for thinking what you're thinking right now. Even though you aren't far wrong.

It's time we talked, Bailey. I've tied up all the loose ends in my life except you. At the risk of sounding pushy, it's time to explore where we go from here.

Love, Cole

December 15, 1991

Dear Cole,
Since when did you start worrying about being pushy?

I'll arrive on December 30 and will depart January 2. It isn't a week, but it'll give us a chance for a thorough catch-up visit and a long ride through the purple sage.

Your comment about me being a loose end concerns me just a little, Cole. I'm not a loose end. I'm what I have always been and always will be—a good friend.

Let's not load up an otherwise enjoyable visit with expectations, shall we? Let's keep it loose. Just two old friends getting together after too long an absence.

Looking forward to seeing you,

Bailey

Chapter Fifteen

New Year's Eve, 1992

Leaning toward the window, Bailey watched Albuquerque slipping past below the plane. Albuquerque appeared larger than she had expected, and there were more trees. Within minutes the wheels of the plane would touch down, and soon afterward Bailey would walk into the terminal where Cole was waiting.

Dropping her head against the headrest, she pressed her fingertips to her temples and asked herself for the hundredth time why she had accepted Cole's invitation. Already she felt the pressure of Cole's expectations and a mounting nervousness due to her own confusion. Part of her longed to see him; part of her wanted to flee. As usual where Cole Tarcher was concerned, her reaction was not clear-cut. Thinking about him sent her emotions whirling into turmoil.

Frowning, Bailey gazed out the window and nibbled her thumbnail, an unpleasant habit she had developed over the past year.

Knowing she would see Cole in a few minutes raised a familiar fluttery feeling in her stomach, an expanding thrill of anticipation. Her muscles tightened, and she felt a flush of heat color her cheeks. Her palms were suddenly moist.

But the decision to fly to New Mexico had also created an unexpected catalyst. Knowing Cole would ask questions and knowing he would reject any glib replies had forced Bailey to acknowledge problems she had been trying to ignore. Though she probably wasn't being fair, she felt she had to justify herself to Cole.

A sigh lifted her breast as the plane touched down and swept past the terminal building, then slowed for the turn at the end of the runway.

Oddly, one of her most disturbing problems was the lack of labels. For so many years she had possessed a comfortable, safe set of labels with which to describe and define herself. Wife, congresswoman, committee person, community leader, commuter, contributor.

Now these labels no longer applied. All the accomplishments she had taken pride in lay in the past. At present she was spinning her wheels, going nowhere at a furious pace. And there didn't seem to be anything she could do about it. She dreaded admitting any of this to Cole.

Aside from the sale of an occasional article—bland pieces that assumed no particular point of view—her writing had not proven particularly successful. Bailey didn't seem to have her finger on the pulse of women's magazines.

Therefore she had switched gears and had begun a novel lightly fictionalizing her experiences in Washington, but she suspected the novel wasn't very good. Too much had happened since her days on the Hill, too much had changed.

Bailey released another sigh as the plane taxied toward the gate. Cole, who had always believed in her and who had always expected so much, would be disappointed. He would remember the important congresswoman gliding around Berlin in a limo, the woman who had been too busy to answer letters and messages, then he would look at her now. The odd thing was, Bailey hadn't let herself acknowledge how badly she was floundering until she tried to see herself through Cole's eyes.

Suddenly she hoped Cole had been delayed and wouldn't be waiting. She'd run for the next plane home and flee back to Washington, D.C., without seeing him.

"Coward," she whispered, biting her thumbnail.

Bailey spotted him the instant she stepped into the terminal, and her heart flipped over in her chest. He was smiling eagerly, holding a single crimson rose, a silver-haired cowboy dressed in jeans and a denim jacket. Cole hadn't changed, he was as stunning now as he always had been, still powerfully attractive, focused and in control. When he spotted her, he stepped forward and opened his arms. And Bailey felt a burst of pride that this splendid man was waiting for her.

"Good Lord! You just get more and more beautiful!" He embraced her, leaving her dizzy from the physical contact and from the spiced scent of his after-shave, then he held her at arm's length to examine her.

"Do I pass?" she asked when his steady inspection began to make her nervous. With great effort, she restrained an impulse to fuss with her new short hairdo and check her lipstick. Immediately she felt overdressed in a silk blouse and wool suit cut along severe lines.

"You pass in spades, Kansas," Cole answered in a gruff voice. "I was trying to decide about your hair. It's very chic, very back-east."

Bailey laughed. "And very asymmetrical. That's what's bothering you." One side was cut short over her ear, the other side was trimmed to jaw length.

"Then it's supposed to be like that?"

She grinned. "Yes."

After she accepted the rose and Cole picked up her overnighter, Bailey had a chance to examine him thoroughly as they walked through the terminal.

Cole's hair was as thick as ever, but nearly all silver now. The contrast between his deeply tanned skin and light hair was strikingly attractive. Prematurely gray men always seemed to draw attention, and Cole was no exception. Bailey noticed several women staring and casting provocative glances in his direction.

What surprised her most was how comfortable he seemed in his jeans and boots. That was how he had grown up dressing, but Bailey had never observed him in anything except suits or expensive vacation wear. Maybe it was his attire, maybe it was a new life-style, but Cole seemed more comfortable than he had in years, more at ease with himself. It occurred to Bailey that she was seeing the real Cole Tarcher. He had come full circle. He had returned to a way of life that ran deep in his blood and in his roots. He didn't need to assure her that he was happy. She saw it in his stride, in his relaxed expression, in the confident careless way he carried himself.

She wondered uncomfortably what he was thinking about her defensive power suit, her prim pearl earrings, her plain no-nonsense pumps. What did he think of her tight little smile and the nervous hint of apprehension behind her mascara?

Cole tossed her overnighter in the back of his Jeep, then opened the door for her, glancing at her legs as she slid inside. When he was seated beside her, he gazed at her for a moment before he said, "I'm glad you came, Kansas. You'll have a chance to relax during the drive between Albuquerque and Santa Fe. If you're interested, I thought I'd give you a brief tour of the town before we drive on out to the ranch."

"Ranch?" she said, smiling and lifting an eyebrow.

"I'm afraid so." His wide mouth curved in a grin. "Not a cattle ranch like the old Tarcher homestead, but there's enough work to keep me busy."

During the drive he explained that although he didn't run cattle, he was drifting into horse breeding a little more each year. "Not fancy show horses, more the garden variety. Workhorses, pack horses, trail horses, ranch horses. That kind. The kind of horse a man might choose to check his fence lines or just for the pleasure of riding.''

"But no ring horses," Bailey said, thinking of Hillendale and of Marsha.

"No. No show horses." Then he grinned. "Strictly speaking, I guess that's not quite true. I entered a pair of Morgans in the trailer-pull contest at the fair this year. I guess that could be considered showing. Or showing off."

"Did you win?"

"Nope," he said cheerfully, then he winked at her. "Maybe next year."

"It sounds like you're thriving in this neck of the woods," Bailey said, feeling a twinge of envy. How long had it been since she had attended a county fair? "How are the twins doing?"

"They've taken to ranch life like butter to bread." He was silent a moment. "They're good kids, Bailey. They've been through a lot and they've had to make a lot of adjustments. But they need a woman's influence. Mrs. Sanchez does what she can, but they need more than a housekeeper. They need a mother." He didn't look at her.

There it was, the first salvo. And not too subtle. Bailey turned to the window and bit her lip, staring at the sage and yucca stretching toward a low roll of hills.

"Moving the kids out of Manhattan is one of the best things I've done in years. They were growing up without a yard to play in, driving to private school in a limo. Have you heard about play dates? Parents in big cities arrange dates for their kids to play with other kids. It isn't spontaneous or random. Playing is by appointment and by the clock, and with children selected by the parents as suitable. That isn't what I wanted for Stevie and Shawn. I wanted something closer to the way you and I grew up."

"Why Santa Fe?" Bailey asked, subtly shifting the focus of the conversation.

"Why not? It's good horse country, for one thing. The town is small, but not too small. The people are friendly and involved in the community and the world at large. There's a thriving colony of artists and writers." He shrugged and adjusted his grip on the steering wheel. "I haven't experienced a single moment of regret for leaving Wall Street and the big city behind. It's good to get back to the land, Kansas. Maybe the kids won't want this land any more than I wanted Dad's ranch, but they'll have the choice. They'll have something more substantial and more personal than a trust fund. In addition, the move has been great for old dad. I have a whole new set of challenges. Wall Street was right at the time I chose it. But this life is right for this period in my life. I'm doing what I want to do. I feel like I've come home."

"I'm glad for you, Cole," Bailey said softly, meaning it.

"How about you?" For a moment his gaze left the highway. "Are you doing what you want to do? Are you happy, Bailey?"

"More or less," she replied, lowering her face to inhale the fragrance of the rose.

"What kind of answer is that?"

"I'm not unhappy, okay?"

They drove in silence, watching Santa Fe's city limits come into view. "I'm not sure how to interpret that," Cole said finally.

"Look, cowboy," Bailey said, trying to keep her voice light. "Let's not turn this into one of those let's-reform-Bailey's-life sessions, all right?"

His tone was as deliberately light as hers. "No need to get prickly or defensive. I'm just trying to learn what's going on with you, that's all."

They had always been honest with each other, and there was no point in changing the rules now. Besides which, Bailey had learned long ago that she didn't excel at deception. Her face always gave her away. She drew a breath and turned to look out the window.

"If you were to plot my life on a graph right now, I guess it would be a straight line. Which isn't so bad. I have a nice apartment that I like, good friends, enough of a social life that I don't feel lonely but not so much that I feel hassled. I keep in touch with a few people on the Hill so I don't feel completely out of sync with what's going on in the world. It's not an exciting life, but it's comfortable." She shrugged. "I suppose that sounds pretty dull to you, but there's a lot to be said for contentment."

"You didn't mention a job. Are you working?"

"At present I'm trying to write The Great American Novel." Her laugh sounded forced. "And before you ask, it's not going all that well. I'm considering abandoning the project."

"That's not surprising," Cole commented, slowing as they entered the outskirts of town. "You trained to be a journalist, not a novelist." The next time he spoke, he did so without looking at her. "You aren't wearing a lapel button, Kansas. And that does surprise me. Is the world perfect now? Have we run out of things to protest or to support?"

"Hardly." A humorless smile thinned her lips. "I think I've finally outgrown lapel buttons. They seem pointless somehow. After all, who cares?"

"You used to. You used to care about damned near everything," Cole said as he eased into a parking spot near Santa Fe's central plaza. After cutting the engine, he leaned back in his seat and stretched an arm over the seat backs, studying her. "What happened to the passion, Bailey? Now that you're no longer in Congress you don't have to worry about stating your position loud and clear. You don't have to consider past favors or lobbyists or the majority opinion of your constituents. Now you can take a stand for or against whatever you feel strongly about. You didn't used to shrug off fighting for what you believed in."

Bailey narrowed her eyes and tried not to think about his fingertips touching her shoulder like tiny bolts of electricity.

"I didn't know you felt so strongly about lapel buttons," she said in a level voice.

"I don't. But I thought you did. I thought the point of getting out of Congress was so you could fight the good fight on your own turf. Now I wonder. When was the last time you spoke openly and honestly about an issue without couching the statement in diplomatic terms? Have you done anything since leaving Congress?"

"Come on, Cole. Aren't you coming down on me pretty hard?" This wasn't the welcome Bailey had expected. He seemed almost angry. "I served my time, I did my part. Someone else can carry the torch."

He studied her in silence, letting his fingertips rest on her shoulder. "I remember a girl who gave up part of her New Year's Eve to protest pay toilets in the women's johns. Comparatively speaking, that wasn't a burning issue to a great many people. But the injustice of it mattered to her. That girl believed it was important to address injustice of any magnitude. She wasn't willing to look aside and let someone else carry the torch. She wasn't indifferent."

Bailey stared at him. She hadn't unpacked yet and already she felt as if she had failed his expectations, as if he were judging her and finding her deplorably deficient.

"That was a long time ago," she said finally, sitting on her temper. Trying to appear casual, she eased away from his fingertips, disturbed by how easily his touch aroused her. As always, her body operated at a level unconnected to her thoughts. Her body didn't know that she was irritated with him. Her skin sensed his touch and sent powerful signals to her nervous system, to her pulse, to her mouth and muscles.

Annoyed by Cole's effect on her, Bailey shifted to gaze out the window. After a moment she realized she was staring at a For Sale sign in the window of a building facing the plaza. Her eyes flicked to the gilt letters curving over the top of the window. The Santa Fe Gazette.

"It's a weekly newspaper," Cole explained as if he were reading her mind. "I understand the *Gazette* used to be a fire-breathing issue-oriented newspaper with statewide circulation. Five years ago the current owners bought it and turned it into something so vanilla-pudding bland that it wouldn't offend anyone. Circulation fell. Now the *Gazette* reports who married whom, who had a baby, and more than you ever wanted to know about high school sports events."

Anger pulsed through Bailey as the realization gradually dawned that he had not chosen this parking space by accident. "What's your point, Cole?"

"Let me ask you something, Bailey. What happened to that girl who marched against pay toilets? It looks to me like she went to Washington, started making compromises, then disappeared altogether."

"That isn't fair. You know how the system works and how discouraging it can be." Pink flooded her cheeks and she felt herself getting angry. Adrenaline surged through her body like a pep pill. It had been a very long time since she had felt strongly enough about anything to get really angry. "I didn't vanish in Washington, damn it. I made a contribution!"

"I don't doubt it." Cole studied the color rising in her cheeks. "But what are you doing now? When was the last time you took the bit in your teeth and fought for something you believe in? I'm talking about a good clean, hard fight. In print. Like you used to do for the *Radcliffe Underground.*"

Bailey stared at him, her eyes flashing.

"Do you know how it looks from here, Bailey? When your marriage fell apart, you did, too. You could have run for reelection—by then you and Brendan were finished—but you didn't. You threw in the towel and ran away to nurse your wounds."

"For God's sake, Cole. Thanks to the gossip columnists, everyone on the East Coast knew Brendan was cheating on me! How would *you* like to face a roomful of voters knowing every one of them probably knew more about your personal life than you did?"

"I understand what you're saying, Kansas. And I know you weren't all that satisfied being a congresswoman in the first place. So, okay. You decided not to run for reelection. What I don't understand is what you've been doing since. You've been hiding out like a whipped dog."

The pulse was pounding behind Bailey's temples, her fingers trembled. "What's going on here, Cole? Why are you attacking me?"

Instead of answering immediately, he nodded toward the entrance of the *Santa Fe Gazette*. "There are thousands of little newspapers all over the United States, Bailey. Just like that one. You can buy one of them for a song. With your talents, you could turn a weekly into whatever you wanted it to be. A voice of protest against everything that's wrong in the world. Or a rallying cry for those people or events whom you believe merit support. The point is, you can make a contribution. You can make a difference. And you can do it right now. Once upon a time that mattered to you, before you decided a woman who fails in marriage or who fails to reproduce isn't worth a damn!"

Bailey recoiled as if he had struck her. The stem of the rose snapped between her fingers. "I shouldn't have come," she whispered when she could speak.

He met her eyes. "If the truth offends you, then maybe you shouldn't have."

They sat in tense silence, watching Sunday strollers wander through the plaza, pausing to peer in the windows of the shops.

"Some of what you said is true," Bailey admitted finally, not looking at him because she was still angry. "But the truth doesn't offend me. It embarrasses me. A lot of people have trouble dealing with a failed marriage, and I've had more trouble than most. I never believed in divorce. My marriage crashed and burned in public, and that was humiliating. It wasn't a private pain." She drew a long breath. "That's behind me now. You're wrong if you think I'm moping around thinking I'm not worth a damn. I know I have a lot to contribute and a lot to give. I just haven't found a focus for my energy and talents yet. But eventually I will."

Cole cast a pointed glance toward the *Santa Fe Gazette*. "You might consider starting here."

"Aside from the obvious, that you always think you know better than I do what's good for me...what's going on here, Cole? What's the hidden agenda? And don't tell me there isn't one. What I do with my future doesn't merit the harshness you're displaying. What's going on?"

He watched the people in the plaza for a moment before he turned back to her. "You've been divorced almost a year. Every day for a year I've been waiting for you to pick up the damned telephone. You said you needed time, and I respected that. But time passed and still you didn't phone. I don't understand that, Bailey. Maybe it hurts a little. I thought I made my feelings clear in Berlin. I thought I understood your feelings. I would have bet everything I own that I'd hear from you after your divorce. Why the hell didn't I?"

Bailey dropped her head and picked at the rose petals. "I've been busy—"

"No good, Kansas. I don't buy it. What happened to the honesty I've always loved in you?" Leaning forward, he jammed the key into the ignition, then swerved the Jeep out of the parking space. In a moment, they were driving away from town, leaving a tunnel of cold dust spiraling behind them. "You've been too damned busy to make a phone call? The hell you are. You're avoiding me because you're afraid, and I'm mad about it. I expected more from you."

Bailey stared at him, tight-lipped. "What gives you the right to 'expect' anything from me? From the moment I met you, you've been 'expecting' things from me, and I resent it! In Berlin you said I didn't know Bailey Hanson. As if you did. Well, you don't, Cole. You've always seen me as bigger, brighter, better than I am. I can't live up to your expectations, I don't know if I even want to try. Did you know that I almost dread seeing you because I know you're going to judge me against your expectations and I'm afraid I'll disappoint you."

He took his eyes from the road and stared at her. "I didn't know you felt that way. I apologize. If I expect the best from you I guess it's because that's what you've always given. I don't recall ever being disappointed. Maybe this problem is more in your mind than in reality."

They drove the rest of the way in angry silence, not speaking again until Cole stopped the Jeep in front of a log gate. Tarcher Ranch was burned into the sign arching above them. Beyond was a sprawling ranch-style house made of glass and adobe, capped by a red tile roof. In summer the patios and terraces would be overhung by thick leafy branches. At present, a plume of smoke curled lazily from one of the chimneys, scenting the cool air with the tang of wood smoke. Behind the house and immediately to the right was a large picturesque barn. Beyond the corral a dozen horses grazed among the sage and yucca. In the distance near the barn, Bailey thought she glimpsed one of the twins riding a pinto in the ring.

As if they both acknowledged there were things to be said, things to be settled before they surrounded themselves with other people, they stepped out of the Jeep and stood beside the log poles, looking toward the house and barn.

Bailey crossed her arms over her chest, glared at him, then turned her face back toward the house. "Are you claiming you don't expect anything from my visit?" she challenged, feeling him step up beside her.

"Expect is too strong a word," he said after a minute, speaking near her ear. He stood so close that she felt his body warmth radiating against her rigid back. "Hope is a better choice. I'm hoping you and I will reach an agreement as to where our relationship goes from here."

Turning, she faced him and moved backward a step. "Why does it have to go anywhere, Cole? Why can't we continue as we always have?"

He stared at her, and his dark eyes caught the winter sunlight as did his hair when he removed his hat and flung it toward the Jeep. "Damn it, Bailey, you're afraid of me. And you're afraid of yourself. Especially you're afraid of us! And that scares the hell out of me." He gripped her shoulders and gave her a little shake. "You and I have been given a second chance, but I'm afraid you're going to screw it up by convincing yourself that you want to go right on playing it safe!"

She gasped when he touched her, and she felt the old chemistry explode into life and bubble in her veins. Wrenching out of his grasp, she stumbled backward another step.

"I don't know what you're talking about," she snapped. But of course she did.

"You married Brendan because Brendan was safe. He didn't challenge you, he didn't expect anything from you. All he wanted was an heir. That marriage ended the day you lost your baby and learned there couldn't be any more."

Anger exploded behind her eyes and she would have slapped him, but he caught her wrist and held it between them.

"The way I see it, Bailey, you stayed in an empty marriage because even a lousy marriage was safer than the uncertainty of building a new relationship with me or with anyone else." He released her wrist when she jerked away, but followed when she stormed to the fence. "That night in Berlin...your marriage was dead in all but name, and I needed you. You needed me, too. But you wouldn't risk getting involved." His dark eyes raked across her face. "Why did you say no in Berlin, Bailey?"

She gripped the log rail until her knuckles turned white against the wood, and she stared up into his handsome angry face, understanding exactly where he was leading her. When all the rhetoric was swept away and nothing but truth remained—she had said no in Berlin because she was afraid. She was afraid that going to bed with Cole Tarcher would be so wonderful that she'd lose her senses and do something impulsive and foolish. Her entire life would change. She had also been afraid to admit the possibility of loving him because love brought expectations and there were no limits in Cole's world. She didn't know if she could live up to grandiose expectations.

"There are many reasons why I said no," she said after a lengthy pause.

Cole stepped up to her, so close she could feel his breath fanning her cheek. "You played it safe with Brendan. You've always played it safe with me. You've hinted that you played it safe during your terms in Congress."

"Cole—"

Once again he gripped her arms and turned her away from the fence, staring down into her pale face. "I'm asking you to stop playing it safe. I'm asking you to take a chance on a future that isn't mapped out. There are no guarantees, Kansas. The future can be whatever we make of it. What's important is that we build our future together.''

Bailey swallowed and swayed on her feet. ''If you're saying what I think you are...''

''You know I am.'' His dark eyes made love to her, even though his mouth was still tight and angry. ''I need you, and my children need you. I think you need us, Bailey.''

''I'm not ready for this,'' she whispered. ''Please, Cole, I didn't expect this.''

His fingers tightened on her shoulders and he pulled her against his body, overcoming her weak protest and pressing her against hard thighs and flat stomach. His hand traced the contours of her back, then his fingers tangled in her hair as he pulled her head back. For an instant he gazed into her eyes, then his mouth covered hers in a hard deliberate kiss that scalded her illusions and made it impossible for her to doubt why she had come to Santa Fe.

When his lips released hers, leaving Bailey shaken and weak-kneed, he whispered against her parted mouth. ''Tell me again that you didn't expect this.''

She spread her hands on his shoulders and dropped her forehead to his chest. Deep inside she had known that by accepting his invitation, she was accepting an inevitable confrontation. After all these years, they were both single again at the same time. If ever they intended to redefine their relationship, that moment had arrived. Naively Bailey had believed she could control the situation, that she would be safe because...

She lifted her head and shock widened her eyes. Safe.

Still holding her against him, letting her feel his arousal and his need for her, Cole nodded toward the ring and the knot of people watching Stevie ride the pinto. ''My children need a mother. I'd like that mother to be you, Bailey. I think you'd be marvelous at it.''

The heat of his need and her own explosive arousal seared her, and Bailey pushed out of his arms, moving to stand beside the Jeep. She passed a hand over her forehead and dropped her head. "The twins might not even like me," she whispered.

"I think they'll love you," Cole said from behind her. "But if it doesn't work out that way, we'll find a solution by working it out together."

Bailey's senses still whirled from his kiss. She couldn't think with Cole standing so close to her.

"Listen to me, Bailey. I want to buy the *Santa Fe Gazette* and install an editor who feels passionately about today's issues and who isn't afraid to shake people up. That person is you. Most of all, I need you. I can't think of anything more wonderful than being married to my best friend. And God knows I love you. I've waited most of my life for you, and for the opportunity to say this to you."

Because she was afraid he would kiss her again—afraid because she *wanted* him to kiss her again—Bailey opened the Jeep door and slid inside. Cole stood looking down at her, then he walked to the driver's side and drove onto the grounds and past the main building before he parked before a guest house, which was larger than the home she had grown up in.

For a moment Bailey didn't move. "You have it all figured out, don't you, Cole? You have my life all arranged. You're offering me a husband, a family, even a career. Just like that." She snapped her fingers. "All I have to do is move halfway across the country, return to a small town and become a rancher's wife. All I have to do is change my whole life, risk everything comfortable and familiar on the belief that you know what everyone needs."

He turned on the seat and rested his forearm on the steering wheel. "I'm asking you to make a choice."

She stared at him. "I haven't seen you in two years, and an hour after I step off the plane, you want a commitment to spend the rest of my life with you. How do I know if—"

"If we don't know each other by now, we never will. You aren't going into anything blind. But there aren't any guarantees, either." He returned her stare. "Once you said you wanted it all. A husband, children, a stimulating career. That's what I'm offering you."

"Like you're some kind of fairy godfather! Like you've decided I need these things, so here they are for the taking."

"That's what you said you wanted—I can offer it to you. The choice is yours." Opening the door, he slid out, retrieved her overnighter, then walked around the Jeep to open her door.

"Yes, there's risk involved," he said, looking down at her when she stepped out beside him. "I'm not an easy man to live with. A year from now I could be standing here trying to persuade you to come explore the Amazon with me. Or asking how you'd feel about moving to Alaska. And raising kids is no cakewalk, either. Kids bend your heart in a dozen places, then they turn around and aggravate you half to death. I imagine you have a few irritating quirks, too. And it won't be easy to take on a small-town newspaper, if that's what you decide to do, and turn it into something vital and exciting. None of what I'm offering is going to be easy."

But it could be so wonderful, Bailey thought, her gaze going helplessly to his exciting mouth. On one level she was reeling from the swiftness of his approach. On another level, she was responding to the sweet seductiveness of his offer.

Turning away from him, she faced the corral and watched Stevie slide down from the pinto's back as Shawn waited impatiently to take his place. Could she be a real mother to them? Would they grow to love her?

Unlike her marriage to Brendan, life with Cole would be turbulent and exciting. There would be arguments, upsets. Wonders and small miracles. Obviously he expected her to cope with whatever obstacles came their way. But what if she wasn't as strong and infallible as he seemed to think she was? Could she bear to fail in front of him?

"I love you, Bailey." His hands slid down her arms, then around her waist, and he held her against him, resting his chin on top of her hair. "I want to spend the rest of my life arguing issues with you, cheering in the New Years with you. I want to watch your beautiful hair turn as silver as mine. I want to watch your editorials turn this town on its ear. I want to make love to you every night and wake each morning to find your head on the pillow next to mine." Gently he turned her to face him. "We're both starting over, Bailey. This time, let's do it right—with each other."

"You had it figured right, cowboy," Bailey whispered hoarsely. "You scare the hell out of me."

He smiled. "A simple yes or no is more the answer I was looking for."

Raising her hand, Bailey touched her palm to his cheek. "Please, Cole. Let's slow down. Before we go any further I think the twins and I should have some time to get acquainted." She shot a glance toward the corral. "We don't know how they might feel about having a new mother foisted off on them."

"I've spoken to them about you."

"You have?" She stepped backward and stared at him in disbelief. "Cole—"

"Calm down, Kansas. We simply had a general discussion about whether we wanted a new mother at all. We agreed we did. To put it in terms the kids could understand I reminded them how we'd interviewed several people before we chose Mrs. Sanchez as our housekeeper. Then I explained that you were my first choice in this instance and they would be meeting you this weekend. I mentioned you had known them from the time they were babies."

Bailey considered this information. Only Cole Tarcher would conduct interviews to select a wife and mother. She didn't know whether to laugh or to throw up her hands.

"Who is your second choice?" An arrow of jealousy struck hard and deep. Bailey realized her emotions were swinging like a pendulum. Irritated by her reaction, she shoved back her hair and straightened her suit jacket. "Never mind. I don't want to know."

"The twins aren't going to be a problem, Bailey. They're prepared to accept you and love you. At this stage they aren't very complicated. In no time at all, you'll know them almost as well as I do." His dark eyes studied her expression. "What else is bothering you?"

Bailey felt as if someone had tossed her onto a roller coaster that was picking up speed, hurtling around corners. She raised a hand and let it fall, gave her head a shake.

"What else...okay. I'm not sure how to say this, but...I can't imagine agreeing to marry someone with whom I haven't..." Crimson flared on her cheeks and a tremble appeared in her fingertips. She swallowed and thought of his kiss beside the log gate. "You know..."

"Slept with?" A smile widened his lips, and the look in his dark eyes sent a hot shiver sliding down her spine. "That occurred to me, too, Kansas. I thought we'd have dinner, then spend some time with the twins. Afterward I thought we might return to your guest house for an after-dinner drink. Then we'll let nature take its course and see what happens..."

He had it all figured out. Bailey gazed up at him with a helpless expression and felt her mouth go dry. The naked desire flaming in his eyes made her muscles go as limp as tissue paper. But if physical desire had been the most important thing in a relationship, they would have become lovers twelve years ago.

There was more. And that was the part that was so confusing.

Chapter Sixteen

"You were terrific with the twins. I knew you would be." Cole pushed off his shoes, then crossed his ankles on top of the coffee table. His dark eyes traveled slowly from Bailey's feet to the nape of her neck, lingering on the flare of her hips, the provocative curve of her waist. "Already you have them wrapped around your little finger." He smiled and loosened his collar. "I don't believe I've ever heard Stevie offer to let anyone ride his horse, and I thought we'd never get Shawn peeled away from your side and off to bed."

Bailey stood in front of the patio door, gazing outside as she turned a snifter of amaretto between her palms. Nerves fluttered in her stomach as she watched a fat wet snowflake float past the porch light and melt on the Mexican tiles.

"It was a wonderful evening," she said softly. The twins were dark-eyed and dark-haired, bright and vivacious, bubbling over with eagerness to claim her for their own. Their innocent mischievousness had captured her heart from the start.

Slowly she turned to face into the room, to face Cole, and when she met his steady gaze all thoughts of the twins fled her mind. Nervousness dampened her palms and turned her body alternately hot then cold. She saw pinpoints of candlelight flickering in his dark eyes like tiny flames. She watched him pull to his feet and knew the moment she had been waiting for, longing for, for twelve long years had finally arrived.

"Nervous?" Cole asked softly. He stood beside the sofa, watching her, his hands lifting to pull off his tie and toss it aside. He opened the buttons on his shirt exposing an arrow of tanned chest and crisp dark hair.

"Yes," Bailey whispered, placing a hand on the back of a chair to steady herself. Since college she hadn't been with anyone but Brendan. And she hadn't been with him for over a year. Tension tightened her muscles and her throat felt as if she had swallowed sandpaper.

"Darling Bailey, we've been leading up to this moment for twelve years."

"Maybe twelve years of foreplay is a bit too much," she said with a wobbly smile. "It's great for anticipation, but it sure puts a lot of pressure on the actual event."

"We'll go slowly," he promised in a husky voice, walking toward her. After removing the snifter of amaretto from her shaking fingers, he set it aside, then lifted her hands and slipped them inside his opened shirt.

When her palms flattened against his hot smooth skin, Bailey sucked in a deep breath and closed her eyes. The scent of soap and after-shave filled her nostrils, and she thought her legs would collapse. But he caught her around the waist and held her close against him, letting their bodies sway in time to the soft sweet music floating from the stereo.

While he kissed her eyelids, slowly, deliciously slowly, her hands moved tentatively, exploring the texture of his skin, the coarse hair on his chest. Their hips moved in concert, tantalizing with every motion.

"I love you," he whispered against her lips. His hands slid up her arms and cupped her face, then he almost kissed her. His mouth, his sexy exciting mouth hovered above hers, teasing, a heartbeat away.

Bailey leaned in to him, thinking she would faint if he didn't kiss her now. But he edged away, tantalizing her until she understood the tease. And when he would have kissed her, she too pulled back, not letting him claim her mouth, spinning out the tension.

Pressing her hips hard against his, she leaned back, drawing him over her, groaning when he licked her lips, traced their contour with his tongue. His hands moved down her body, cupped her breasts, then molded her waist and hips. She felt his fingers sliding her silk skirt up, passing over the tops of her stockings and garters, gripping her hips to pull her roughly to him.

And suddenly the teasing was over, ended in a titanic eruption of raw, pounding passion. They stared into each other's eyes, then clasped each other fiercely, a single unit, and covered each other's faces with frantic kisses, hot urgent kisses that sought to claim and possess. Their hands flew, touching, stroking, seeking. They broke apart only long enough to tear off restrictive clothing, then flew into each other's arms again, gasping at the sudden scalding thrill of naked skin against naked skin, of deep urgent kisses, of hands that enflamed and urged.

And the urgency was desperate and overwhelming, the need so powerful and driving they could not part for the few seconds required to race into the bedroom. Cole lifted her up and onto him and Bailey's legs circled his waist, her lips clinging to his. And she cried out when his demanding fullness penetrated her and thrust forward. Arching, she lifted her breasts to his mouth, and as her body closed around him, taking him deep inside, a shudder of joy racked her body.

"Say it," he murmured hoarsely against her breasts. "Say it, Bailey. I've waited so long to hear your wonderful deep voice cry my name."

"Cole," she whispered against his hair, gasping as a dewy heat dampened her skin. "Cole, Cole, my darling Cole."

Afterward they stood in each other's arms, covering each other with tender kisses that swiftly flamed into renewed passion. Once could not satisfy them, perhaps after so long a wait they would never have enough of each other.

Cole swept her into his arms and carried her into the bedroom. After he placed her gently on the sheets, he stood over her, drinking in the sight of her high firm breasts, the feathery softness between her legs, the sweet curves and shadows of her. And before she lifted her arms to him, she saw her effect on him and smiled with joy.

"Slowly, darling," he whispered after kissing her so deeply that her senses tumbled and soared. "Slowly this time. I want to taste every inch of you." His mouth slipped to the pulse thundering at the base of her throat; his tongue traced a path to her hard nipples, circled, teased and gently sucked. His hand danced across her stomach, slipped lower to stroke and caress and coax her into a wild frenzy of desire. When his mouth followed where his fingers had explored, Bailey moaned and, unable to wait another moment, pulled him on top of her and arched to receive him.

In the next hour they discovered their own unique rhythms, their own pace and their hunger for each other. They gloried in the uncharted delight of discovering how to give the greatest pleasure, where to stroke, when to tease. Then finally, like a symphony drawing into perfect harmony, they met in a crescendo of fever and magic and the earth whirled around them in glorious eruption.

Afterward, they lay sated and exhausted on the damp sheets, fighting to catch their breath, letting the chill air dry the perspiration from their bodies. Cole raised up on an elbow and smiled down into her glowing face.

"You are the most beautiful woman I have ever known. I could make love to you every night of my life and never grow tired of looking at you."

Laughing softly, Bailey pushed him down on the bed and snuggled her head on his shoulder. Drowsily she murmured, "I had no idea it could be like that, that it could be so...spectacular."

"Neither did I," Cole said gruffly, holding her.

"I was so afraid I might disappoint you..."

He stared at her incredulously. "Never! You were wonderful!"

Bailey sensed he was waiting for her to tell him she loved him. And she wanted to. But she also knew those three little words carried dizzying implications. Once she said I love you, there was no taking it back. She would be committed. And that commitment would result in an upheaval the likes of which she had never experienced. Everything in her life would change.

Before she fell asleep, she lifted her mouth near Cole's ear and whispered, "I..." but her courage failed. She swallowed and finally said, "I'm so glad I came to Santa Fe."

WHEN BAILEY AWOKE the next morning the bedroom was filled with pale wintery light. The snow had stopped during the night, but the sky was still gray and hazy, and a bank of dark clouds widened across the southwestern horizon.

Cole had dressed and gone, but a note was pinned to his pillow.

Dearest Bailey, You're the most wonderful thing that ever came into my life. I love you.

Cole.

P.S. There's a fresh pot of coffee in the kitchenette.

Ring the main house when you're ready for breakfast.
I love you.

Smiling, Bailey dropped her head against his pillow, inhaling the scent of him, imagining she could still feel his warmth. A pounding at the door interrupted the heated memories stealing through her mind, and before she could get up and put on her robe, the twins burst through the door, ran through the guest house and threw themselves onto her bed.

"Hurry up," Stevie urged, tugging her hand. "We can go riding. Dad said you could ride Ophelia if you want to. I want to take you to McGill's Draw and show you my hideout."

"Isn't it too cold outside to go riding?" Bailey smiled and cast a doubtful glance toward the window.

"It isn't far to McGill's Draw. Honest."

Shawn gave her a shy smile. "Did you know us when we were babies?"

"I sure did. You were the prettiest babies I ever saw. And you both loved strawberry ice cream."

Shawn looked happily surprised. "We still do!"

"I'll tell you what, guys. Give me a minute to get dressed, then we'll go up to the house and see if Mrs. Sanchez needs any help preparing for the party tonight. If she doesn't need our help, we'll go for a ride."

Mrs. Sanchez insisted all was in readiness. The food was being catered, and two girls were coming out from town to lend a hand with the cleaning and last-minute preparations.

"Is Cole here?" Bailey inquired, gulping a second cup of coffee before she let the twins herd her outside. She hoped she wouldn't embarrass herself; a lot of years had passed since she last rode a horse.

"Mr. Tarcher had some errands in town," Mrs. Sanchez explained. "He said he'd return about two o'clock."

Bailey smiled, deciding Cole was pretty transparent for an old wheeler-dealer. It didn't require any genius to understand he was giving her and the twins a chance to get acquainted.

Bailey enjoyed every minute with the twins. As it turned out, Ophelia was mild-mannered enough that Bailey didn't embarrass herself during the lively tour of the ranch. The twins chattered every minute, telling her about school and about Miss Dolby, whom they adored. They talked about their best friends and their favorite horses and told in great detail how Stevie had broken his arm shortly after school started. Bailey admired Stevie's hideout, inspected the corner of the barn where Waffles had had her kittens, and praised Belle Jesse's new foal. When Bailey noticed Cole's Jeep parked in front of the main house, she glanced at her watch in surprise. It was almost three o'clock.

"Hey, guys, do you know what time it is? We missed lunch."

The twins blinked at her in disbelief, then laughed. Mrs. Sanchez's husband took their horses, then they walked toward the house, suddenly starving, trying to appease their tummies by catching snowflakes on their tongues.

"Maybe we'll get snowed in," Stevie said hopefully, looking up at the sky.

"That would be great!" Shawn smiled up at Bailey and squeezed her hand. "You could tell us stories."

Cole was waiting at the door of the main house. "Did you guys have a good time?"

"I had a terrific time," Bailey said, meaning it.

"Mrs. Hanson rides real good, Dad."

"I thought she might," Cole said, smiling into her eyes. His smile was intimate and private, recalling last night and the wild joy they had shared. Bailey gazed up at him and felt herself grow weak with wanting him again. She hadn't known lovemaking could be as thrilling or as fulfilling.

Gently Cole touched the pulse beat at the base of her throat. "I also think Mrs. Hanson might want a nap. We were up late last night, and we'll be up late again tonight. Does a nap sound appealing, Kansas?"

The heat in the kitchen glowed against Bailey's cold cheeks and coaxed a yawn. She wished he could join her in the guest house. "A nap sounds wonderful. What time does your party start?"

"Not until eight. You have plenty of time."

Bailey glanced at the snow falling past the kitchen curtains. "Won't this weather keep everyone home?"

Cole grinned. "You've been away from small towns too long. A little snow and ice isn't going to discourage anyone. They're all curious to meet you." Before Bailey could decide how she felt about being placed on display, Cole slipped his arm around her waist and walked her toward the door. "Before you return to the guest house, ask me what I did in town."

Bailey examined the excitement smiling over his face. His dark eyes twinkled; he was bursting to share his news. "Okay, cowboy. What did you do in town?"

"I made an offer on the *Santa Fe Gazette*. My Realtor thinks the owners will accept it." He pulled her next to him and held her tightly. "It's yours, Bailey."

Stunned, Bailey tried to understand what he was saying. She pushed back and stared up at him. "You're taking a lot for granted. I . . . I don't know what to say."

She was genuinely speechless. Some men bought flashy engagement rings. Cole Tarcher bought a newspaper. If she spent the rest of her life trying, she would never be able to second-guess him.

"You don't have to say anything. Not yet."

But she understood she would have to say something soon. Very soon. The expectation was there. And the pressure.

THE GUEST HOUSE was quiet and toasty warm but Bailey couldn't fall asleep. After tossing and turning, she made an irritated sound, then pushed her pillow against the headboard and leaned against it with a sigh.

What was she going to do? The pressure was building, both intentional and unintentional, pushing her toward a decision she didn't want to make on the spur of the moment. Frowning, she tried to sort through a confusing tangle of emotions.

There was something unnerving, almost frightening, about having everything you ever wanted suddenly handed to you on a silver platter.

It was impossible not to speculate, and the possibilities were wildly exciting, almost intoxicating. Bailey could almost see herself as the twins' mother, and the daydream was warm and wonderful. Moreover, from the first moment she had noticed the For Sale sign in the *Gazette*'s window, her mind had played with shaping editorials and arranging type fonts. As for Cole, the prospect of spending a lifetime with him took her breath away.

The frown deepened on her brow as she turned to watch the snow blowing past the bedroom window. Long ago she had learned if something seemed too good to be true it usually was.

The problem with someone giving you everything you ever wanted was that the same someone could take it all away just as suddenly.

What if it didn't work out between her and Cole?

Once upon a time she had believed in another man and in another marriage. That man hadn't meant half as much to her as Cole did, yet the failure with Brendan had been so devastating it had effectively brought her life to a standstill.

She didn't think she would be able to endure it if she invested all her hopes and all her love in Cole and a family and then the marriage didn't work out. And this time there would be children involved. Bailey's mind flashed backward to her own childhood trauma when her parents had divorced.

A tide of panic overwhelmed her. Her hands shook and her lips suddenly went dry. Could the twins endure losing a second mother? Closing her eyes, she pressed the heels of her palms against her forehead. It was terrible to want something this much and to be this afraid.

In the midst of her anxiety she recognized that the panic she was feeling now was only a tiny taste of what she would experience if she failed to build a successful life with Cole and the twins. Another failure would tear her heart out.

Throwing back the blankets, Bailey jumped out of bed, wild-eyed and shaking. She couldn't stay here. She was only giving everyone false hope, only torturing herself. Cole believed he was solving everyone's needs. What he was really doing was asking everyone involved to risk terrible pain.

Sensing that she acted out of panic but unable to stop herself, Bailey dashed into the living room and called a cab. She had to dial twice before she got the number right.

"Pick me up at the gate to the Tarcher Ranch," she instructed in a shaky voice. Her teeth were chattering.

Hurrying, pausing only to wipe her eyes, she dressed in a warm pantsuit, then threw her clothes into her overnighter. It was too cowardly to leave without a word, but she couldn't bear to face Cole. After rummaging through the desk she found a pen and a sheet of paper.

Dearest Cole,
I know you won't understand this. You've offered me everything I ever wanted and I'm afraid to take it. The risk of hurting everyone is too great, and I couldn't bear that. Now I know why I always insisted I had small ambitions. If a person fails in small things, the pain is small. But if a person fails at being a wife and

mother, the pain would be huge and devastating.

Please forgive me.

Bailey

Tears sluiced down her cheeks as she shut the guest house door behind her, then struggled toward the road through the blowing snow. Staying well away from the main-house windows, she dragged her overnighter down the driveway. When she reached the gate, she sagged against one of the posts but she didn't tighten her scarf. She let the icy wind and snow flow over her hot face hoping it would cool the panic pulsing through her blood.

Finally the cab loomed out of the snow and descending darkness, and Bailey jumped into the back seat and rubbed her frozen hands over her cheeks.

"Nasty night," the cabbie commented.

"I need to go to the airport in Albuquerque."

The cabbie hooked an arm over the back of the seat and looked back at her. "If you're trying to get somewhere for New Year's Eve, miss, I don't think you'll make it. I heard on the radio that the airport is closed down."

"Please," she said, peering back toward the light shining from the windows of the main house. "Just go." Fresh tears blinded her.

"It's your nickel," the cabbie said with a shrug.

It was warm and dim inside the cab, a safe womb. Once the snow and darkness had blotted the Tarcher Ranch from view, Bailey discovered she could breathe again. The panic began to recede from her throat, and she steadied her hands against her knees.

By the time the cab passed through Santa Fe and turned onto the snowy highway leading to Albuquerque, she was rational enough to wonder what in the hell she was doing.

"Do you believe in astrology?" she asked the cabbie. Maybe she wasn't so rational after all. Without waiting for a reply, she babbled on, speaking more to herself than to him. "I didn't think I did but there's no denying I fit the description." Disgust thinned her voice. "Gemini is the sign of the twins. We want two different things at the same time. We want the safety of absolute guarantees, which don't exist, and we want the excitement and adventure of the unknown. We want to go to the moon, but we don't want to risk flying. We want to be happy, but we're so damned afraid of losing it all that we won't take happiness when it's offered."

"I know what you mean," the cabbie said over his shoulder.

Bailey stared at the back of his head. "You do? I don't even know what I mean." She shoved back a lock of hair. "I've never been more confused and upset in my whole life!"

"My granddad had a chance to buy a hundred shares of Coca Cola back when it was selling for about a buck a share. But he was afraid he'd lose all his money so he didn't do it. He had these big dreams, see, about getting rich but he didn't want to risk losing his nest egg. Maybe he was one of those Geminis. Turns out he lost it all anyway. He might as well have bought the Coca Cola stock. The worst that could have happened is he'd have ended up the same as he did, but he would have had a hell of a good time along the way. Is that what you meant?"

Bailey nodded slowly. "That's about it. Being so afraid of losing what you want that you don't take what you want."

If she took a risk and married Cole she might end up unhappy. But she knew for sure that she'd be unhappy if she didn't marry him.

The farther the cab drove from Santa Fe, the more appalled Bailey became at what she was doing. Without stopping to think, she had responded to a knee-jerk panic and she had run away. A shudder of self-disgust rippled down her spine. Not only had she behaved like the worst coward, but she had thrown away a twelve-year friendship in the process.

Horror widened her eyes as she gradually realized that was exactly what she had done.

There were some acts that a friendship could not withstand, and this was one of them. The odd thing was, she knew Cole would understand her panic. But their friendship would not recover from it. Not only was she rejecting the man she loved and the miracle of a family, she was about to destroy the most important friendship in her life.

"This is the stupidest, most self-destructive thing I've ever done," she whispered, staring through the windshield at the blizzard blowing across the highway. She'd been thinking that everything depended on Cole, that he could take away what he had given. But that was wrong. "Everything depends on *us*. On both of us." She looked at the cabbie. "What would you say if I told you I was running away from everything I ever wanted in my life?"

The cabbie laughed. "No offense, miss, but I'd say you're crazier than a bedbug. Why would you do something like that?"

"Because I'm an idiot. Because I don't think I deserve to have all my dreams come true. Because I'm afraid I'll screw everything up. Maybe because I couldn't stand the pain if everything didn't work out wonderfully."

"Hey, there's no rule that says dreams can't come true. As for the rest . . ." The cabbie shrugged. "You just do the best you can. If things don't work out the way you hoped, well you pick yourself up, dust yourself off and try again."

Bailey stared at him. It might have been Cole speaking.

"Please," she said in a whisper, "turn around and go back. Before I make the biggest mistake of my life."

The cabbie glanced over his shoulder and shrugged. He slowed, swerved to the side of the road, then swung the cab back toward Santa Fe. Thick snow danced in front of the headlights, hissed past the windows.

"Can't you go any faster?" Bailey asked, leaning forward.

"I'm going faster than I should right now," the cabbie started to say. Then suddenly they were sliding, spinning, hurtling sideways down the ice-slick highway.

Bailey gripped the edge of the seat and stared in horror as a dark shape loomed out of the blowing snow.

There wasn't time to scream before the impact.

COLE DIDN'T KNOW she'd run away until the phone rang.

"Cole, this is Bill Pooley at Mercy Hospital. The ambulance just brought in Mrs. Bailey Hanson. A cabbie said he picked her up out at your place. Is there someone we should notify?"

Cole stared at the telephone in shocked disbelief. He couldn't make himself believe what he was hearing.

"What? Bailey? It can't be Bailey. She's in the guest house napping. Unless..." Straining, he leaned to the window and tried to see the guest house through the snow and darkness. Unless she'd run away. He felt as if he'd just received a hard blow to the stomach. "Bill, are you absolutely certain it's Bailey?"

"That's the name on the driver's license. It's a George-town address. That sound right?"

He collapsed against the wall next to the window. "What happened?" he asked through dry lips, staring at the light shining into the snow from the guest-house window.

"Car accident. Between here and Albuquerque. Apparently the cab hit a patch of black ice, slid, and slammed into the only tree within five miles. With this weather, we're going to have a lot of nasty accidents before the night is over."

Cole wet his lips. "How badly is she hurt?"

"She got banged up, but nothing too serious. A broken ankle, a couple of broken ribs, enough cuts and bruises that she's not going to feel like celebrating the new year. We're

going to keep her here overnight. Make sure she doesn't have a concussion. The cabbie got off light, only broke his wrist. Listen, I've got a handful of forms someone needs to sign, is there anyone we can call?''

"You just did," Cole said grimly. "I'll be there as soon as I can get into town."

After he hung up the telephone, he stood for a moment trying to understand. What on earth was Bailey doing in a cab on her way to Albuquerque? But deep down he knew. And it hurt like hell.

"Mrs. Sanchez?" He pulled on a sheepskin coat and pushed a hat down on his forehead. "Call the guests and tell them we're canceling the party due to the weather." Bending, he kissed the twins, hoping his expression didn't frighten them. "It's after seven. Why aren't you scamps in bed?"

"Mrs. Hanson said she would tuck us in," they protested.

"Not tonight, guys." Not ever. Bailey had made her decision. She'd run away. "We'll talk about it in the morning."

Part of him still refused to believe it could be Bailey in the hospital until he walked into the guest house and felt the silence and the emptiness. Until he found her note.

When he finished reading it he crumpled the paper and slammed his fist against the wall. On some level he had always recognized the possibility that Bailey might cut and run. For all his talk about how alike they were, he knew they were also different in fundamental ways, and those differences scared her. They always had.

Moreover, he understood how she could be afraid of happiness, so afraid of losing it that she couldn't bring herself to grab it in the first place. He'd had a little trouble with that one himself. He had thought long and hard before he was willing to risk their friendship on the possibility of something more. Now what he had feared most had

happened. He'd moved too fast, he'd scared her, and she had run away. He knew better than to hope there would be another second chance. They had reached the all-or-nothing phase. And Bailey had chose nothing.

The pain was like a knife in his heart. Smoothing out the note, he read it again, then slowly tore it into little pieces and let the pieces flutter to the floor.

"Damn it, Bailey," he whispered, covering his eyes with his hand. "What makes you think it's all your responsibility to make a marriage work? You can't fail unless *we* fail." Striding angrily to the window, he watched the snow falling for several minutes before his shoulders dropped in resignation.

If that was the way she wanted it, he wouldn't fight her. He had done everything he knew to convince her they belonged together. He didn't have any magic tricks to pull out of a hat. The tragedy of the whole thing was he really believed they could have been happy together. But she didn't love him enough to try. Hell, maybe she didn't love him at all.

Angry and hurting, Cole slammed the guest-house door behind him, then climbed into the Jeep and shoved it into gear. By the time he reached the hospital, his anger had settled into a dull throbbing pain.

But his pride had kicked in. He'd be damned if he would beg her to do something she clearly didn't want to do. He'd be a gentleman about the whole thing. Cool and polite. He'd make it as easy as he could on both of them. And eventually—if he lived long enough—he'd get over her. Or so the theory went.

Inside the hospital, he went in search of Dr. Pooley.

"I tried to phone you, but you'd already left," Bill said, waving aside the forms. "It doesn't look like Mrs. Hanson has a concussion after all, she was able to handle the paperwork. So, do you want to see our patient?"

"No," Cole said. He turned his back to room 226. "I'm probably the last person she wants to see right now." He resisted the urge to satisfy Bill's obvious curiosity. "But I want to leave a book for her at the nurses station."

"Hi, Mr. Tarcher."

"Hi, Cindy." Cole summoned a thin smile for the girl behind the nurses' counter. Occasionally Cindy baby-sat for him. "What are you doing here on New Year's Eve?"

"I'm a volunteer." She shrugged and smiled. "My boyfriend had to work tonight, and I didn't want to stay home alone on New Year's Eve, so I figured what the heck. I might as well see if they needed me here."

They talked for a minute, then Cole placed the astrology booklet on the counter. "Will you see that Bailey Hanson gets this when she feels up to it? Room 226."

"Sure," Cindy said, glancing at the booklet. "It's too bad about Mrs. Hanson. Frank said she was in a terrible hurry to get back to Santa Fe. Said he was probably driving too fast for the weather."

Cole was halfway to the door before Cindy's words registered. Turning on his heel, he returned to the nurses' station. "Who is Frank?"

"Frank is my boyfriend's father. He was the cabbie driving Mrs. Hanson."

Cole frowned. "Cindy, it was my understanding the accident happened on the way to Albuquerque. Did you just say that Mrs. Hanson was in a hurry to get back to Santa Fe?"

Cindy nodded and leaned on the countertop. "Mrs. Hanson was going to the airport but then she told Frank she'd changed her mind. She wanted to go back. She said something about a letter she wanted to get before someone else did. I don't know. It's kinda confusing."

Cole spun to face down the corridor, and a slow smile transformed his face. "Well, I'll be damned," he said softly. "She changed her mind." A great weight lifted from his chest.

He grinned at Cindy, then picked up the astrology booklet and slipped it into his pocket before he walked out the front doors and ducked his head against the flying snow, trying to remember where he'd parked the Jeep. There was something he needed to pick up.

BAILEY ACHED all over. Whatever Dr. Pooley had given her had eased the worst of the pain, but she still ached. Her ankle throbbed beneath the cast; her chest felt as if it were on fire beneath the wrappings. There were bruises on her arms, other bruises in other places that she couldn't see.

She wondered how late it was and wished she could see a clock. Did Cole know yet that she had run away? God, what had she done? What was he thinking?

A painful sigh lifted Bailey's rib cage and caused her to grimace and clench her teeth. She cursed herself for a cowardly idiot and felt like weeping. Once Cole read her note, once she had hurt him that deeply, how could he ever forgive her?

Her door opened and a silvery head covered with snowflakes leaned inside. "Hi, Kansas."

"Cole!" Wincing and panting with the effort, she struggled to sit up, her eyes searching his expression. "You shouldn't be here. What about your party?"

He strode into the room and stood over her bed, inspecting her cast, bandages and bruises. Bailey thought he had never looked as handsome, even if she couldn't read what he was thinking. How could she have been so stupid as to think she could live the rest of her life without him?

"I canceled the party after discovering the guest of honor had taken a hike."

"I'm sorry," Bailey whispered. "I started thinking about the twins, about you and me, about...everything, and I panicked." Her eyes begged him to understand what she didn't fully understand herself. "I know I hurt you, Cole, and I'm sorry."

He sat beside her and his wonderful dark eyes swept her silly hospital gown and studied her face. "So where do we stand, Kansas? Are you coming or going? Staying or running away?"

"Do you still want me?" she asked in a small voice.

Now he leaned forward and finally he touched her, stroking his fingers down her cheek. Bailey's eyes closed, and a tear leaked from beneath her lashes. She pressed his hand against her cheek and felt a joyous burst of relief. It was going to be all right. She had seen it in his soft eyes.

"I've always wanted you, Bailey. I always will." He brushed her tears away with his thumb. "Don't you know yet how much I love you?"

"Oh, Cole, I've been lying here thinking how my stupid fear just about ruined the best chance at happiness that I ever had."

"That *we* ever had." His face softened, and he brushed his fingertips over her lips. "I love you, Kansas."

"Listen to me, cowboy, I'm about to say something important and you need to hear it." She gazed up at him with shining eyes. "I love you. I love you so much that it scares me to death to think about ever losing you. So I'm not going to." Her eyes locked to his. "While I was thinking about all this, I thought about what I'd do if I was given another chance. What *we'd* do. And, Cole—" she gripped his hands "—we're not going to hurt the twins, not ever. If you aren't going into this marriage thinking it's forever, then get out now. Because this one is for keeps, for ever and ever."

His laughter made her smile. "'Atta girl, Kansas. That's the kind of talk I love to hear. You and me—forever."

"There's more." She drew a breath and brought his hand to her breast. For a moment the look in his dark eyes dazzled her, and she almost forgot what she intended to say.

"I'm going to wear huge lapel buttons and I'm going to write blazing editorials that change the world. Maybe just a tiny piece of the world, but that's okay. I'm going to be a terrific wife and mother and—" she leveled a mock frown at his grin "—I expect you to be a terrific husband and father. I expect you not to interfere with whatever I do at the *Gazette*. You can argue and you can attempt to persuade, but you can't interfere. Think you can handle that?"

He raised his hands in surrender, then bent to kiss the corners of her lips. "I'll try."

"And I want a promise that this is the last time we'll tear up our lives. We're going to put down roots and build a stable, semipredictable life."

"Sorry, Kansas, I can't promise that." Cole's dark eyes twinkled as he kissed her chin, the edge of her eyebrow. "We're going to leave all options open. I'll promise wholeheartedly to love, honor, and cherish—but I won't promise to play it safe." He dropped a kiss on her nose.

Somewhere deep down, Bailey would have been amazed—maybe even a tiny bit disappointed—if he had said anything else. Their eyes met and held, and she saw that he, too, was remembering last night and the passion they had shared. His expression promised that last night was only the first of a lifetime of magical nights. A faint blush brightened her cheeks.

As if reading her mind, Cole asked in a thick voice, "Is it possible to give you a real kiss without hurting you?"

Bailey drew a breath and opened her arms. "I'll risk the pain to have the kiss." She got both, but his kiss was long and tenderly exciting and filled with promises she knew they would keep together.

When they reluctantly parted, Cole reached inside a paper sack she hadn't noticed until now and withdrew her astrology booklet, a bottle of Tattinger's, two crystal glasses and a pair of paper hats.

"Champagne?" Her gaze darted toward the door, then she burst into laughter that brought tears to her eyes. "Cole Tarcher, you're impossible! And wonderful. So wonderful. I love you." She turned the silly paper hat between her hands, then moving carefully, blinking at tears of happiness, she placed it on her head.

"Bill said one glass of champagne won't hurt you. We have a lot to celebrate."

While Cole poured the champagne, Bailey glanced at her horoscope booklet. Outside the night exploded in honking and fireworks. Someone blew a noisemaker in the room next to hers. It was midnight, the beginning of 1992 and a new life.

Sitting on the side of her bed, Cole leaned over and kissed her gently instead of taking her into his arms as he longed to do. "Happy New Year, dearest Bailey. We are never going to spend another New Year's Eve apart, not for the rest of our lives."

Twining her fingers through his, Bailey gazed at him with shining eyes. Already she was planning next New Year's Eve with her family. With her husband and children. She hadn't known it was possible to be this happy.

"Happy New Year, darling," she whispered.

From the corner of her eye she noticed the astrology booklet and the first line on the page it had fallen open to: "Geminis should prepare for a roller coaster of a year." She laughed as Cole leaned over and kissed her again and again, sending thrills through her body.

The astrology booklet was wrong. Her roller-coaster ride had already begun.

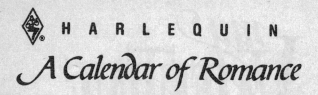

◆ H A R L E Q U I N
A Calendar of Romance

Be a part of American Romance's year-long celebration of love and the holidays of 1992. Experience all the passion of falling in love during the excitement of each month's holiday. Some of your favorite authors will help you celebrate those special times of the year, like the romance of Valentine's Day, the magic of St. Patrick's Day, the joy of Easter.

Celebrate the romance of Valentine's Day with

**#425 VALENTINE
HEARTS AND
FLOWERS**
by Muriel Jensen

Read all the books in *A Calendar of Romance*, coming to you one each month, all year, from Harlequin American Romance. COR2

my VALENTINE 1992

Celebrate the most romantic day of the year with
MY VALENTINE 1992—a sexy new collection of four
romantic stories written by our famous Temptation
authors:

> GINA WILKINS
> KRISTINE ROLOFSON
> JOANN ROSS
> VICKI LEWIS THOMPSON

My Valentine 1992—an exquisite escape into a romantic
and sensuous world.

Don't miss these sexy stories, available in February at your favorite retail outlet. Or order your
copy now by sending your name, address, zip or postal code, along with a check or money
order for $4.99 (please do not send cash) plus 75¢ postage and handling ($1.00 in Canada),
payable to Harlequin Books to:

In the U.S.

3010 Walden Avenue
P.O. Box 1396
Buffalo, NY 14269-1396

In Canada

P.O. Box 609
Fort Erie, Ontario
L2A 5X3

Please specify book title with your order.
Canadian residents add applicable federal and provincial taxes.

 Harlequin Books

VAL-92-R

Harlequin Intrigue®

It looks like a charming old building near the Baltimore waterfront, but inside 43 Light Street lurks danger...and romance.

Labeled a "true master of intrigue" by *Rave Reviews*, bestselling author Rebecca York continues her exciting series with #179 ONLY SKIN DEEP, coming to you next month.

When her sister is found dead, Dr. Kathryn Martin, a 43 Light Street occupant, suddenly finds herself caught up in the glamorous world of a posh Washington, D.C., beauty salon. Not even former love Mac McQuade can believe the schemes Katie uncovers.

Watch for #179 ONLY SKIN DEEP in February, and all the upcoming 43 Light Street titles for top-notch suspense and romance.

LS92

Take 4 bestselling love stories FREE

Plus get a FREE surprise gift!

ABOUT THE AUTHOR

Like Bailey and Cole, the characters you'll meet in *Happy New Year, Darling*, Margaret St. George has her own tradition for this most festive of holidays. She and her husband spend the evening alone in their Colorado mountain hideaway, with no TV and no distractions. They reminisce about the year just past, and they dream about the year to come. And, Margaret says, they make the same resolutions each year: eat less, exercise more, learn to ski, take more vacations—and stop making resolutions!

MGCOR

HARLEQUIN
PROUDLY PRESENTS
A DAZZLING NEW CONCEPT IN ROMANCE FICTION

One small town—twelve terrific love stories

Welcome to Tyler, Wisconsin—a town full of people
you'll enjoy getting to know, memorable friends and
unforgettable lovers, and a long-buried secret that
lurks beneath its serene surface....

JOIN US FOR A YEAR IN THE LIFE OF TYLER

Each book set in Tyler is a self-contained love story;
together, the twelve novels stitch the fabric of a
community.

LOSE YOUR HEART TO TYLER!

The excitement begins in March 1992, with
WHIRLWIND, by Nancy Martin. When lively, brash
Liza Baron arrives home unexpectedly, she moves
into the old family lodge, where the silent and
mysterious Cliff Forrester has been living in seclusion
for years....

WATCH FOR ALL TWELVE BOOKS
OF THE TYLER SERIES
Available wherever Harlequin books are sold